The Asturian Campaign

Guy Arthur Simpson

Published by Guy Arthur Simpson, 2022.

This is a work of fiction. Similarities to real people, places, or events are entirely coincidental.

THE ASTURIAN CAMPAIGN

First edition. January 6, 2022.

ISBN: 978-1916106154

Written by Guy Arthur Simpson.

Also by Guy Arthur Simpson

The Ministry of Flowers
Hoodwink
Immig's Work
John Eyre
Parasite of Choice
The Life and Death Performance of Tony Bedowie
The Man Who Died
The Sweet Teeth of God
The Asturian Campaign
Citizens of the Night
Four Stories
El ministerio de las flores

Watch for more at www.guysimpson.com.

Table of Contents

For my Spanish friends

The Asturian Campaign

ALL SHE HAD TO DO WAS press the button strapped to her thigh. She sat dripping perspiration, her heart thumping. The long weeks of carefully rehearsed preparation with the team were as nothing compared to these last, stifling, lonely minutes.

She had, or imagined she had, a minor tremble in her right hand. I'm not alright, she realized. There's no air in here: I need more air.

Do it, do it, answered her breath, fast and shallow.

She couldn't pull out now. She had to go through with it. Wait for the moment, squeeze the trigger, and her work would be done.

Erica sat in the target location in full burqa, feeling voluminous and petrified, hoping only that fear and the oxygen-starved heat inside the cotton hood wouldn't cause her to faint and fail, while her nails were painted what the beautician called "love pink." It was the new, breathable polish, the girl in winged spectacles was telling her, which could be safely left on for daily prayers since it allowed water to penetrate to the nail during *wudu*.

The pre-prayer purification of arms and hands, the imams insisted, included a woman's nails.

"You're sure it's *halal*?" Erica asked from behind the brown gauze of her head cover.

Yes, she was promised.

An older Arabic woman, reading *Hola* magazine in a corner by the shop door, snorted derisively. It was typical of European converts to Islam to aspire to out-ritual her own kind.

After which, in the cheap boutique, in the suffocating Madrid summer, conversation died away. A wobbly fan succeeded only in pressing the tedious heat against them. A plastic clock on the wall continually tried and continually failed to advance, a spent battery causing its second hand to flicker and shudder repeatedly in the same spot. In the high wall mirrors, nothing happened.

Erica's eyes strained at their peripheral limit to watch the door of the shop, while her reflected image in the mirror looked back mockingly. The woman in the corner licked a finger and turned a page.

As the moment of asking approached, Erica's mind went numb. She remained alert and set to act, but that was all. Any sense of self beyond staring eyes and a dry mouth was lost and forgotten. She remembered her training and what she might have to do —the slim pair of hairdressing scissors on the shelf in front of her would make an ideal close combat weapon— but she didn't really know why, or what it meant. There was no wider world beyond these four walls. There was just waiting.

The spectacled girl finished one hand and asked for the other, turning around at the same time to switch on a radio. Erica put her newly decorated left hand where her right had been, so that the tip of her longest finger rested on the firm lump that the mechanism made under the burqa. She tried not to panic, panting the hood's exhausted air, aware that the hand which she now offered up was quivering suspiciously. The radio reported news of another boatload of illegal immigrants, drowned as they had attempted to enter Spain, and the appointment of a Ku Klux Klan sympathizer to the White House staff. Neither item elicited a reaction from the two women, both of whom Erica knew to be Moroccan. She also knew their names, ages, relationship (aunt and niece via an arranged marriage) and their supposed affiliation to a particularly uncompromising Islamic order: supposed only, since beauty salons were condemned by the order as the work of the devil.

A man came in carrying pizzas and two-litre bottles of Coke in a plastic bag. He passed through the shop without a greeting and went to a door in the rear, where the wall was lined with shabby carpeting. To unlock it, he had to put the Coke down on the floor and punch a code into a security panel. The moment he pulled the door open, Erica hit the button under her robe.

It took two full seconds for helmeted police, responding to the signal, to burst in from the street. Two bulkily equipped agents hammered the man with the luncheon take-out to the floor, while another prevented the steel door in the rear from closing. Erica already had an arresting grip on the beautician and was pouring fast words of warning into her ear. That left only the magazine-reading aunt, who raised the alarm by ululating as if possessed until the back of a heavily gloved hand put an abrupt end to it. The door in the back of the shop was held open for more armoured black jackets bearing semi-automatic weapons to bustle through, taking their prisoner with them. There were echoed shouts from within that suggested a measure of resistance, but then, during the strangest of intervals, the cramped space filled by crouching armed men in assault gear, an unconscious old lady, a demolished fan, scattered ointments and brushes, and a young woman held forcefully to the floor by another in burqa and pink nail varnish, was perfectly quiet. Not even the radio, whose plug had become dislodged in the mêlée, disturbed the riotous silence that ensued in the beauty parlour.

It seemed like the end to an embarrassment when sirens finally broke out in the street, collapsing the vacuum to claim the local territory with their demoralizing howls.

• • • •

JUST UNDER AN HOUR later, Police Officer Erica Sánchez was off the scene, making her way home to change clothes before reporting back at the station. Her mental faculties, if not her composure, had been restored as soon as the raid had gone into action. Her sense of relief, on the other hand, was far from complete and her footsteps were as brisk as her mind was busy with what she had just seen, trying to figure out whether there was more to it all—if the real fireworks were yet to be unpacked—or if the long, tense anticipation had culminated in a damp squib. Hot and bothered, soaked in sweat and anxiety and still confined within the burqa, having dressed only in bra and knickers beneath it, Erica hurried down a steep, narrow street, looking up at the old apartment buildings, whose neighbours declared their allegiances with national and republican flags, gay rainbows and anarchist slogans. The upper storeys, painted by the brush of Madrid's inimitable light, were presented in the same shocking clarity of detail as the recent events in her mind's eye.

As the police operation's only Arabic speaker, she had been led quickly through the breached security door and down a corridor to a windowless space as high as a small warehouse, in which industrial sewing machines were set on trestle tables, along with spools of fabric and what turned out to be a heat transfer press for logos. The squad leader was haranguing the bewildered women there, five of them, in Spanish that they clearly didn't understand. Assault rifles were trained on them and on the only male, who cringed on his knees on the cement floor, hands already cuffed behind his back. Everywhere one looked there was sportswear, spread out on tables, hanging on walls: football shirts and shorts in particular in Madrid and Barcelona colours, but also tennis gear, embossed with Nike and Adidas insignia. Dozens of cardboard boxes and polythene bags were massed along one wall, and a desk in a small office was stacked with wrapping tape and marker pens.

In spite of a clatteringly busy air conditioning unit, the place was rank. There was a primitive shower and WC, but the rancid smell emanated from another room, if you could call the featureless cubicle a room. Foam rubber mattresses lay on a floor strewn with sheets and clothes that hadn't been washed for weeks, perhaps months. A single bulb hung from its ceiling and a few photos were taped to peeling walls. Erica fought back a wave of nausea.

The armed agents, having reported the situation secured, were searching frantically, filming and photographing everything, but making no finds.

No explosives, no bomb-making materials, no guns or incriminating documents. No ISIS or other extremist literature.

A laptop in the office was open at a page in Arabic that Erica looked at eagerly before informing the lead detective that it was health advice for body rashes.

"Copy the URL anyway," he told her. "And check through the hard disk contents."

He seemed disappointed, she thought. More dismayed than relieved to find no evidence of a terrorist cell. He was right, she thought also, to assume that the true operation might yet be concealed beneath the outward show, but all the visible evidence—the fact that the women were chained to the trestle tables by the ankle, one of them just a young girl—suggested that they had busted nothing more than an illicit production of fake sports fashion, a worse-than-average sweatshop.

Erica hurried as fast as the burqa would allow, past a shuttered late-night bar and a guitar maker's workshop, and emerged onto a local square that was one of the few public spaces in Madrid where her garb would go unremarked. She would have preferred to stride straight through the multiculturality and blank it out entirely, but she was still high on adrenaline after the raid, still in full operational mode. No matter that her vision was hampered by the gauze mesh of the veil, her eyes were taking in every detail, every move, every face. Any hurried dissimulation, any urgency of tone, especially in Arabic, could be a lead, a hint that the raid, which would certainly be known about down here already, had meant something big.

Instead, she found the barrio to be its usual, tentatively nonchalant self. On the street corner to her right, the usual bunch of young Africans, Senegalese, maybe some Nigerians and Mauritanians as well, were hanging around selling hashish, stolen mobiles and shoes. Or just pretended to, trying to look tough. To her left, a bench jammed with very drunk eastern Europeans, their sole prop a radio playing loudly on the ground, made a similarly unambiguous statement about territory and lifestyle.

Whether Erica Sánchez Morales belonged here, in the centre of her country's capital, was a moot point.

The square was shaped like a large wedge of pie, narrowing down to the Metro entrance to which Erica was heading. Lining the square like proud, serried teeth stood tall buildings, their balconied façades wearing a hundred years of Spanish elegance, save for one ugly gap where a healthy incisor had been pulled by order of the city council and its socket left to decay, accumulating graffiti and dog excrement. In nearby streets, the story was the same or worse. The municipal authorities had earmarked the historic area for a brighter, more vibrant future, which meant that eviction and demolition were in full swing. While Erica approved the mayoress's chastisement of the immigrant-ridden district, it troubled her to see the traditional face of the city being brutalized for property developers. It was with mixed feelings that she noted how the old residential area still retained a solidity of character, one that seemed to embrace and even encourage its diverse inhabitants. Either side of the gaping hole, Chinese one-euro shops, Maghrebi retailers of electrical goods, Bangladeshi grocers and curry restaurants all persisted and even flourished. The only Spanish business she could see, an outdated hardware store, stood out for having closed for lunch.

In the centre of the square, casual trash had fetched up against the bright primary colours of a playpen's low picket fence. A few infants played on the slides and see-saws, watched solicitously by Latin American families, Ecuadorean, Colombian or Cuban, Erica couldn't be sure which and didn't care. The whole neighbourhood was a jumble of what she considered an interracial mess. I am an out-and-out racist, Erica nodded to herself. Several of her fellow officers shared her views, but few were quite so intolerant. The trouble was, she couldn't find it in her to kindle any fellow feeling toward her Spanish compatriots either, who somehow still made up the majority of the residents here. Erica's discrimination appeared to be indiscriminate, extending to all those she saw about her: a hard-pressed shopper with kids in tow, a gay couple with a diminutive dog, seedy-looking men, an old lady in her dressing gown asking passers-by for coins. The defeated and the dreary poor. She somehow blamed them all for being party to a generalized disintegration, for succumbing to it, for being nobody that she could take any pride in even if it was not their fault. If changing times and the fierce summer were making this low-lying district into a social crucible, all she saw was scoria.

A disoriented middle-aged couple, clearly tourists who had strayed from the nearby museum route, were staring at a creased map. They stood in front of a giant poster that occupied the entire side of a newspaper kiosk. Such was the scale of the publicity image that it looked almost as though they were part of it. It showed a Spain that they really should have opted for, Erica thought, rather than here. If it really or still existed. Mountains in a bounteous spring and a smiling young woman surrounded by wild flowers and brown cows under a pure blue sky. Another country, another time altogether.

ASTURIAS. CRÈME DE LA CRÈME, declared the poster's slogan.

It looked so free and fresh and implausible, a lost truth that had no place here, one that Erica simply couldn't know. Here it was saris and headscarves, African voices raised in argument and overweight Latin girls in tight shorts, aspiring to husbands who would take them in shiny cars to go spend the day in a shopping mall.

At least the bars and the banks are still ours, she told herself, and it was outside one of these, the Santander Bank next to the Metro entrance, its windows shuttered against acts of political vandalism, that a kerfuffle caused people to scatter away across the road to the safety of a theatre forecourt. Police officers supported by patrol cars were rapidly joined by more, whooping their sirens, flashing blue lights, and by an unmarked van out of which helmets poured.

It was clearly a planned and coordinated intervention, a round-up, and initially Erica was gratified to see the rule of law being enforced. It was about time. Wasn't it enough that they had all these somehow legal people here? Half the young people in the country out of a job and now EU Romanians and Bulgarians were flooding in, willing to work for a pittance. Did they have to tolerate illegals as well? The decline had to be addressed and she, for one, had voted for a government which promised to deport illegals without papers.

But then she felt incensed. This was far too close to the beauty salon. The municipal police had failed to comply with procedure and desist from action within a five-hundred-metre radius during a five-hour period, while her own force went in on the suspected terrorist target. It was serious mismanagement that someone at high level had either overlooked or condoned.

The burqa had become a nightmarish contraption. It conspired with the midday heat to smother her. She walked towards the commotion barely able to breathe, sustained only by a combative stubbornness. A handful of young people gathered together in feeble protest were quickly outnumbered by private security agents from the van, whom the police, often with misgivings, were now being obliged to employ as accredited associates and whose lack of proper training was substituted by an eagerness for brutality. They soon created a defiant, baton-wielding periphery around the point of disturbance.

When a girl attempted to film the ongoing detention with her mobile, they arrested her as well. She was grabbed, pulled inside the bristling ring and thrown to the ground, where her mobile was crushed by a boot. Her companions retreated to the pavement opposite outside the theatre, while other impromptu protestors made themselves judiciously scarce.

The city police had a tall, powerfully built black man backed up against the bank.

"I have come to be with my people," Erica heard him say in loud, clear English. She looked straight at the man, who rose imperiously high over the Spanish policemen, larger than life in an extravagant white-and-gold robe, his lips pursed in indignation—and recognized him.

Erica was still nominally undercover on the terrorism case, even if that description was looking rather doubtful. She didn't dare identify herself here and intervene. In any case, it wasn't her police corps and she didn't frankly give a damn. But Sebastián might. And her boyfriend's boss most definitely would.

Madrid was, for the umpteenth time, and ignoring all counsel to the contrary, promoting its candidacy for the Olympic Games. Sebastián, her boyfriend of five months, was a chauffeur attached to the Ministry of Education, Culture and Sport, and this gaudily dressed person was one of three dignitaries that he had had his photograph taken with and shown to her; all three being members of the International Olympic Committee, who were being shown around the city as VIP guests and enjoying a number of privileges commensurate with Heads of State.

Erica lipread the arresting cop speak into his mike: "The individual has no ID." As he listened for instructions, the officer stared at Erica's amorphous brown form with that consummate professional blankness that she knew meant complete contempt, and was surprised to find herself look away, as if ashamed.

She got out her police-issue mobile and called Sebastián.

"How fast can you get here?" she asked, telling him why.

And then, having been parched with thirst and fixated on an ice-cold Coca Cola ever since she saw the man carry the two-litre plastic bottles through the beautician's (bottles which had rolled free on the linoleum floor only to be bagged as evidence), feeling too stupid to enter a bar wearing the burqa and troubled by all the events of that morning, she got into a waiting taxi and headed home.

• • • •

THE NIGERIAN OFFICIAL, tall and aloof in his fine robe, stared mutely ahead as one who does not deign to interact with his interlocutor as the Spanish Sports Minister apologized, explaining away his apparent arrest as a complete misunderstanding. The Olympic delegate heard out the rationalization in the presence of an embassy attaché from his country, whose smile suggested that a greater price awaited to be extracted, whether their vote for Madrid 2024 was granted or not. The minister scoffed at any notion of detention and described the police engagement as a function of dutiful protection, since the esteemed gentleman, the honoured guest of their government, had opted to enter unescorted and, it should be noted, without his IOC credentials, one of the city's slightly more inconsistent urban areas.

They stood in a gilt saloon at the Ritz Hotel, to which a ministerial sub-secretary had delivered the delegate in a black

Mercedes driven by Sebastián, after whisking him from under the noses of the bewildered city police.

The Minister would be delighted, should their gracious visitor so desire, to arrange a meeting with the leaders of the Nigerian community in their city, which so prided itself on its friendly and welcoming posture vis-à-vis African nations.

As a mark of attention to his occasional chauffeur, having been pleasurably amused by the young man's resourcefulness, Sebastián's maximum superior had admitted him to the room, where he stood in the background, gloved hands behind his back, itching to get back to the official car from where, concealed behind tinted windows, he could relay his contentment to Erica. He was only delayed, on the departure of the triumphantly injured party, by a gesture from the minister to stay and listen to what he had to say on the phone call that he was already making to the city's mayoress, berating her for disloyalty to the Party, for not taking the capital's Olympic bid with even a pretence of seriousness, using it instead as an opportunity to make lucrative concessions to rival cities, in particular Berlin and St Petersburg, and as an excuse under the banner of security to clear the streets of indigents and undesirables. "Which is all very well but impolitic, señora, and there's the rub." He ended the call and turned to his chauffeur.

"It makes me feel good to know I have a reliable man close to me, Sebastián. A minister's staff are like hyenas round a lion and his dinner, you know. Useless chatterers only good for keeping him on his toes. The driving pool is marked out by its steadiness, but all the same I suspect we've underrated your talents. What did you say your relationship was to the police source? A most timely intercession." The portly man's smile made his round cheeks rounder still.

"She's my fiancée, sir."

"Oh. I haven't seen her at Mass with you."

"She works special duties, sir. Unusual hours." He didn't feel the need to add that Erica was an unbeliever, because he trusted this would change with time. Nor, come to that, that they weren't in fact engaged. To him it was as if they were, even if she had laughed when he brought up the idea of marriage.

The Church was an implicit, almost furtive, private connection that Sebastián shared with a boss who ranked immeasurably above him in the service of the Government. It was his attendance at Mass, at a certain church preferred by a very correct type of Catholic, people who set store by decorum in ritual and fastidiousness in appearance, which had brought him to the attention of the minister, Francisco Villalba. At the time he was still a new recruit to the driving pool, ferrying secretaries and sub-secretaries back and forth in the capital. The minister had spotted him in the congregation, standing erect, firm and nicely shaven, just the right profile. Before he knew it, he was stand-in to the man's regular personal driver.

"She wouldn't mind if we claimed you tomorrow, then? I'd like you to think about junior staff duties." Villalba patted him on the arm. "We'll take the Bentley."

An hour later, Sebastián, feeling on top of his game and thoroughly officially commended, let himself into the tenth-floor apartment he shared with Erica. It smelled of nail varnish remover and onions. He left the heavy bag of Valencia oranges he was carrying in the bedroom and walked down the hallway to the kitchen, where he found Erica in her police uniform rinsing plums at the sink, her dark hair tied high in a bun. A green salad waited to be tossed in a bowl, next to a plate of cold chicken,

He recalled the first time they had met, chauffeur and patrol driver, in a canteen at the ministry, when she had been dressed the same way and he had admired that behind, snug inside the navy blue polyester.

"Want one?" she turned round. She looked, as she sometimes did, testy and expectant.

He took the colander from her, set it down, and reached both hands behind her bottom to pull her up for a full, long kiss. She had a sensibly low centre of gravity for a lithe woman and sank back on her heels.

This was, whether Sebastián realized it or not, exactly what she wanted. It helped her to believe in a normal life, with a normal boyfriend to help shake off the morning's stress and commotion. Soft drinks, a cold shower, and a well-conducted follow-up back at the station had not come close to quieting her discomposure after the raid.

"The Minister said I showed presence of mind."

Erica took a purple-black plum and sucked on it, inviting him with her eyes to continue.

"I think I'm getting a promotion. You're wonderful."

"I know," she said.

"Are you going out to work?"

"No, I'm wearing this just for you. I have been debriefed and am waiting for your strong hands to do more of that." Reaching up to take water glasses down from a shelf, she said, "Can you dress the salad? I don't want to get stained." Then turned round and suffused him with her scent. "I have a six o'clock at the station. A new assignment starting tomorrow that apparently can't wait."

For a moment, they just looked at each other.

"The Islamists! What happened?" Sebastián said with a jolt. He had completely forgotten.

"All over this morning and very quickly," she said. "The terrorist ring turned out to be a sewing circle. We found some Muslims alright, making fake Nike football shirts. Five women, all illegals, in forced labour, a shitload of cash and some stolen mobiles. Almost certainly no ISIS or Al Qaeda or other terrorist connection at all. Just a lame little commercial deal."

"Well you can't be too careful. It could have been the real thing."

"There really aren't that many people out there conspiring to destroy Spain and all it stands for, you know," Erica told his serious mien. "Just a few mixed-up young foreign men who'd soon be cured of their neurotic compulsion to heroism by meeting a nice Spanish girl and having lots of sex."

"You told me before that there's enough of that kind of thing going on already," Sebastián remarked.

"The nation's race being corrupted. Yes, well. Maybe I did. Anyway, you like blondes."

"Not just blondes—"

"So I was right. Who else, besides me?"

The dark-haired officer, asking the questions, catching him out. Not for the first time, Sebastián thought how far too good-looking she was, too alluring, to be a policewoman.

"I don't have to leave for another hour. Are you going to waste police time?"

She laid a gentle palm against his belly.

• • • •

"WE DON'T DO THIS OFTEN enough," he said.

"Thank goodness these don't need ironing," she said, retrieving her slacks from the floor. "But I'm going to need fresh knickers. We don't *see* each other often enough."

Sebastián sprawled out long and dark on their bed and activated the remote for the air conditioning before pulling her back to him. They lay together in the semi-darkness, aware of the new current of cool air, facing a low chest-of-drawers onto which a couple of oranges had rolled out, lodging themselves against Erica's discarded burqa.

"You'll never guess—guess where I'll be this time tomorrow," he challenged.

"Valencia," she said.

Sebastián raised himself abruptly on one elbow. "How do you know that? How could you know that?"

"Because you're a simple soul, adoringly predictable, and you never buy oranges," she smiled.

"It's a Formula One event," he continued, somewhat cagily, letting her comment pass. "To announce a new sponsor. I'm to be included on staff duties. The Minister told me to report to the section chief for security. You've got me a rung up the ladder."

They'll have you valet-cleaning the car next, the cynical policewoman in Erica's head wanted to say. If you knew how many officers were being obliged by budget cuts to double up for other duties, you might not be so chuffed. She fought an unwelcome unease. He looked so cute, like a boy who had won a goldfish at the fair, that she felt prickly. Her sexual hum had gone.

"When do you leave?"

"First thing in the morning. Sunday is dinner at María and Alfonso's. That's unchanged, don't you worry."

It took a second for Erica to realize that he meant her parents. *María and Alfonso*. He'd only met them once. Sebastián was talking about them as if they were some happy family that got together all the time and that he was part of.

"Aren't we meeting your foodie friends tonight?" She preferred not to think ahead to the weekend and her parents. "The ones you've been wanting me to meet ever since when?"

"At nine o'clock," he said.

Erica could almost see the punctual chauffeur in Sebastián shake out his shirt cuffs.

"At a rather special French restaurant. We'll be having a sampling menu that they were recommended by one of Shakira's nannies."

Erica failed to see why someone who cleaned up the orifices of a famous baby would make a reliable food critic, but lacked the inclination to debate the point. She was, she noted, vaguely put out that he hadn't asked if she minded him not being there on Saturday, or, even more unreasonably, not taking her to Valencia with him to see those fabulous cars: as if she could go along for the ride in the passenger seat of the ministerial limousine, chatting to him all the way to the east coast! She found the thought quite comic until she realized what the time was. She gave her boyfriend an until-later kiss and ran for the lift, leaving behind her foolishness and the untouched chicken salad.

• • • •

AT 9:01 P.M., AS ERICA knew he would be, Sebastián was outside the restaurant, elegantly suited and smiling thinly at the doorman, smartphone secreted in his hand.

It didn't vibrate until nearly half an hour later, by which time he was seated at the table with Raquel and Antonio and nodding strongly at anything they said. The maître d' was pursing his lips, eyeing the empty seat at the table for four and as perfectly conscious of the precise time as Sebastián, who had drained his sparkling water and lime twice and hadn't dared ask for another.

"They won't let me in."

"Where are you?"

"Where do you think?"

Raquel's eyes questioned him.

"Excuse me," Sebastián said.

His friends, who had been waiting to meet Seb's girlfriend forever, told only that she was two years older than him, twenty-seven, and claimed by a job that he was not at liberty to divulge, watched him go and then return through the forbiddingly exclusive venue via a slalom of tables filled by socialites and would-be sophisticates, with a girl that they didn't know whether to stare at or not.

The maître found himself in the same dilemma. She was outré and she was late, and could only be a celeb he didn't know or unbelievably common. He took a deep breath, swerved up at their table and found himself unable to speak.

"A chardonnay, very chilled," said the punk fairy in the expensive clinging dress. She had blonde and silver spikes for hair and big black eyes. The eyes smiled at him and he wondered if he was being dared to hold her gaze and not slip his own down to her bosom. "I feel so free tonight." She looked round the table.

Sebastián was finally the one to speak. "The first dish, whenever you wish." He raised his empty glass."And another pétillante."

Erica really did feel free and found herself taking more pleasure in the dinner than she could have possibly imagined. The restaurant's fascination with her was so contagious that an unpractised savoir faire welled up in her and she could do no wrong. By accident and the pressure of circumstance, she found herself doing her job—acting a part—in a private social milieu and strangely enjoying it.

Her new persona, dictated by the nature of the police investigation to which she had been swiftly moved, was as incongruously odious to the real Erica as the orthodox Moslem before it. To her, they were as weird and fake as each other. Unlike the dour religious fanatic, though, the role of nonconformist mystery girl had so much scope that it did indeed release something like a hormone of liberation in her. The emancipated spirit suggested by her fantastic appearance was enough to do the rest. Participating modestly without being reserved, she came across as poised and inscrutable to Raquel, disconcerted the supposedly suave Antonio, and utterly confused her boyfriend.

When she excused herself, Sebastián stole off to the ladies' after her.

"What's this all about?" he caught her at the door.

He experienced a momentary sense of being in command until her tearfulness floored him.

"But I thought you liked blondes," she started to sob.

His look of consternation was, Erica thought, sweet and dim. She waited a few seconds before telling him, in her normal voice: "This is the new me, Seb. I have to look like this. The make-up people went to work on me almost as soon as I got to the station. I'm being moved into position for a new assignment tomorrow. And it's not the kind of look you can slip on and off. Not like that ruddy great sack."

"You've had your nose pierced."

"In three places. But the holes will heal afterwards. You won't notice them. I said no to the barbed wire tattoo."

He looked partially reassured.

"I'm supposed to look rich, vulnerable and young."

She looked, he thought, just that. Like a well-endowed teenager.

"Is it alright to tell them?"

"Antonio and Raquel? No." Erica smiled. Even if her disguise hadn't been one that she had to keep up, the enjoyment of keeping them guessing would have produced the same response.

"Do you think she's a whore?" Antonio was whispering to Raquel.

"Really!" Raquel objected, her brain cogitating at full velocity.

"It would explain why he's kept her hidden all this time. What can be so secret about what she does? Know what I mean? Why the taboo?"

For a few seconds they cast challenging smiles around, as if defying neighbouring tables from entertaining such brazen thoughts themselves.

"She's far too chic," Raquel decided. "Too proper. No ordinary girl comes out to dinner at La Cuvée looking like that and holds her own."

"Of course," Antonio made a nominal show of defending his friend's partner. He found himself desiring her return to their table in the brief summer dress, little more than a negligee, knowing that she unnerved and intimidated him, what with the hair and that assured gaze of hers set above cheeks playful with glitter.

Having missed lunch, Erica was distinctly peckish, not to say downright hungry, but the Entrée, marinated, uncooked scallops, white and slimy and chill, set her stomach chary and it was not placated by the similarly raw veal that made up the Plat Principal. After Plat Surprise, quinoa in squid ink, had left its black stain on their lips, she breathed an inward sigh of relief that there was just the dessert to come and a very drinkable champagne to go with it.

By this time, the restaurant felt flattered to be sharing the evening with the fairy punk princess. It was enough that the maître, arbiter of all that was right in this social microcosm, was devoted to her. Tables in her immediate sphere of influence were too cowed by his unblinking stare to attend to anything but their own meals and restricted themselves to discreet asides. An actress, some confided to those who didn't know. Or somebody's daughter.

Antonio was attentive to the point of frowning and then turning suddenly voluble. Raquel gave up trying to draw her out for fear of appearing crass and she was no wiser for quizzing Sebastián, who stuck to his regular staple of conversation, where he felt safe. It was watching him, as he went so steadfastly about this, that Erica felt a fondness stir in her. Sebastián was rather stuffy, but he was principled. He was well-groomed, correct in his manners, athletic, faithful, sober and not in the force. Everything that Dani, her last boyfriend, wasn't. If only Dani hadn't been such a drunk, such a filthy lout. Such an asshole. If only he wasn't still in her unit. The fourth and last dish was a long time in coming. She finished her glass and started on Sebastián's, he holding forth, she drowsy from wine-tinted benignity and the emotional anticlimax of the morning, whose aftermath hovered in the background of her mind to irk her.

"Four World Champions, no less," Sebastián said. "And the venue will be the circuit itself."

"Wouldn't you like to go, Erica?" Raquel asked. "Brush with fame and maybe get along down to the beach afterwards?"

"Only if they let me have a go on the track in one of the cars," she said.

Antonio laughed. "But Valencia's so common. I see you rather at Monte Carlo, or Abu Dhabi."

"Well, you know I've been seconded to the security detail," Seb leaned in and lowered his voice. "Here's an inside item. You're sworn to secrecy, of course."

Antonio adopted his most serious expression and arched two forefingers at his fiancée as if to impress the gravity of their assurance. Raquel realized that she wasn't supposed to giggle and didn't.

"You all know the new sponsor is an Arabic royal. Well, apparently there's this Scottish journalist, a woman, who's been hounding him halfway around the world. Something to do with a scandal she thinks he's answerable for. Anyway, she's quite obsessed. They think she'll turn up and try to embarrass him at the press conference, and so we've all been issued with her photo and instructions to keep her at bay. It's a silly thing, I know, but the procedure's the same as for dealing with a would-be assassin!"

"How exciting!" Raquel said.

"What's his name?" said Erica.

"Like a bodyguard," said Raquel.

"Will you be issued with a gun?" asked Antonio.

"I haven't taught him how to shoot yet. What's his name?" Erica asked.

"Are you a good shot?" Antonio was prepared to believe it, but Erica wasn't looking at him anymore.

"Wally, Walid something," Sebastián offered good-naturedly.

"Wally?" said Raquel.

"Convicted of rape and murder," Erica said.

"In another country," Sebastián said, confusedly.

"And besides the bitch is dead."

"What?"

"His name is Al Walid bin Zayed, and the journalist is called Carol Sinclair. It's a well-known case. Al Walid was convicted in absentia by a Scottish court and cannot set foot on British soil, but he otherwise enjoys immunity. His billions ensure him a warm welcome everywhere else."

"He got off scot-free," quipped Antonio.

"You think it's funny?" Erica said. "And you'll be shielding him from justice," she turned back to her boyfriend.

"Are you sure?" Raquel hoped she might relent.

"I'm certain."

"But come on. This is politics, and you're being unfair on the boys. We all know full well that if ethical upstanding were insisted on, none of ours would be able to deal with any of theirs. Cast the first stone and all that," said Raquel.

"I'm not talking about being dodgy. He raped and strangled a girl. Yes, in another country, called the United Kingdom. Calling it politics just makes it worse. Makes you an apologist."

Raquel wasn't put out, but she was curious. She tried to read in the other woman's face whatever it was that threatened to antagonize their sociability. There was a contentiousness in Sebastián's girlfriend that belied the kooky look she was wearing.

"In the end," Antonio said. "This man is protected by the law. Spanish law. What do you expect Sebastián to do?"

Sebastián wasn't looking. It was as if he had withdrawn into another place altogether.

"I don't expect men to do anything to stop another man who is a predator on young girls," Erica smiled at Antonio. "I don't expect them to lift a finger unless it's to shove it up their ass."

In the unhappy seconds of silence that ensued, their table's spell was broken and its magic removed. The light that had shone kindly on them now left them feeling exposed. Erica drained her champagne with raised eyebrows and obvious enjoyment, but the others looked and felt plain awkward. A waiter arrived and, with an indefinable attitude, deposited massive, white, square dessert dishes in front of them. At first sight, they appeared to be empty, until closer attention made out five blobs, tiny and pink, arranged in a ring around the centre of the plate. They looked like miniature tits.

"Blood ice cream."

Since no one else was going to, Antonio felt obliged to name it. But the verve had gone from him, and his subsequent explanation—that the ingredient was not only elemental and exciting, nutritious and overlooked, but also a natural substitute for people allergic to egg whites—was received with politeness only.

Erica sat back and watched them attempt to eat their blobs, which adhered to the dish and resisted being scooped up. "Pig?" she asked.

He nodded. "Just like black pudding, for example—"

"Oh really," Raquel put down her spoon.

"Another glass, please," Erica beamed at the maître, whose devotion seemed to have waned with their star, but in whom the need to venerate her person, once awakened, lingered on. "And is there any other pudding? Dessert?"

"There is a new dish, mademoiselle," he drew up at her side. "In my opinion, it's the jewel of the collection. Not included in the meal, but should you wish..."

"How much is it?"

Raquel made a face that Erica knew she was making.

"Bring it. One each," Sebastián said, clearing his throat.

The melon slims had been hard to make out, camouflaged against the bone-white china, but they had all dutifully tasted and swallowed their two lozenges, iced by liquid nitrogen, crowned by a sphere of yoghurt and aerate of carrot.

Erica's query was answered with forbearance. Yes, she was told: air, flavoured with carrot. At that, she had only pouted long and thoughtfully, but when Antonio and the waiter suggested civet shit coffee, explaining that the cats were treated as holy and that the defecated coffee beans were only retrieved from their dung when they were asleep, her snorting laughter brought the meal to an abrupt close.

"You paid for everything! I can't believe it," she exclaimed loudly on the street on the way to the car.

"I was embarrassed," said Sebastián.

"We can't afford it. We're not in that league."

"We can't afford not to be."

"The carrot air alone must have cost over forty euros. Give me the key."

"Uh uh. You've been drinking. Quite a lot."

"Give it to me. You drive like an old man. Like my father. I can't bear it."

"And you're dangerous."

"I am not dangerous! I *drive* the car. I don't steer it like a ship." She fished in his trouser pocket and snatched out the keys.

"Erica."

"*Erica*," she mimicked him.

"You know you can't. If you keep it up, I won't tell you where it's parked."

She stuck out her tongue. Then threw the bunch of keys up into the air as high as she possibly could. There were some other people in the street and Sebastián didn't know whether to push them out of the way or not, before the keys smacked onto the pavement, attracting an indignant "Do you mind?" from a well-dressed, middle-aged couple.

"I can't believe you did that," Sebastián's fingers flexed open and closed on the steering wheel of the BMW. "You just made me a look a fool in front of two of my most valued friends. Why couldn't you just be civil?"

"If they really are friends, it'll be okay. It was me that came across as the weirdo." Erica pulled down the passenger visor to check herself in the mirror.

"Right this minute, I don't know if we're right for each other. You obviously don't respect men for a start."

"Oh Seb, don't be overdramatic, please. I'm sorry, I haven't had a moment to relax between assignments and I was upset about what happened this morning. I'm sorry. I really am." They stopped at a red light. When he turned to her, she reached over and kissed him. It seemed to appease him. He relaxed visibly. Thank goodness for that, she thought. Love's dart. "And that bastard Saudi is guilty as hell."

"What do you mean about this morning? I thought it went OK?"

"The girls."

"The ones working there? What happened? Were they... abused?"

"Sexually, no. We don't think so. Pretty sure not. But when I left the scene this morning, something bothered me. I wasn't sure what it was. I thought it was my reaction to the man we arrested. An immigrant. When I questioned him he was still kneeling on the floor and he looked at me with such disdain. 'I will speak to a man,' he said. 'Police*man*.' And I felt such hate that I wanted to kick his teeth in right there and then."

"Did you?"

"I sent over one of the male detectives."

"So it's alright, then."

"No, it's not alright. A good police officer doesn't fall for elementary provocation like that. I was in a real, violent rage. It was unprofessional. Unacceptable. If I'd been wearing riot gear I might have shown him what it was designed for."

"But you didn't do anything. What's it got to do with the girls, anyway?"

"But I wanted to. I think I still want to. Anyway, when we were about done at the scene and a WPC came to take the women away, one of them went apeshit—and the others joined in with her in a huddle and refused to leave, and they were looking at me, screaming and begging. And when I went to the station this afternoon, it turns out that they'd been there for years. *Years*. Three to four years. Without leaving that room. They think the girl's twelve, so she was only eight or nine when they arrived. They were slaves, Sebastián. Right in the centre of Madrid."

Her boyfriend was silent. He didn't know what to say.

"Tomorrow, before I start being this alternative young person full time, I'll go check on them at the Protection Centre. There's one just for Muslim girls, which says something. Which means I'll have to wear that hateful sack again, goddammit, because I can't risk being seen and recognized in the same area."

"You shouldn't take the name of the Lord in vain."

"You shouldn't be disclosing details about the movements of the Minister."

Sebastián felt the shock of what she said raise bumps on his skin. Holy Mother of God, it was true. If anyone had been guilty of unprofessional contact today, it was him. He'd let a desire to impress lead him into revealing to a third party, friends or not, the day and destination of his delivery of a senior government figure. Not that his attendance at the Formula One event wasn't public knowledge, or that the character of the event wasn't leisurely. That wasn't the point. It wasn't like him and it was wrong.

"I'm going back on patrols," Erica said.

"What? Why?" Sebastián's guiltiness made him wonder if it was somehow his fault.

"Because one can't keep on doing undercover work forever. And because I want to."

"When? What about passing as detective? Aren't you going to?"

"Yes," she said half-heartedly. Probably. I suppose so, she thought.

The fact was that she had only really moved on from working patrols because other people had urged her to. She had liked being out on the highways, driving fast and well, with nowhere to go. Feeling in charge. It was the one thing she knew that she was unquestionably good at. Being on the roads allowed her a sense of autonomy alongside her working partner. Let her feel a kind of freedom. She liked the simplicity of it. She liked taking the smarmy look off the faces of certain men when she stopped them for dangerous driving. They thought they were so charming until she slapped the ticket on them. If she made detective, it would put an end to all that.

"I'm allowed study time and it doesn't matter what one's doing in the run up to the exams. I'm going to be sick."

Sebastián pulled in to the kerb and pushed her door open just in time to save the upholstery and also the paintwork, on which stomach acid could be quite corrosive, from being spattered. She got out and finished puking under a small tree, again and again, shaking a little, until the wretchedness passed. She spat a last time and cleaned her face with Sebastián's monogrammed handkerchief, which he had waited to hand to her.

She was silent during the rest of the journey home. He had put the radio on and was saying, well, that's the drink, I don't think it was the food, you hardly ate a thing, and you had a big pressure day today. She said nothing, but as the car moved slickly along, her mind spoke its innermost thoughts to her.

As she had heaved and coughed, bleary with tears, one hand on the slim tree, sneering at her in the midst of it all were the man's eyes: the bloodshot eyes of the man kneeling on the floor that morning. Sebastián hovering behind her, near her, not knowing whether to touch her or not. *OK? Are you OK?* The man whose teeth remained to be kicked in. Such *fury*. Sebastián had helped her back into the car. Should she explain what lay behind it? Behind what conditioned her still? Tell him? It was half a lifetime ago, yet the impotence and the anger were even now the key to Erica Sánchez. Would he get it? No. Not now. Another time, maybe.

Fourteen years old and separated from her friends, from Bea and Lola and Marisol, wrenched from her life and home, from summer and Spain, where she had been so happy, to a place where she didn't know the language, where nothing and nobody made any sense, where she wasn't allowed to do, like, the most normal things because she wasn't a boy. She couldn't even go to a normal school, like she had some weird disease or something and couldn't be with other kids. With no sisters or brothers, she had only her mother for company. It was the days before social media and people just wrote to each other by email. She had kept in touch with the girls for a while, but the gaps between messages grew longer, and after six months she felt as if she might as well not exist for anyone in Salamanca, where she had lived all her life, where she expected to stay for long, teenage years until leaving school, and where her father had taught Eastern Religion & Philosophy at the university before having the bright idea of accepting a well-remunerated posting to Morocco. All of a sudden, her whole life was gone. She was in a taxi booked for Madrid Airport and a flight to Casablanca, in tears, understanding nothing, aunts, uncles and cousins waving goodbye...

To begin with, an old lady tutor who seemed to hate her on principle came to their residence in Rabat to give her classes, like she was under house arrest or something, until she was finally allowed to go to an all-girls school and the alien planet that was Morocco started to open up to her. She opened, too, if only marginally, to the warmth and the scent of spices, the almond cakes and the plums in tagines, the donkey carts among the cars, the noise of life, the sound of Arabic, and little foreign oddnesses, such as finding Korans in the supermarket aisles. She would go downtown or visit the medina with her mother who, of an unadventurous disposition, had initially opposed the move, but now found she was delighted to be freed from her job in the legal agency. María could afford a housekeeper and spend time shopping for clothes and rugs or a tea service to decorate their house, whose airy, high-ceilinged rooms opened onto a tiled internal patio shaded by tall palms. Erica's father operated an open house to his new colleagues and acquaintances, making it a point of honour and intellectual commitment to invite leading academic minds, writers and political thinkers to soirées that he would host, welcoming them in his corporeal largesse and adopted kaftan. He would sit cross-legged like the rest on cushions as tea was passed round, pitta bread and dips, sometimes alcohol, also. One of the men was young and very good-looking and always smiled under his moustache at her, but another of the regular guests was a fat-faced man who stared but never smiled and seemed almost offended if she walked by in her own house, sometimes in the company of her best friend from school.

Salima helped Erica with Arabic homework and they would make couscous or pasta together, henna their slim arms and hands with red and black traceries, try on tight jeans and listen to rap. One evening, they interrupted a heated discussion of the men by walking unannounced into the room, putting on a Michael Jackson song and performing their own invention of what was supposed to be a meld of traditional dance with moonwalking. When they finished, there was no applause. Erica was put out to see the men not even remotely amused and the short, fat-faced man glaring in his jowls. Her father, discountenanced, rose to lead them out of the room. She didn't dare look back to see if the handsome Malik felt the same way and hurried out with Salima, who looked more than just embarrassed, almost scared, and didn't stay for tea.

After that, the door to the debating room remained closed. Her mother told her not to mention the meetings at school. "Some of these men are important," her father explained to her. "Progressive minds, who want to make Morocco more democratic." Why they didn't like her western-influenced dance, then, didn't make any sense to Erica, but she didn't argue the point and didn't interrupt them again.

Erica made rapid progress in Darija and learned to haggle in the market for her mother, yet she still struggled to feel at home in what remained a foreign land to her, no matter how used to it she became. She fantasized herself as a doomed exile, a Spanish patriot, whose time and return must surely come. Once in a while, when they strolled the Kasbah and she looked out to sea, a homesickness would take hold of her and she would press her mother to go and spend a typically Spanish day at the beach with fried fish and ice cream.

Alfonso, Erica's father, was in his element in Rabat. While no convert in the religious sense, academically and intellectually he was a wholehearted islamophile. He would treat his wife and daughter to a generous allowance and spa treatments at a hammam, but also to lengthy discourses at mealtimes on the cultural pre-eminence of Islamic culture in the establishment of Al-Andalus in the Iberian Peninsula. The Catholic reconquest, he let it be known, was the end of enlightened culture in Spain and the country had never properly recovered since. Erica let it wash over her and went to her room to dance to techno. Salima, who was now a regular visitor, became her source of information about real culture, and the more she found out, the less she agreed with her father. Whenever Erica protested against the way Salima's family discriminated unfairly against her in favour of her brothers, her friend would always say, "But they don't care what I think. I'm just a girl. I'm lucky they let me come here." She took her clothes over to Erica's house so that they could play at dressing up. They both loved the pink and turquoise djellabas and the different ways they could wind colourful headscarves around their hair. They would parade and pose in the long mirrors in Erica's beautifully big bedroom.

One day, at Erica's request, Salima brought over traditional Muslim costume. It was a burqa, which her mother owned but would never have worn in the mild Islamic climate of the country, any more than a Spanish woman would unbox her mothballed first Communion dress and go out dressed in it. When her friend put the burqa on to model it, Erica took an instant and intense dislike to the item.

Salima wasn't there anymore. She had been turned into a monster.

It wasn't so much that it made her friend disappear inside a formless cloak: it was the closed hood. The burqa's head cover with its oval mesh hid her classmate's face and eyes utterly, in a cruel kind of way. It reminded Erica of the scary story of The Man in the Iron Mask. It was clothing designed to punish. At last it came off and the smiling Salima reappeared. After some insistent prodding from her friend, the Spanish teenager reluctantly donned the same outfit, all the while knowing that it wasn't a good idea. The experiment lasted for less than ten seconds, by which time Erica had torn the thing off, head cover and all, and was coughing and gulping air, red-faced. The sensation of being thickly imprisoned had brought on an instantaneous claustrophobic terror, a tendency and reaction to being shut in that she had only guessed at previously and had now had confirmed.

Shortly before his first year of tenure at the university was about to conclude, with summer holidays in Spain beckoning and both women in the house eager to go home for an extended stay, Alfonso announced that he would be away from home for two weeks running, a conference in Marrakech to be followed directly by a series of lectures in Seville. There was no reason for them not to continue with their normal weekly routine and he would be back in time to accompany them on their long-awaited family vacation. The Wednesday meetings at the house could continue without him and they should let the gentlemen come and go as they pleased. María and Erica heard him out, already mentally packing for the big trip.

The second Wednesday Alfonso was away, the men filed into the house and took up their usual positions in the room off the patio, helping themselves to the mint tea and sweet cakes that

Erica's mother had left on a tray outside. After about half an hour, Erica and Salima were playing a noisy computer game in her room when the door opened and three of the men stood there. Erica silenced the racket the computer birds were making with a click of the mouse and apologized. She didn't think they would hear them downstairs. The men walked in. One of them grabbed her and clapped a hand over her mouth. The other two caught Salima. One pinned the girl's arms to the floor and the other tugged the western jeans and knickers off her kicking legs, got on top of her, and raped her. Erica couldn't move and her screams were muffled by the fat hand over her mouth. When it was over, she managed to bite the hand and received in return a thwack to the head that left her dizzy. Malik, her favourite, who had raped her best friend, spat on her on his way out of the room. Erica went to Salima, who had been silent throughout the assault and remained so now in total shock. She got a towel to stem the blood and went running in rage to her mother. When María called the police, they refused to do anything until her husband was present.

Unsurprisingly, Salima wasn't at school the next day; nor was she the day after, or the following week, which was when Alfonso returned as scheduled. He reacted to the news with shocked silence. Two days later, Erica's mother told her that she was not to contact her friend and that her father had been to see the girl's family.

"Your father's very upset," she said.

"*He's* upset? When are the police going to arrest them?"

"I don't know, dear," her mother said, looking anxious.

That evening, Erica's father sat her down in the kitchen for "a little chat."

"It's not easy," he said.

"What do you mean 'it's not easy'? Malik—that's his name, isn't it?—nice, smiley Malik raped Salima and the other two helped him. What's not easy about it?"

"In Morocco," he said. And she felt ire rise in her, a bitter fire that would never be put out. "A woman, a girl, can be punished for leaving home on her own. As this is the case, and she was with an unrelated man without a male relative present, the police do consider her guilty of..."

Erica stormed out of the room without waiting to listen to the rest. It took a letter signed by Salima to persuade Erica not to publicize the case across the internet and campaign for her. If she didn't keep quiet, the typed letter insinuated, Salima would be shamed and might even be obliged by law to marry her rapist.

The only time Erica heard her mother raise her voice against her father was when he suggested the next morning that they ought to "stay and work through this as a family."

"Stay? Are you out of your mind? That plane leaves for Madrid in six days from now. If you want to come back after the summer and carry on as if nothing ever happened, we're finished. You're on your own. *It could have been your daughter!*"

"But it wasn't."

"Ah!"

Erica pulled open the kitchen door to find her mother trying to beat her heavy-set father with both her fists, him holding her by the wrists, looking bewildered.

"Stop it!" shouted all the pain in her fourteen-year old self, and the terrible sound echoed from wall to wall until the whole house, even the birds in the patio, fell silent.

An hour later, Erica heard a knock on her bedroom door. When she opened it, her mother stood there with her arms crossed, quivering.

"Get your things," she said.

Erica grabbed her in a desperate hug and wouldn't let go.

Alfonso insisted on accompanying them to the airport.

"Thanks for leaving me to take care of everything," he said to his wife. "I will ship everything over and join you after I've talked to the rector. I hope you're satisfied," he turned round to address his daughter in the back of the taxi. "I will be losing my job and career and cannot promise to be able to support you in the luxury to which you will now be fully accustomed."

"I hate you," she told him. They were the last words that she would speak to him in over three months.

Erica channelled her teenage anger into moodiness and ditching boyfriends every time they got too sweet on her. Neither did she form close friendships with girls of her age group, whom she found collectively as childish as the boys were dim-witted. She mixed with everyone and respected no one. A practised defensiveness kept them all at bay. Unhappy and occasionally livid with her uncomprehending parents, for her mother now sided with her father in playing down what had happened in Morocco, she chose for her seventeenth birthday a course in judo, which she hoped might bring her a certain equilibrium and peace of mind. When, after intensive training and dedication, it did nothing of the kind, she gave it up. Any satisfaction in her purple belt and knowledge of grappling techniques felt hypocritical when it wasn't accompanied by anything approaching inner harmony. And if there was one thing she couldn't abide, it was hypocrisy.

Six years on, after a series of aborted jobs and relationships had bought a questionable independence from Alfonso and María, Erica applied to join the national police corps. There wasn't so much an avenging desire for justice in her decision. It resulted rather from a recommendation by her best friend Marta, who worked as a sex counsellor and always knew how to weigh someone up. Yes, Erica agreed. It would suit her temperament and could turn out to be a stable career move. It might, as a bonus, piss off her liberal father, now comfortably ensconced at a Madrid university's Faculty for Islamic Studies, but that was by the by.

She was told to her face by a recruiting officer that she was too attractive and a psychological test showed her to be contradictory in empathetic reactions, but they couldn't argue with her written papers or her ability to handle herself physically. Accepted on a probationary basis, Erica Sánchez Morales outshone ninety per cent of the male rookies on driving skills to earn a place on security details and patrols. With that, she settled into a regular professional life which palliated the typically unsettled private one that she had grown used to, and then, after two ill-advised and untidy relationships with fellow officers, she met a handsome young chauffeur at the Ministry of Education, Culture and Sport and found they had a job in common to talk about.

Cars were such a safe subject. Sebastián proved to be surprisingly conventional, even dull, but that was what fascinated Erica about him. She was intent on a relationship that promised steadiness and reliability and when he proposed that they go out together, she jumped at the chance. He was so correct, unperturbed and sane. And he had a BMW, not an Audi.

Although she considered that she had long ago moved on from the events in Rabat, Erica maintained a somewhat obsessive habit of keeping tabs on high-ranking sexual offenders in Arabic countries. It was a harmless, if arguably pointless, practice. When a certain Yemeni eminence came to spend the summer in chic Marbella, resort of choice for the big spenders, and Erica gifted the local press and women's associations with a documented portfolio of his crimes, she wasn't dismayed when they published not a single word. She knew that there was nothing she could do to bring men like him to justice, but it was a point of honour with her not to forget Salima.

After two years on patrols, budget cutbacks reduced her highway schedule to part-time duties, and the prospect of being dragged down into administrative work raised its ugly head. So that when a friendly senior officer suggested that she try undercover police work, Erica decided to give it a go, even if she intuited that being selected for her looks to bust prostitution rings smacked of the same sexist abuse that it promised to combat. She convinced herself that the new work offered a chance for promotion and the protection of the innocent. And when the opportunity of being involved in an anti-terrorist operation presented itself, she volunteered immediately, although it was with distinct unease that she found herself having to brush up on the Moroccan dialect of Arabic that she had spoken as an adolescent, only to be told that she would have to don a burqa for the purposes of the operation. Being encased and enclosed, all alone with a bad memory, leaving only slits for her anxious brown eyes, had suffused her with childish horror.

But she had made it through the ordeal, played her part in a successful raid that would have made national headlines had the suspected terrorist cell been a real one, gone home and had sweaty if muted sex with her boyfriend, been transformed into another person altogether by the undercover unit, and got drunk at a ruinously expensive dinner engagement.

How could so much have happened in one day?

Being switched in appearance and persona into a hippyish girly, just the kind of intentionally naive creature that she couldn't abide, had proven unexpectedly liberating for the duration of an absurd dinner, but she hadn't been able to keep it up beyond the third course and now here she was, thoroughly sober again, enduring the conscientious driving and silent censure of a boyfriend who liked her new character even less than she did. At the sedate speed Sebastián drove, she reflected, it was hard not to be sober by the time they reached home.

• • • •

THE FOLLOWING MORNING, Sebastián waited with uneasy concern to use the bathroom while Erica threw up again, this time in the toilet bowl. His watch told him he couldn't wait any longer.

"Pucker up, girl," he said, patting her gently on the back, and stepped past her into the shower.

Erica arrived for the definitive briefing by the Chief at police headquarters with no breakfast inside her and only seconds to spare.

"I'm taking you off undercover after this one," he said. "That's no reflection on you, Sánchez, quite the contrary. Your action in the raid yesterday was exemplary. Commendable even. It's just that the next undercover operations are centred on drug trafficking and that scene calls for a look you just don't have.

We're better off using a real druggie. An officer who tries to imitate the way they dress, the ill-fitting clothes because they're always losing or gaining weight, it just looks phony, a dead giveaway. And although I've seen you look better," he paused. What the hell is a good-looking girl like you doing in the corps? He had always wanted to know. "I can see you're trying to make an effort with that sickly look, but you're never going to have those sunken eyes, that pallor. You're too healthy, Sánchez."

"Yes, sir. Sorry, sir."

"I'm expecting you to pass for detective in October. Until then, I will support you in whatever you choose to do, within reason. With your flair for languages, there's interesting work being done in electronic surveillance these days. I could probably wangle you a small office of your own. A geek or two at your command."

"I'd like to go back on patrols. Highways."

"Patrols."

"Yes, sir. Before getting stuck behind a desk."

The Chief looked displeased, but when he shook his head it was in acquiescence. "Alright. As you wish. Now, this last assignment. You will liaise with D.I. Pastori and you'll have the usual back-up to count on, but it's a passive role and there's just one order I want you to follow. Would you like a mint, Sánchez?" The man winced, taking a roll from his desk drawer.

"Thank you, sir, no thank you."

"Dyspepsia. Comes with the job, they say. You know, the astonishing thing is that in spite of the permanent misery, public education in ruins, hospitals—it gets you right in the base of the stomach—the people most affected in this country, the impoverished and exploited millions, react by doing absolutely nothing at all. Pusillanimous, bamboozled, call it what you like, but the autocrats have engineered utter hopelessness and apathy. So what's the worst social problem we have, Sánchez? It's like a long, slow burn that you can't put out."

"Drugs, sir?"

"Almax, Omeprazole: yes, I know, I've tried them. Somehow I just like sucking on the mints. Disrespect. Disrespect for authority. And then, of course, sooner or later the long-term desperate poor are going to realize that they have nothing to gain and nothing to lose and we've got a rumpus on our hands. So what? you might well ask. When it kicks off, we'll just send our boys into their neighbourhoods and give them a kicking. Al very true. But to postpone that day, the powers that be—in this case the City Council—want to pre-empt any bother and disband or put down any opposition that might gather support and prove troublesome. It's all in their bureaucratic minds, you know. There isn't any effective resistance in the offing: we know that. In that respect, the electronic age really has been extraordinarily good to the forces of extreme order. If there was any serious subversion out there, we'd know about it. But the mayoress likes to think she's ahead of the game even if there isn't one. In this instance, her municipal police don't have the resources we do and the national government is happy to do her a favour and have the matter under its own control, especially as the lady has a tendency towards procedural unsubtlety."

Arresting Olympic Committee VIPs, for example, thought Erica.

"In short, we are going to put into effect selective infiltration of anti-system groups in Madrid and other major cities in the country. Yours will be a non-aggressive, information-gathering role over the next ten weeks, at the end of which you can go back to being your real self and patrols. I'll make sure you have one of the new Nissan Qashqai. However—"

"Thank you, sir."

"*However*, Officer Sánchez, that's not what this briefing is about. We already have very close tabs on these so-called radicals and know them to be about as dangerous and organized as infants in a playground. In that respect, your workload can be as light as you like, as long as you keep the reports coming in, which we will duly dress up for the mayoress's consumption.

"You will have another job to do. Your real remit, which neatly kills two birds with the one stone of your new persona, is another affair altogether. The teenage daughter of a well-connected industrialist has, as such girls are wont to," he pushed a file across the desk for her to open. "Rebelled against her father's wishes and values. It seems she's defiant in a passive-aggressive kind of way. We don't think she's experimenting much with marijuana or speed or poppers like other girls, but she's bunking school and any movement that's anti-capitalist, any alternative philosophy or bunch of non-conformists, and the weirder the better, and she's onto it. That's her drug. She is heavily into her own sweet, half-baked self. You know: the usual. She's fourteen, about to turn fifteen. The businessman father in question is the president of a major cement company and if you don't grasp the wealth and political influence behind such a figure, you'd better brush up on your national economics. The girl has taken to hanging out with a variety pack of social discards and crusties, also Africans, who she says are 'misunderstood.' Makes you want to vomit, doesn't it? Anyway, they never know where to find her. It's a serious concern and that's official. From the top."

"Why don't her parents just gate her?"

"When they did that, she cut herself and refused to eat. She's quite a determined young lady. And she tells them she wants to die. They're powerfully rich parents, but parents all the same and they don't know what to do with her. They'd rather give her some rope and make sure we're on hand to make sure she doesn't hang herself with it."

"So that's the assignment?"

"The girl turns fifteen next month and the family have planned the usual big party for her, which she has refused, surprise surprise, to attend. Me, I have annual leave starting tomorrow. If, when I get back, the girl is safe and unharmed, you will have one very pleased police chief. If you can manage to get her to turn up for her party, at which I myself will be a guest, there are big brownie points going. The only slightly embarrassing thing is that she hasn't been seen for a while. Just phones her mum to say she's okay and staying at a friend's. Which is why it can't wait. You'll have to find her. It's the summer holidays," his fingers drummed the desktop involuntarily. "And for the three days prior to her birthday she's booked herself onto a summer camp, even though it's in the city and behind closed doors. We understand the camp sells rip-off trendy bullshit about achieving nirvana with secret disciplines, or some such crap. Inspector Pastori and her people will fill you in on any other background we have on the girl, plus alternative young person vocabulary and behaviour to prepare you for being one. I just want the subject kept out of harm's way. An intervention team with medics is available. Any questions?" He took his mobile and car keys from the desk and stood up.

The subject, so far, was little more than a name on the printed pages in the file that Erica was now looking through. Zoe Iris Urquizo Fuentes. 'Zoe Iris' was a pretty combination, she thought. The photos showed evenly balanced features with a sullen look that matched the profile she was learning about. Erica guessed that the thick, heavy eyebrows were a genetic gift from her father.

"Does she have a boyfriend? Close friends? Anyone she listens to?"

"Not of her own age, no. No romantic attachment that we know of. No one at all apart from this alternative person who signed her up for the summer camp. The girl's essentially a loner, which may play into your hands or not. Depending on how you play it. Tell my wife to remember the dog muzzle," he said into his intercom. "For the beach," he explained to his secretary and Erica, who wasn't looking at him.

"What does she call herself? Zoe Iris?"

"Just Zoe. Apparently she hates the Iris. Just Zoe. Get her to the birthday party, Sánchez."

In an adjoining room, Detective Inspector Pastori ran through Zoe's social networking (minimal), her pet hates (countless), her favourite music (death metal), her inspirations (Sylvia Plath and Marilyn Manson) and her flirtation with self-cutting and bulimia. When Erica's early morning indisposition threatened to return, an unimpressed Pastori sighed and agreed to a coffee break.

Sipping a Coca Cola, Erica looked at the brooding senior officer to whom she would be reporting. "Is anything wrong,

Detective Inspector? Apart from Zoe's teenage rage and unfortunate taste in the arts?"

Pastori looked back at the cute punk pixie, whom she was finding difficult as hell to believe in as a bona fide police officer. The obvious answer was that any safe and successful undercover operation took time and careful, if not painstaking preparation. Not twenty-four hours. The Chief was doing someone a personal, private favour with this one, and if it went wrong, she'd be the one to carry the can.

"The boss is back in a fortnight," she said finally. "Just make sure the girl's alive and in one piece and I'll arrange for your general surveillance of anti-social elements to be wrapped up, too."

"Yes, ma'am," responded Erica with genuine enthusiasm.

"The summer camp—'Field of Light' it's called—is the typically esoteric kind of event the girl might go for. Kind of elitist, really. No phone number or email or Facebook page. You have to be proposed, it seems. As Zoe's under age, the application had to be signed off by a parent, so the mother was able to give us the name of the person who put Zoe's name forward: a certain Olga Vanderveldt. There's your lead. You, Carina Delgado Ruíz, as you will now be known, are going to have to locate the females and find your own way into the Camp."

"'Not for everyone,'" Erica said.

"What?"

"Nothing. Something I read once."

Pastori handed her an ID card and a mauve mobile with yellow spangles.

"#100 gets me, #900 is emergency medical back-up, and it's encrypted for anonymous personal calls. Well, how do you feel? Ready to go in?"

"How do I feel? Out of sorts. Tired. Confused."

"Fine. Goes with the persona, Carina."

"Call me Cari," Erica flashed her superior a disconcertingly believable smile.

• • • •

BY MIDDAY, THE JULY heat in Madrid had hiked up to a formidable 41°C.

While the rear view mirror in the Bentley showed an air-conditioned Sebastián to be the very image of groomed correctness as he conveyed the Minister for Sport to the jolly in Valencia, Erica sat on the burning-hot ground of a small and dusty city park, where she was attending an assembly for disaffected citizens looking believably disgruntled and the worse for wear. It was not only abnormally, powerfully hot, but perfectly cloudless besides, so that the sun beating down baked everything in its gaze. The red bandanna tied around Erica's forehead looked like the wrapping on a birthday cake, from which the blonde spikes of her impish hair protruded like candles, ready at any moment to catch into flame.

Erica fanned herself while the first half an hour was taken up with procedural detail and smiled weakly at those sitting closest to her. She strained her ears to listen to a man who didn't realize he had to talk into the megaphone to make himself heard. As far as she could make out, he was telling the thirty or so present and spread out haphazardly before him that the proposal to form a Working Group to action the proposal to post minutes in

Tinipad had been turned down owing to a prior reformulation of the proposal in order to further define the term "Working Group" with reference not to the Working Groups of the District Assemblies of Madrid but to the Working Groups of the Madrid Coordinating Commission, which was made up of various Assemblies, not just one. The proposal had as its aim to open the Coordinating Commission to cross-organizational Working Groups and Assemblies and thus refute claims that the Commission was operationally vertical.

She swallowed down a mouthful of lukewarm water from a small plastic bottle that she had brought with her and hoped devoutly that the Ibuprofen she had taken with it would relieve a mounting headache.

There would be a sale of house plants in aid of evicted families, the man announced, before pausing to consult a frizzy-haired woman behind him. The postponed session of crystal healing, he resumed, would take place in a changed venue, which would be announced later but they had, together, to carry out a counter-offensive against a kleptocratic regime in the pay of big business which used unconstitutional strong-arm tactics and repressive legislation to deny basic rights and freedoms.

Erica took a look around. The women were almost all dressed in a low-key, nondescript fashion. In fact, only she and a couple of teenage girls were overtly flaunting what they had. It was the men, young men in their twenties and early thirties, who had dandified their image and clearly dedicated a lot of time and thought to self-grooming. A coiffured beard was almost de rigueur, as were spectacles. It wasn't possible that a generation of males had suddenly developed shortsightedness, so she assumed that a lot of the lenses were made of plain, unrefracted glass. Their air of self-preening was quite repulsive. One beard was decorated with daisies. Erica wondered whether this was what happened in a country after a protracted period of peacetime. Women carried on the patient struggle, as always, while men had no reason to act manly and degenerated into self-absorbed peacocks.

A thin woman took over the megaphone which now boomed so loudly that people instinctively looked up at apartments in a nearby block to see if anyone was being disturbed and coming to the windows to look for the source of the noise.

"Sisters and brothers, we need to revolutionize our language to redefine and refind ourselves in a non-sexist future. Why is day, the light of our life, masculine, while night and darkness are feminine? Our language may now allow for female lawyers and authors, but what about power, legal rights, time and the ego? These and so many more are male: male privileges and a male exclusivity. While they remain so, discrimination of women will continue, and cleaners and whores are destined always to be women. Our speech defines and assigns roles and the time has come for change that will recognize the full gender spectrum."

The woman went on to demand a syntactic reorganization of the Spanish language that would put the two better known biological sex genders on a par with a broad variety of sexual orientations and gender expressions from androgynous and asexual to genderqueer, LGBT and pangender.

The bold proposal for a wholesale and wildly complex rewriting of verbs and nouns and their articles took a bit of digesting, but was remarkably well received, Erica noted, by those present, who waggled their hands in silent but vigorous approval.

The megaphone was then claimed by a dishevelled man with a red face, who made it abundantly clear that he was of the opinion that the government was run by uncharitable and, moreover, disreputable individuals, who sought only their own advantage. It was also abundantly clear that he was very drunk. The man was eventually interrupted when his vehemence overstepped an unspoken rule and arms crossed in the air indicated that a change in speaker was in order.

The event struck Erica as a terribly unpromising first step on a trail that might lead to Zoe Iris Urquizo, but Pastori had insisted that it was her best bet and that she had to be there. Associates of Olga Vanderveldt were known to occasionally attend the Assemblies and also, by recording the proceedings on her police mobile, taking photos and asking questions, she would be gaining material for the analysts to work on in her ostensible role as an undercover infiltrator for the City government.

The agenda dragged on for another forty minutes until the Assembly finally agreed to utterly transform the existing political structure and then broke up. Erica hung around by the speakers' area, asking a couple of people how she might get involved and do more. Was a girl called Olga here? One of girls was suggesting a women's collective, "They're cool and that, really," when a man interrupted with a kind of snigger and started to bring up the debating points with Erica in particular, ignoring the other girl completely. He wore a grey robe from head to toe, clearly designed to suggest a certain depth and seriousness, even if it looked like a dress. The contrast with Erica's skimpy summer wear was quite salacious. As he talked and she looked away with feigned thoughtfulness, she felt his eyes roam over her.

When she complained that they weren't going far enough, he agreed completely. Wasn't there anyone more radical?, she wanted to know. He could, he said, bring her into contact with a group of people who were going "much deeper and much further with all this" and suggested they go for a drink. By this time, the other girl had already turned away.

"I'm Carina," she remembered. "Cari," she offered ingenuously and essayed the kind of pert body language that might suggest a keen, sexual nature beneath a vulnerable and sincere self.

"Fernando, but they call me Badu. Yeah."

Do they? She wanted to reply. *Or did you make up a nickname to make yourself sound more interesting? Yeah?*

They walked together towards the park exit. Erica shaded her eyes against the sun. "Can we go to a place where these people you're talking about get together?"

"It's a bit early. They tend to be, huh, night people."

"Oh, by the way, do you know a girl called Olga? I was told she could tell me about a thing going on this summer called Field of Light." She had her head turned innocently to one side, from where she could study his reaction with some precision.

He didn't know one or the other.

"I could find out."

Almost certainly a dead end on all counts. He was just some dickhead trying to get her in the sack. It was too much to expect anything else, really.

"How about later on, then? What time do they get together?" She turned a smile on him. "I have to go see my mum."

"Cool, cool. Cool." A slow shake of the head, thinking she was fobbing him off, deciding she might not be. "Ten o'clock's good."

"Ten o'clock? Where's the meeting place?" She sounded hopeful. "There's so much to talk about."

"Near San Bernardo." There was a hint of second thoughts about Badu Fernando's eyes, of having suggested something he shouldn't, that made her think she might not be wasting her time completely after all.

"Call me?" She got out the mauve police mobile and he told her his number, which she punched in and made him a missed call before waving goodbye.

She had a long wait until ten, but unless and until she got sucked into an undercover scene that might cause her movements to be monitored, or her domicile known, Erica could make off home and rest there, even sleep in her own bed.

Before that, though, she had a personal commitment to fulfil. After quickly quenching her thirst at a noisy café filled with immigrants, where one of them tried to chat her up, she took a stairwell from street level down to Sebastián's BMW, which she had borrowed while he commanded the ministerial Bentley, and drove from one underground car park to another, masked all the way by its tinted windows. From the basement of their apartment building, she took the lift up to the tenth floor, where it opened not onto a shared landing, but directly onto the front door of their flat. It was this small but crucial discretion that made her agree to move in with Sebastián at what was, for her, an unnecessarily expensive address. Her curious job spec and its abrupt physical transformations ruled out chance meetings with the neighbours.

In the bathroom, after a long pee, she peered at the face in the mirror with scant recognition. She looked so lightweight. For some reason, the silver glitter on her cheeks made her feel almost tearful. She massaged her breasts, which were tender, even a little sore, and then took the brown burqa, pulling it down over her head and body. This time, instead of producing instant anxiety, the sensation of confinement was offset by the image of the thing in the mirror. She even felt a faint amusement. The stubby spikes of her hair raised tiny bumps in the cotton hood, so that she looked like some freaky comic book character. Octopuswoman, she decided. She took the lift down and exited the building anonymously, using an emergency door from the parking area, and hailed a taxi to take her to the Centre for the Protection of Muslim Women.

• • • •

THE PRESS ROOM FILLED up quickly and a calmly professional buzz set the tone. The backdrop to a high stacked stage was dominated by a life-size photograph of a Grand Prix automobile, sporting the new racing team's green-and-gold livery and emblazoned with sponsorship logos. Sebastián stood at one end of a long table that was backed by seven chairs and set with as many microphones and bottles of water, the manufacturer's labels faced forward for the cameras. He looked over the heads of the accredited reporters to the rear of the hall and a voice in his ear told him that the doors were now closed and that Nessi, as they were calling the importunate Scottish journalist, hadn't shown. Taking quiet pleasure in his new role, he looked down upon the clutch of photographers crouched directly below the stage as if in obeisance, before he disappeared behind the display to perform his sole responsibility for the occasion, which was to tell the dignitaries that everything was ready.

The guest of honour, berobed in traditional Middle Eastern fashion, was listening to the Sports Minister without shifting his eyes from a line-up of girls wearing gold hotpants, green tops, peaked caps and radiant smiles. On his only other visit backstage, Sebastián had already seen the Prince ogling the Valencia Grid Babes and very clearly coming to some kind of agreement with one of the event organizers. Sebastián waited for a nod from Francisco Villalba before filing down to the Press Room floor to take his seat in the centre of the front row, just as the overhead stage lights came on.

The familiarly tousled mogul of Formula One began by announcing a great day for motor sport and Sebastián, after ascertaining that concentrating didn't help to make English any more comprehensible, resisted a temptation to cross his longs legs and relax. He would remain alert and composed.

Some of Sebastián's colleagues, including his superiors, believed that Elcano relished breathing the intoxicating oxygen of power, but those who knew him best would have told you that it was the elegance. Sebastián loved the daily stylishness of pressed suits, Ministerial savoir faire, the waxed, black cars, and a job well done. He had that confidence which comes from knowing that you are in the right job and made for it. This, combined with an earnest adherence to moral integrity, lent him a presence which, even more than his lofty physique and flawlessly suited appearance, discouraged the general public from approaching his official car when he was standing by it and secretly overawed some of the older, more experienced chauffeurs. Elcano overlooked the vulgar language and not infrequent peccadilloes of the politicians he served out of the elegance of loyalty and he took pride in contributing to the poised protection that was the due of legal authority. Francisco Villalba was quite right in recognizing him as a faithful servant in every sense.

It would not be too much to say that Sebastián was proud of reality, for his sense of the deep rightness of things, of another order underlying the visible world, explained to him with a sufficiency unto itself how he had come to rise to where he now was, to have promise and respect, to have a smart and commendable, even if strangely fractious, fiancée who needed his guidance, and to be well remunerated to point of having a clothes allowance. And to preserve the balance in this invisible harmony, to make firm and sound his reward before God and honour Him in his heart, Sebastián had faith in his ability to do the right thing when the time and challenge came, all of which gave this frankly good-looking young man from a modest but hardworking household both seriousness and the advantage of clarity. The world, however, and the people in it, did have a capacity for complexity that could catch him out in ways that seemed unfair.

When Prince Al Walid bin Zayed was introduced and the level of expectancy in the Press Room rose, so to his discomfort did the voice of Sebastián's conscience, as he recalled Erica's vehement denunciation of the man and why, so that his sense of completeness was hedged round by misgiving.

The Prince spoke into a microphone about his new Safi team, with which he planned to unsettle the dominant Mercedes, not to mention the Red Bulls, Ferraris and Maclarens. The public figures on stage looked extremely pleased with themselves.

Nessi! Nessi!

Sebastián felt suddenly hot in his suit. The device in his ear confirmed that the indefatigable journalist had somehow gained admission to the room. Although he was effectively along for the ride, Elcano was officially on the security team and he felt a flush of responsibility.

"What does Prince Al Walid think his team will bring to the racing scene?" asked a Dutch correspondent from the seats.

Eight rows back, five seats in from the right. She is dressed as a man.

Sebastián swallowed and kept his eyes trained forward on Al Walid. In the seat next to him, Villalba was looking contentedly composed. A dread of shame made Sebastián feel keenly protective of the Minister.

"How many races before you get your first podium?" asked an Italian reporter.

The Prince smiled indulgently. "We will have a long learning curve, but we have a winning team. We want to win."

"When will—" The woman had wrenched the microphone away from the Paris Match correspondent. The microphone went dead, but one could still hear Carol Sinclair insisting with her question. "When will you stand trial for the rape and murder of Maureen O'Keefe?"

The security detail that had moved into position either end of row eight went for her, but the first of them came up against unexpected resistance from one of the seated journalists whom he had he barged aside and whose indignant shove in return threw him off balance.

It gave Ms Sinclair a few extra seconds. She pulled off a sturdy shoe and flung it straight and hard at Al Walid bin Zayed's scornful and now suddenly alarmed face. Sebastián, who had already been getting to his feet in the front row, reached up a hand and caught it in mid-air, before hurrying instinctively away from cameras that switched en masse in his direction and could capture only his dark-grey suited back. Sinclair was detained to prevent her from commenting to her colleagues from the world's Press, and the conference was brought to as rapid a conclusion as dignity and the pretence of normality would permit, upon which Al Walid similarly disappeared from view.

When the hero of the hour was presented later to the Prince at the latter's wish, the small-eyed man asked him what he would accept as a gift. To make such a gesture was not just a custom in his country, he told Sebastián, but a matter of honour. He should speak and not be shy.

The Minister and the Prince's entourage waited for the young man to overcome his embarrassment. Sebastián's mind was awhirl. At a fateful loss, he finally managed: "For myself I ask nothing. But perhaps the Prince might make a simple contribution in his handsome name to a centre in Madrid for the protection of Muslim girls."

There followed a significant silence.

Under any other circumstances, most any proposition would have been recorded by a lackey, attended to, and that would have been an end to it. But in the context of the Prince's personal history, which was officially known to no one present but unofficially known to them all, such a particular request from the mouth of a government servant could only be one of two things: either inadmissibly ignorant, or daringly insolent.

It hardly mattered which, because the ambiguity on its own was unacceptable, but Sebastián, in his artless way, was in fact guilty on both counts. He was convinced that he was doing the potentate a favour. It gave Al Walid the opportunity to demonstrate his support for Muslims in the host country, while recognizing a more enlightened expression of Islam within the framework of Spanish law.

Never mind that such a law did not overlook the rape and murder of women and girls.

If the pitfall of righteousness is tactlessness, Sebastián had walked straight into it. He had blundered into the ultimate high-stakes game called diplomacy, whose first and cardinal rule is that the power players alone are allowed to play. Surely, thought the Prince, it was unthinkable that this minion, who had moments ago saved his face and was now being granted a boon, could respond with effrontery. In Al Walid bin Zayed's palace, a servant who aimed an affront at his master, let alone his master's guest, simply did not value his physical well-being for the rest of his miserable life. But one way or another, he had been put on the spot. Everything now hinged on his personal interpretation. To recognize the request as impudence would be tantamount to admitting certain things and oblige him to a defence of his honour. He would have to take abrupt leave of the country, shaking the dust of Spain from his feet, and withdraw from the Formula One sponsorship altogether. Not to mention a certain armaments deal worth two billion.

If the Saudi's eyes that bore into Sebastián gave nothing away, the Minister's most certainly did. Elcano had overstepped a diplomatic mark by a mile and Francisco Villalba turned a look of murder on him.

• • • •

"HI, BADU. WHAT HAPPENED to the cool robe?"

He seemed quite a lot shorter without it and Erica hardly recognized him to begin with. It entertained her to see him look so unimpressive without it, the more so since she had got rid of her own equally shapeless garment on the way there, tossing the brown burqa into a skip after leaving the Centre for the Protection of Muslim Women.

She had been warmly received by the two Lebanese women who evidently ran the place on a shoestring, but so indifferently by the women whom she had been responsible, if only in part, for saving from slavery that she wondered why she had bothered going. All they had wanted to know was what she could do to improve the food there. For the first and last time, Erica had been grateful for the burqa, which concealed her face and its expression. She had turned and left, glad to put behind her the inadequate refuge which advertised itself as Residencia La Paloma, and its depressing, run-down atmosphere. It was hard to imagine how the goofy security guard on the door might offer any real protection from an enraged husband who knew where to come.

Anyway, Badu it was. The conceited look on his face, reinforced by regulation glasses and an attempt at a beard, marked him out as the same creep she had met at the Assembly that morning. Even his walk, shambling and supercilious, feet falling languidly inwards but chest pushed out, was a studied way of letting you know how self-satisfied he was.

"It's total now," said Badu, in what Erica imagined was supposed to be an arcane manner. He then took a new fifty-euro note from his pocket and slowly tore it to bits in front of her eyes, letting the pieces fall to the pavement. Unbelievable. The guy had to be the biggest twat she had ever met. The look on a passer-by's face said much the same thing. Badu took out some more banknotes.

"Stop it," she said. His extravagant littering was attracting attention.

"They're not real," he said. "We've started to make them. What more eloquent way of showing up the lie on which the financial police state is based? We are going to leave them in public places, hundreds of them, thousands. In shops, in Metro stations, in government offices, until people wake up to the grand hoax played on them. Until they reject the bogus money that the government prints. Here, take some."

They were surprisingly good counterfeits on quality paper. She had to hand it to them, whoever they were. If their strategy were equally sophisticated, they would be quite a formidable outfit. But Badu's plan of action was on the level of a schoolboyish prank, one for which he faced a good eight years in prison. Erica pocketed the neat, shiny bills for the forensic lab to examine later. The police mobile she carried with her had the GPS function enabled, allowing Pastori's small team to follow her movements, and she now messaged Pastori to let her know that she should pinpoint her next stop.

Going to meet some cool guys! Hope they're with the programme. Haven't heard from Tanya, have you?

Tanya was their codename for Zoe.

Hey Cariiii!! Hope they're cute with it haha! ☺ Tanya sez she'll be @ Transformer Fair 2mro. Don't miss it!! BTW, any idea wot the White Door is??

The White Door? She had no idea. But if Pastori was asking, then it mattered.

Badu led her into a squatted building, where cheap bottled drinks were sold from a crate in a sort of reception room that was otherwise filled with a jumble of notices and people and a nervous dog. Erica, now Carina, let herself be invited by Badu to a disappointingly warm bottle of beer. They climbed a rickety staircase to the third floor, from where a landing offered four identical doors. Before they went in to meet the supposed plotters, Carina placed a hand on Badu-Fernando's shoulder and he turned around brusquely, as if shocked. His desirable acquaintance raised her small bottle and clinked it against his own in camaraderie.

"One, two, three, four, one, two, three, four," she danced a finger round the doors. "Hey, Badu, do you know what the White Door is?"

"Huh, yeah, well, it's where you pass through to, you know, the White Door, to be free of the ego and that. I'm really interested in that, too. We should get together on that. We're in here," he motioned, knocking.

The room had a window open to the hot, dirty night, a few small tables and a single chair, which was occupied by a guy staring at a laptop screen, while another looked over his shoulder. A girl with a sour expression was rolling a joint and a fourth member of the group—if it was a group—corpulent in an ill-fitting black T-shirt, stood by the window wearing a sardonic smile or a sneer. Erica couldn't tell which. She was struck by how none of them returned Badu's greeting or took any interest in herself. The two guys at the computer exchanged mumbled comments about what they were looking at. Badu led her to one side to half-sit on the wooden tables. They reminded Erica of school desks. To her frustration, Badu now decided to be interesting.

"I think one has to grow on different fronts without limiting oneself to just one aspect." He made a little *huh* by means of suggesting that what he had just said surprised even him with its insight. "Yeah, I'm thinking of going back to the guitar." When she didn't prompt him, "Classical and bass," he went on."They kind of feedback each other in an ongoing dialogue."

"So where's the action?" Carina said out loud to the room.

Fernando's shoulders were hunched in a questioning shrug. She didn't seem to be following his line of creative reasoning.

"I said, where's the fucking action, Badu? You told me there were people getting radical with shit and all I see is a couple of anal geeks, a pothead and a dummy in the corner."

"Tsss," countered dummy and the girl made a gesture with her hand as if physically wounded.

"No, that's okay," said the fellow standing by the computer, whose oddly angular face really did make him look geeky. "That's what we're looking for. What's your name?"

"Carina."

"What's your angle, Carina?"

"Fight back. Let them know we won't take it lying down. The system's rotten all the way through. We gotta act or it'll rot us, too. And I don't mean play with Monopoly money." She waved Badu's spurious banknotes in the air.

"Fucking yeah," said the girl. The stink of marijuana coming from her made Erica want very much to break cover and arrest her. Fortunately, Erica's fierce stare made Carina look all the more defiant.

"It's so fucked up, man," said Badu.

The smile or sneer at the window was silent but unchanged.

"You want action? Tonight we have action. You in?" said the guy sitting at the laptop, who lent back in his chair and sounded serious. He was quite muscular and had a tattoo of a piranha on his neck.

"If it's serious: yes. What's it all about?"

"We're going to leave our mark on a bank."

Ten minutes later, Carina had the meeting place and time for the action. She had even joined their WhatsApp group. It was so facile—they were so naïve—that she felt suddenly depressed. She would meet them there, she said, going to the door, and held a hand up when Badu made a move to accompany her.

She found a café-bar on the next block where she could sit alone and plan her contribution for later that night. To delve deeper into the underground anti-system scene, if such a set-up really existed, she would have to earn some respect. She took two long gulps of an energy drink and used the mobile to retrieve some notes that she had taken during a training course on counterinsurgency. The owner, who had been eyeing the punk warily ever since she sat down by a window near the exit, sent his Ecuadorean waiter to her table.

"That's two euros twenty. He says to pay now," the waiter requested gently.

Erica put her phone face down on the table, rather than leave in open view instructions on how to make an incendiary device, and gave him the coins out of a zipped cotton purse. The summer evening had turned dark and her face in the window was superimposed on shadowy passers-by in the street. For some reason, tiredness perhaps, she half-expected to see Badu Fernando go by dressed again in his cool-bestowing robe.

She picked up the mobile and reread the instructions in her notes. The hardware stores were closed at this time of night, but the Chinese one-euro shops stayed open until eleven and she could get the missing ingredient she needed from their garden supplies. After which, she still had a long wait. She wouldn't be meeting the others until the middle of the night.

What could she do? Her back ached and her breasts felt sensitive again. She felt a real need to stay in character and had already decided against going home and seeing Sebastián, who should be home from Valencia by now. In any case, she felt somehow ashamed to face him, the model of rectitude, planning what she was planning to do; having to listen to him as he told her about his day with the Formula One celebrities, having to sound interested and ask questions. On the other hand, she didn't feel like being alone and she also needed a hand from someone who wouldn't ask awkward questions. Being on assignment meant she had to forget all about her meagre handful of friends and family. Her parents' was the very last place she could go. The next day, she remembered, was Alfonso and María's anniversary dinner, although there was a good chance the job might excuse her absence. That left nowhere and no one. There was Dani. Absolutely no way, she shook her head at the thought of her previous boyfriend, but then punched his number.

"I'm coming over," she said and hung up.

As she left the café, she typed #100 into the phone to request that Pastori divert police patrols away from the bank they were going to hit between three a.m. and five a.m., but then didn't hit the call button. She wasn't sure that she could justify damage to private property and Pastori might order her off it.

Before she took the Metro to Dani's apartment block, she stopped at a Chinese store to buy a sack of fertilizer, making sure that it had a high urea content.

• • • •

SEBASTIÁN SAT ON ONE of the straight-backed dining chairs in their apartment and stroked his nose, a gesture he knew he only made when he was severely perturbed. One of his feet, at the end of a crossed leg, wouldn't keep still either, twitching an impatient tempo. He had taken his jacket and tie off, but his dangling foot still wore a dark grey sock and a shiny black shoe.

He knew that he shouldn't expect to see her, but that didn't prevent him feeling resentful. The fact that he couldn't call Erica during an undercover operation riled him and a sense of frustration and abandonment now took hold of him in their empty home. Sunken deep in private shame, he didn't really want to tell her about the shocking blunder he had made, but neither did he want to be left alone with it.

The good news was that the sponsorship deal was going ahead as planned, but Sebastián was still in the doghouse. A ministerial aide had instructed him to come up with the details of the centre for Muslim girls, which Al Walid was now honour-bound to take into consideration. It was a deplorable predicament. Even after setting aside certain unmentionable matters, the Prince's personal profession of Islamic faith saw the existence of such a facility, however small, as an abomination in the eyes of Allah, who desired women to serve their menfolk. An independent woman was a disobedient woman and punishment was her means of correction. Heaven forbid that her misdemeanours be rewarded with food and shelter.

But Sebastián had cornered him and he had to keep his word. In the car, all the way back from Valencia and upon leaving him in Madrid, the Minister had not addressed a single word to his driver.

• • • •

AT 3.30 A.M., THEY parked around the corner from the bank in a side street. The target was situated in the city's financial district, where there were very few people out on the streets and even fewer reasons to be there. Residential apartments, such as there were, occupied higher floors above the commercial premises, and their occupants hid away in routine anonymity.

It had been decided that four of them would take part in the action: two boys and two girls, pretending to be couples. Carina was told in the car that her boyfriend, the overweight guy in the black T-shirt, whose name was Osvaldo, would spray-paint a slogan on the wall of the bank while the other three covered him and kept a look-out. Badu wasn't included, or even mentioned.

The bank was at the far end of the street, where it occupied a corner with a broad avenue, along which an occasional car or taxi passed. They approached it walking down the side street lined with parked cars, but otherwise deserted. Osvaldo went straight to work, stencilling large black capital letters above the ATM in the wall of the side street.

THE BANK WILL PAY

It was all over very quickly.

"Let's go," he said and three of them started walking quickly back the way they had come.

Carina let them go. She remained at the ATM machine directly beneath the slogan and placed on its metal keyboard a pouch made from newspaper. In it were four hundred grams of fertilizer and from a scrimped opening at the top there protruded a wad of cotton wool.

"Hey, come on!" Miguel, the guy who she thought of as the group's leader, spoke in a low voice from twenty yards up the street. The others had stopped, too.

Erica took what had been a vinegar bottle out of her shoulder bag and unscrewed the top. As she poured a little gasoline from it onto the cotton wool, some of it spilled onto the ATM's tilted keyboard and the newspaper pouch slipped down a little. She moved it up again carefully with her finger nails until it lodged against the screen.

The others were coming back to her. She gestured urgently to send them away. A car went by in the avenue and the driver looked at her, but didn't slow down and kept on his way.

She stuffed a length of ripped-up Pink Floyd T-shirt into the neck of the bottle and tipped it upside down. It leaked more than she expected, wetting her fingers with petrol and dripping onto the pavement. She dabbed her hands quickly on the other, dry end of the T-shirt. It was old and full of holes already, but Dani had been loath to part with it.

The other three were still hovering halfway down the street, not knowing if they should abandon her or not. After wrapping the long end of the ragged cotton strip under the bottle, she hurried to the corner to look up and down the avenue for people and vehicles. It was all clear. No pedestrians and just couple of cars passing by on the far side. Erica returned to the ATM on which the newspaper pouch looked like an unwanted kebab.

She stepped carefully back into the street between a parked car and a van. Squeezing a lighter out of a tight shorts pocket, she flicked it alight with a shaky hand. As soon as the strip of T-shirt fizzled, she threw the bottle at the brick wall of the bank and ducked behind the van. Her companions, who were already concerned and about to be horror-struck, saw it hit the wall a good metre wide of the ATM.

It was a poor throw and the bottle failed to break, but the petrol inside caught alight and exploded its glass container before it hit the paving. A flash fire ran up the building and ignited the home-made bomb Erica had made in Police Sergeant Daniel García's bathroom before her ex-boyfriend's disbelieving eyes, booming a clap of splintering sound that caused the air around their heads to shudder. Erica was shoved violently to the ground, not by the explosion itself but by the van she had sheltered behind and which rocked sideways onto two wheels before thumping back down to its original position, its windows shattered. Car alarms woke up and went off. She could see three backs disappearing round the corner to where the car was parked and she managed to get up, but her knees wanted to betray her and her lungs were hot. She tried, but with the shock she couldn't run properly. An echoing clap was reverberating its angry way down the street, from wall to wall, like a startled firebird. There was blood. Her face and legs and arms and scalp were hurting. Now cars were stopping and a municipal rubbish truck with a flashing yellow light. She hobbled to the corner and the car braked for her ten metres from where it had pulled out. Frightened faces in the car let her in. Lights were already on in a score of apartment windows as they made a right turn and shouted about where they could possibly go.

• • • •

THE REST OF THAT STIFLING night was spent tediously incarcerated in Jaco's poky apartment. When he opened the door, Erica recognized the ratty features of the computer geek from that afternoon. He was still awake, if not expecting them, and soon grew as excited as his *compañeros* as he heard about Carina's daring exploit.

They went over the whole thing ad infinitum and also extremely rowdily, since the blast had left them all not only charged up, but also partially deaf. At one point, a hammering on the ceiling from the apartment upstairs seemed to challenge how heroic they really were. They continued in urgent whispers that soon rose again into loud disagreement.

Carina's fellow conspirators had been unhurt in the explosion, except for Miguel twisting an ankle, but they were by no means indifferent. The group was split into two camps. Carina's act was either unforgivably foolish, or bold and magnificent, depending on who was doing the talking at the time.

Miguel and Zeta were adamant that Carina had exhibited fascist unsolidarity in ignoring the democratic dynamic and had put them all in danger. She had had no right to decide for them all.

Jaco, on the other hand, was crooningly enthusiastic. "We are the Bankía bombers, you bastards. It's real. This is it. It's manifest."

Osvaldo was clearly nervous that his car might be identified, but he was inclined to go along with Jaco and claim a famous blow for their cause.

Carina herself was silent, hearing most of the discussion from Jaco's bathroom, where she lay for a long while submerged in a bathtub filled with cold water. She had been lucky, but not that lucky. The van had shielded her from the worst of the fertilizer bomb blast and the flying glass and masonry, but not all of it. The petrol flare of her Molotov cocktail had curled around the parked vehicles and scorched her skin. Jaco's flat had no cosmetic cream and no air conditioning, either. The bathtub was her only refuge. How much was burn damage and how much was superficial, she couldn't tell. Parts of her were burning red and blood tinged the water. The overhead light hurt her eyes and she called Zeta to extinguish it, sinking then deep into the water, where she lay in the dark with only her mouth and nostrils clear of the surface.

The shocked mind behind her watery eyes was at a loss to explain what the hell had got into her. To get kudos in the anti-system network? To get further in? But the Chief had made it clear that there *was* no insurgency. A passive role was what he had instructed. And to look after the girl. The girl was the mission. Today was Saturday already and Pastori had told her to look out for Zoe Iris at a fair called Transformer. As if that wasn't enough, Jaco's airless hole of a flat and the endless reiteration of the same arguments in the living room were making her claustrophobic.

She wanted badly to get out of there, but she dared not leave empty-handed. Her job was probably on the line. The one factor she had in her favour was that the other three were somewhat in awe of her. At eight a.m., she got out of the water and walked dripping and naked into the living room. The others stopped their arguing.

"There are things that I want," she told them croakily.

Her shockingly pink face, singed hair spikes and ample breasts over seared arms and legs made her look like a character in a porn horror flick. Miguel gave up his chair for her and she sat down. Zeta offered her a pungent joint before realizing her mistake and waving its smoke away from Carina's face.

"Three things. One: if you're the part-time wimps I think you are, you're no good to me. I want in on the real people. Who are they? Where do I find them? Two: a woman called Olga Vanderveldt. I need to find her. Three: phone calls. If I don't check in, people will start wondering and that's not good for us. If you have a problem with that, fuck you, because I'm going to make them anyway. Don't worry, my mobile has no GPS fix," she said truthfully, having disabled it temporarily so that Pastori couldn't interfere with her plan.

They had no idea who the Olga woman was, or anyone committed to the hardcore direct action that Carina espoused. Jaco, though, as if waiting for this invitation, brought over his laptop and set it up in front of her, whereupon his speechlessness at the sight of the pubes between her uncrossed legs turned into jabbering about how the real revolution was the invisible revolution and the nameless warriors hacking deep into the heart of the iniquitous system.

"Babylon," said Zeta.

"This code takes me into the Treasury site," said Jaco.

Erica spluttered a cough of genuine astonishment and cleared her throat. "You can hack the Treasury?" *Good grief!* "You can see what's going on? Payments? You can hack them? Alter them? Move money?"

"Not the Treasury itself," Jaco admitted. "It's the public page. And I can't access their algorithms but I can totally block the page. Block all public access with a message that fills the entire screen. We're just waiting for the moment."

Erica fought back her disappointment. Just when she thought she had uncovered a serious threat to national security and a face behind the hackers' Anonymous masks, it turned out once again that she was dealing with amateurs. All Jaco could do was impede members of the public from visiting an official government website that had no usefulness whatsoever other than streamlining income tax payments via the downloading of the standard form.

Oh well. It would have to do. They would all have to take their chances.

"The moment has arrived," she said.

Jaco's eyes lit up. "Are we agreed?"

They were. Troubled by the impasse in which they found themselves, the conspirators put hope in an action that might be construed as purposeful. Even Zeta and Miguel saw that they might later be hailed as the instigators: that they really might be message of change.

Carina went to the bathroom to get dressed and get her phone. By the time she had got through to Sebastián, the Treasury's Homepage had been replaced by a yellow and black error message and their adopted declaration:

THE BANK WILL PAY

• • • •

"IT'S ME."

It was Erica, calling from an unidentified number. She hadn't made it home at all that night.

After an early morning work-out at the twenty-four-hour gym where they were both members, Sebastián had read the Saturday papers online and, all in all, felt a lot better about the world than he had the previous night.

The headlines were divided between a corruption scandal and the first bomb attack in Madrid since 2004, when an Islamic cell had blown up commuter trains, although this time it was clearly little more than escalated vandalism. His intervention to protect the new Formula One team sponsor was also deemed to be newsworthy, however, and even being triumphed as an act worthy of Clint Eastwood. "*In the Line of Fire,*" proclaimed the press. He had gone to bed fearing for his job, but now he realized that the Ministry's diplomatic embarrassment was a media hero. And the media mattered.

"Have you seen the news?" he asked. "I'm a bit famous."

Silence on the other end.

"Wait till you see. Well, it can wait until tonight."

Her parents, she remembered. The long planned-for dinner.

"Listen, I probably can't make it tonight."

"But it's their anniversary. We promised."

"I'm not well."

"Well, you should make an effort. We can always leave early. Are you working?" Worry threatened to mutate into jealousy in Sebastián's mind.

"Yes. I have to go. Look, I'll call you back, OK?"

• • • •

SHE IMAGINED THE AFFRONTED expression on his face and looked round at the silent figures of her companions in the darkened apartment. For some reason, they seemed to think that lowering the shutters would conceal their whereabouts.

"Fucking amazing," murmured Miguel, checking the screen image and its blunt three-word message against the url of the government website.

Jaco had hacked it alright.

"We should celebrate," Jaco said.

"There's no food," said Osvaldo, whose body odour had for some time been dominating the apartment's twenty-five square metres. "I guess we can get pizza."

Jaco got out half a bottle of peach brandy and a full one of gin, but there was only heavily chlorinated tap water to mix it with and nothing more than a tin of frankfurter sausages to share between them.

Erica made a second call, this time to Pastori.

"Carina, sweetie! How are you? I never see you anymore. What's happening with you? We must meet up. We really must."

The over-ebullience in Pastori's tone said it all.

"Hi, yeah, well, maybe later. I got real bad sunburn and I can't bear anyone to see me until it wears off."

"I know what you mean. Just imagine the photos!"

Pastori told her agent everything she needed to know. The city police had recorded images from street CCTV, or people had taken photos of them as they ran to the car, got in it, drove away. Fuck. The car would be found and the trail would lead to them in the apartment. They had hours at most. Maybe minutes.

"Can you wait until tomorrow?" *Hold off. Give me a chance to salvage something from this.*

"Not really. Don't forget Tanya's expecting you at the fair, but come by and see me first, okay?"

When Carina said she had to leave, Miguel, the one with the piranha tattoo, and the girl, Zeta, said no. They had to stay together and lay low. In any case, leaving the flat looking like the way she did would compromise them all.

"Jaco, what do you say? Osvaldo?" Carina asked.

"She's a fucking hero. She can do what she wants," Jaco said. He had been her staunch supporter ever since they had holed up in his dingy digs in the north-west of town.

Osvaldo, clearly keen to be out of there himself, agreed.

Erica called Sebastián again, going to the window and raising the corner of a shutter. "I need you to do something important for me. Pick me up as soon as you can. Corner of Calle de Leñeros and María Pedraza. There's a furniture shop. Wait there and I'll come to you. And one more thing: drive like I do."

"It's not safe here," she told the others after she'd clicked off. "Get out now. I mean it. We should split up and communicate via email. We'll use this account." She wrote down the day's date followed by xyyzzz@yahoo.com and a password, but an inertia seemed to have overcome the others in contradistinction to her urgency.

Jaco lent her a long-sleeved shirt to cover her pink skin and she went to the bathroom to see how she looked. Horrendous. For a third morning running, she felt sick to her stomach. It was becoming a habit. She hadn't slept. None of them had. She stopped tears from forming in her eyes by scooping cold water into her face and dabbing them dry with Jaco's only towel, which he never washed and smelled foul.

When she emerged from the bathroom, her frizzled hair shaved off and ready to leave, they were crowded round the laptop. Osvaldo pointed at the screen. An early morning news photo showed their graffiti slogan above the blackened hole of the bank's ATM. Fire officers and police had cordoned off a section of the street that appeared to be covered by leaves from the trees blown off by the explosion, only the leaves were too regular and there were too many of them. It was money, she realized. The blast had expelled cash from the ATM machine onto the street, where the paper notes lay looking as meaningless as Badu's counterfeits.

The bank will pay.

Her vandalism hadn't quite made the national headlines, but after Jaco's little publicity stunt just now, by lunchtime it certainly would.

Erica waited by the window until Sebastián's BMW arrived and stopped outside the furniture shop. As she made for the door, Zeta offered Carina one of five shots of neat gin poured to toast their success, but she refused.

To the girl's offended look, she said: "I'm pregnant."

Her burned skin chafing beneath the shirt and a floppy hat, Erica crossed the street and got in the car.

"Just drive," she said to Sebastián.

"Darling," he lent across to kiss her anyway. "You'll never guess what happened. Or have you seen the papers? I'm not sure I have a job anymore. Are you alright?"

Sebastián glanced over to his girlfriend to see that she was shaking with laughter. For some unimaginable reason, she found his momentous news, which he was about to rationalize at some length, hilarious.

"You look a bit odd," he said.

"Take me home," said Erica.

Sebastián stopped at a chemist's when Erica, quiet and self-contained in the passenger seat, asked him to buy some aloe gel. He came back from the shop with a tiny tube of gel, which he asked her not to put it on in the car.

"If it stains, I don't know, it might be permanent. We'll be home in three minutes."

Sebastián opened the front door and she went straight to the bathroom. She took off the floppy hat, shook the silly little tube from its plastic bag and squeezed out the entire contents to smooth over her face and neck. Her skin was screaming out for it. "Would you like a drink?" she heard. "Water," she said loud and clear. Then she found a blue-lidded pot of cold cream, almost full, plenty enough for the rest of her. She even smeared the cream over the parts where she hadn't been scorched. Belly, bottom, nipples, aching back, everywhere. Then she sat on the loo, put her head back and breathed in the air-conditioned coolness. Under the salve and lotion she felt helpless and anointed, like a sacrificial offering. Erica looked down at her pudenda, which she had exhibited to the four hapless activists like some untouchable Amazon queen, then up at the mirrored bathroom cabinet, possessed by an urgent need to know. Seconds later, she had ambushed it and was sitting down again with a pregnancy testing kit. The excuse she had made to Zeta in order to avoid having to drink warm, neat gin now reminded her of an array of symptoms she had been experiencing recently. She peed on the stick for seven or eight seconds. Sebastián called her name. "Just a minute," she sang. As she waited the five long minutes that the test tortured a woman with, she messaged Pastori. *Hey, where's the Transformer gig?* The reply, a park in the south of the city, pinged into her mobile with emphatic abruptness and a smiley face.

She looked at herself in the mirror and felt her skin. It was going to be alright. She must have been on the outer limit of the petrol flash. It looked worse than it really was. She checked the time and then the test stick.

Two purple stripes said: "Positive."

He looked, she thought, like a hopeful dog, standing outside the bathroom door with her glass of water. How long had he been there?

"You've shaved your hair off," he said.

"Come and lie with me," she said, and when it hurt her skin to be touching his, she went to the kitchen and made them a breakfast of eggs and fruit and coffee. She was hungry again. She sat down in a gossamer negligee and clicked on the TV. When the news item Sebastián was hoping for didn't come on to give him the cue he now felt he needed to tell her about Valencia, he retreated behind a copy of Esquire magazine. Erica, though, as if reliving a bad dream, listened to the newscaster report a two-pronged attack by unidentified terrorists who had bombed a Madrid bank and simultaneously targeted a government website. "An unprecedented terrorist attack on civil liberties," said the government's vice president in his gravest tone and Madrid's mayoress declared: "These people are terrorists and murderers. On a Sunday morning, people are preparing to go to church. We will defend Madrid for decent people and their families."

"She got it wrong," Sebastián said, looking at an advertisement for a watch he was fairly sure none of the other drivers had.

Yes, thought Erica. The website hack wasn't simultaneous. It was an afterthought.

"It's Saturday," Sebastián pointed out.

The news broadcast ended with the weatherman standing next to a map scattered with yellow suns and temperatures in the high thirties, looking apologetic. He ran through the familiar daily ritual of predicting unchanged summer heat throughout the country.

Erica went over to Sebastián's armchair and stood behind it, mussing his thick hair and kneading his scalp with her fingertips.

"That's nice." He closed his eyes and let the magazine rest in his lap.

The first TV commercial was for Natural Asturias. The lightest of touches of hands on percussion, accompanied by a single flute, was joined by melodious bagpipes as a sequence of brief videos presented lofty mountains, chamois deer, alpine flowers, dancers with hands held high, blue sea beneath high cliffs, a placid, stumpy horse on a heath thick with mist, an exquisite, stone-built hamlet... Erica found herself drawn into it, following the flute's peaceful invocation which desired to rescue her from any suffering that was past or might become, and deliver her into an eternal present in which eagles are flying high, a woman serves from a vat of rich bean stew at a fair, a family walks the trail of a scenic canyon and mock dinosaurs pose outside a museum by the coast; elsewhere, boats bob at a fishing village and canoes fill a broad river on a day of pageant, where a waiter holds a bottle above his head to decant cider into a tumbler. The bagpipes broke into to a jaunty rhythm as an emblematic peak filled the TV screen, a brown bear reached into a tree for berries, water gushed down from Covadonga's high cave, visitors admired art in the Niemeyer Centre, the sea lapped gently at a sandy cove and a milkmaid held up a glass of fresh cream from the cow.

Erica was spellbound. She felt safe. Safe like a little girl in a playworld, where promises were sacred. This is your country: it does exist, a conviction told her. It ended, and an advert for car insurance began. Erica reached for the remote on the arm of the chair and silenced it, but the conjuring illusion was lost already and would not return. She recalled the poster she had seen from inside the burqa, in the square. The brown cows and the healthy smile of the girl. The tourists blind to it, staring at their map.

The land in the north seemed once again to be somehow forbidden to her. She felt inexplicably saddened by it, unworthy of it, suspicious of it. Reality was what she had to deal with. The campaign by the Asturian Tourism Board might have been clever and captivating, but her mind had switched back to police mode.

Sebastián had dropped off. Left on her own in the silent apartment, concentration returned to her like an unexpected visitor. She wasn't confused. She certainly wasn't Carina. She was Erica Sánchez Morales and she was going to get her head screwed back on, no matter that it was now bald, no matter that she hadn't slept. Before she left for the Transformer Fair, where she hoped to find Zoe Iris and have some mitigating, if not career-saving, news to deliver to Detective Inspector Pastori, she took a notepad from Zoe's folder to jot down a chronological account of her actions of the previous day and her expenses.

She couldn't really claim for the ingredients of the bomb, which had only amounted to a bag of fertilizer, anyway. The cotton wool and the petrol had been provided by Dani, and in the dirty excitement of the hour spent at his flat, after measuring the fertilizer, pouring it onto the open pages of an old football newspaper and twisting it closed, ripping up his old T-shirt, after pouring the petrol into the empty vinegar bottle and tightening the cap, spilling a little as they had no funnel, the fumes stinking in their nostrils in the evening heat, she had fucked him, all the time thinking that she was buying his connivance and silence, knowing very well that she might incriminate him, and it had turned her on in a way she had never imagined. She would have felt despicable, but the feeling had been somehow deferred.

She wrote down 2.20 € for the coffee, together with the place and time, omitting the twenty-cent tip she had left for the courteous barman, which would have been improper. She took a long look at Zoe's picture and made sure the police mobile was charged.

Meet you here at 9 pm before going to my parents. Hope you had sweet dreams xx, she wrote for Sebastián on two coloured post-its and went to check her appearance for a last time in the bathroom mirror. Blotched, she thought. Bright pink in patches, and the abrasions on her knees and forearms from falling on the road were bruising up purple and yellow. She looked involuntarily at her belly in the reflection, put on a floppy hat and slipped out the door.

••••

THE TRANSFORMER FAIR was being staged at an exhibition centre, spread out between two indoor pavilions and marquees erected in an open-air park which was also lined with stalls. For an event aimed ostensibly at New Agers and alternative types, it was drearily commercial. She even had to pay to get in. There were a few free attractions, where one could learn to juggle, do face painting, discover one's chakras or make holistic soap, but even these were linked to some product or other that you could subsequently buy.

There were up to a couple of thousand people, all rather standardized and conventionally trendy, and Erica decided that Carina would make a body fashion statement by removing her hat, only to put it straight back on as the sun burned fiercely into her scalp and face.

She dipped inside a tent for African Awareness where Senegalese music was being played, reasoning that she might luck upon Zoe here, given her sensibilities. There was no band, only a sound system and a choice of charities signing people up for monthly donations by direct debit. Zoe wasn't here, or at the Aromatherapy Bliss, or in the excruciatingly hushed felinotherapy room, where a strictly limited number of people were paying twenty euros to sit or lie on cushions for half an hour, while cats did the same or walked round, allowing themselves to be meaningfully stroked or ignoring the po-faced humans altogether. All in all, Erica thought, I've seen happier people at a police station.

The Fair was filling up. The temperature was rising by the minute and the best business was being done by a stall selling eco-cocktails. But for the queue, Erica would have coughed up for an over-priced bio-mojito because her gruelling night was catching up with her and she was feeling blearily irritable. The young crowd, her own generation, was alien and irritating to her, complacently lost, self-infatuated and witless, lining up to buy experiential satisfaction and personal growth as if they were burgers.

The next tent was busier. It was dedicated to Universal Creation and those present sat cross-legged on the ground in concentric rings while a man, standing at their centre in a long robe, told them how to do it. Erica scanned the group thinking initially of Badu and was relieved not to see him, but there, in the second row back from the speaker, was Zoe Iris Urquizo, looking very intense, and very young.

It was an unthreatening scene, posited on peaceful togetherness. A promising place to establish a contact. Erica looked around, feeling good about her chances. She felt like a predator about to circle before moving in on the kill. Towards the exit of the tent there was a trestle table with books and CDs for sale, and those who so desired could contribute two euros to sound a Tibetan gong in the cause of world peace and light an incense stick. The robe invited the audience to participate and left the stage to sit down in a space set aside for him.

A man got up and stepped between two seated girls into the intimate centre circle.

"It can't wait. The time is now. We have to be curing ego with love and sending that love out into the world. What people don't understand is..."

Erica bided her time. As soon as he finished, sitting back down in the crowd to appreciative clapping, she made for the spot he had vacated. She was hissed and shushed at by more than one person, causing her to suspect that the event was staged, but she ignored them and occupied the centre where all eyes were turned on her, even if there was still pockets of low talk in the tent. She took off the broad, floppy hat.

"My name is Carina and I hurt myself."

She held out her scorched arms and the murmuring stopped.

"Yesterday. I don't know why. I had to do something. I just wanted to scream, but I knew that if I did, I wouldn't stop. I would die screaming. They would say I was mad and take me away, but I would still die. My family isn't a family. I hated everything: and now this. I'm sorry and I'm not sorry, you know? But it's over now. Now I have renounced violence. I'm ready for this: for change. When I saw the name of the fair, I knew I had to come. 'Transformer.' And now this. I had to be here."

She stopped, genuinely lost for words, and some applause, encouraging or nervous, accompanied her as she went and sat down next to Zoe, who made room for her compliantly. The woman on Zoe's other side leaned forward to look across at her. She had large, cordial eyes.

When the session of sharing concluded, the gathering did not break up immediately, as people purported to be nice to those in their immediate vicinity. Erica stood up, looking at the girl next to her and blowing out her cheeks as in relief. To her satisfaction, Zoe smiled, however weakly. But it was the other woman who spoke. "I'm Olga. Would you like to have a drink with us?"

It was as easy as that. She followed them out of the tent, pausing with them to be given a leaflet about the principles of Universal Creation and make a kind of reverential curtsey as she received it.

They walked over to a drinks stall, where Zoe Iris bought them all some iced lemonade but then stood back diffidently.

"Tell me about yourself." The woman called Olga had a beaming smile that Erica found disconcerting. She was thirty-something and very good-looking, but more than a little intense. Her eyes shone like floodlights and Erica was tempted to stare her down, but as Carina she looked instead into her plastic cup.

"I'm just lost. Nobody really understands. You heard me but you don't know me. Nobody can know anyone. When I do try to tell them they just want to put me on drugs to shut me up. I've got nothing."

"Don't try to tell them. Forget the world. The world is deaf. But there is a way."

Erica didn't need to look up to feel the confident smile on her.

"This?" She looked, unconvinced, at the leaflet.

"Zoe?" prompted Olga.

Zoe made a dismissive sound with her tongue. "It's kind of it's not me, you know? I am not the problem, right? 'I' is something different. But the light dissolves everything, so nothing can be wrong." Zoe frowned up at Olga, whose open face told her she could say no wrong. "It's like God without God. I don't know. You're older than me."

"But I think your soul may be older than mine," sniffed Carina, and received a look of surprise that told her she had won a friend. She looked again at the leaflet and sighed.

Before they parted, having agreed to meet again at the Fair the next day, Olga suggested they take a selfie threesome. Carina objected that she looked awful, but Olga insisted that the surface image was irrelevant.

"And I have the P6," Zoe showed her a baby pink mobile. "It kind of gives instant facial support, gets rid of spots and that."

The girl looked, Erica thought, rather grateful for her unexpected new friend. Olga's unequivocal support would no doubt fill more than needy emptiness, but the woman's flawless self-assurance must be intimidating.

"Do you want to smoke something?" Zoe said.

"I can't. I have problems. Met this guy—I think I'm pregnant? Can we talk tomorrow?" Carina's look was pleading.

"Sure. Fuck!"

"Cari," Olga gave her a massive hug that she wasn't ready for.

"Ah!" she recoiled in unfeigned pain. Olga threw a horrified hand over her mouth, but Carina told her through smiling tears that it was okay and waved a weak goodbye as she left.

• • • •

"YOUR FRIENDS ARE IN the cells," Pastori greeted her. "As would you be, if I had my way. Charged with criminal damage, sedition, terrorism, endangering public safety: the list just goes on."

Erica intuited something important. "But. There's a 'but,' isn't there?"

DI Pastori let the tone of her speech express her displeasure. "Even our Lady Mayoress, or her advisors at least, can see when a political opportunity has been handed to her on a plate. She's just gone on television to claim the credit. The most nefarious of threats to the nation has been put down within hours of the attack thanks to the brave and incisive action of a special police network set up by her personally. You were, were you not, seconded by the Chief to the city police? In your 'passive role?'"

"Officially, I am reporting to both police authorities: national and municipal."

"Which makes you doubly responsible: for committing the principal crime and for helping to apprehend the alleged perpetrators. The mayoress is not interested in hearing that the arrested suspects shopped you immediately for the bomb attack and has decided, in her wisdom, to allow you to continue. Under strict supervision. Even she's not that stupid."

"I'm not sacked? Not even any disciplinary?"

"I know. There's no justice. But that's just the mayoress: the Chief may have other ideas. Supervised or not supervised, you're off anti-system surveillance, which my report will justify on the grounds that you are the tendency's most serious offender. You stay on the babysitting duties on condition that you come up with a positive result on the girl within twenty-four hours and report in to me twice daily. Put one foot wrong, however, Sánchez, cross the faintest line, and it will be my pleasure. Is that clear enough for you?"

Erica got out the police mobile and showed her the picture taken earlier that afternoon. "I don't need twenty-four hours. This is my new friend," she said. "We're meeting up again tomorrow at Transformer."

"You found her. Count yourself lucky. What the fuck," said Pastori, "got into you last night? What the fuck were you doing? Why?"

"They included me in on an action against a bank and I thought I ought to get into it. Show them I was the real thing and then use that to get to know the real subversives. I never thought they could be so wimpy. Just leave a dumb graffiti, you know?"

"But when you did see that they were just a bunch of asshole amateurs, you went ahead on your own anyway. Don't try and tell me anything different. You know that entire area is on CCTV." Pastori stood up. "I don't get you, Sánchez. I think you're a problem. Your friends don't think much of you, either. They snitched on you without being asked, not that it'll do them any good. The Government will want to make an example of them."

"They're just a bunch of dorks. They're innocent."

"Well, you should have thought of that before playing Patty Hearst. They're going to get eight to ten years. And you know something else? You're no longer the station looker. More like a boiled egg with ketchup stains."

• • • •

"DON'T TOUCH: SUNBURN," Erica said to her mother in the entrance hallway. She wore a beret and a light summer dress that covered her arms and reached down below her knees.

"Darling," her mother still wanted to be hugged. "But you never burn. Oh, well. He's through there. Hallo, Sebastián, do come in. You must be parched, what with this heat. What will you have to drink? Beer? G&T?"

"Just a tonic, thanks, María."

"I'll mix my own, Mum," said Erica, knowing that it would otherwise come with five per cent spirits.

Her father was pretending to be busy with something in order to be surprised by their appearance in the living room of his chalet, which opened onto a garden illuminated by burning torches from IKEA.

"Oh, you're here. How wonderful. Erica," he let himself be kissed on both cheeks by his daughter. "Your mother's in the kitchen. Sebastián," he growled. "The man of the hour. They tell me you'll be playing in goal for Real Madrid next season. Here we are." He stood them in front of the TV.

Sebastián's shoe-catch had been quickly forgotten by the news channels, but a video of it recorded by a French journalist had gone viral on YouTube. Erica's father clicked a mouse and it played out on the TV screen, which was connected by cable to his laptop. The video captured the incident from the floor of the Press room, just three rows back from Carol Sinclair.

"Again," said Erica, watching more carefully the second time, and Sebastián realized that she hadn't seen it before. There it played again. Of all the people at the promotional event, the one person who had defended the brutal Al Walid from the vengeance of the crusader journalist was her boyfriend. He waited for her anger.

She shook her head, choosing her words. "That was so cool," she said.

And it was. A fine-looking young man, impeccably attired, in a single movement and as if on cue, rises from the front row, reaches up a hand, and a shoe flies into it to stick fast like a ball in a baseball glove. He turns and disappears into the wings, as if it had been a practised move that he had been expecting all along.

"But do we call it a Christian act, I wonder?" Alfonso knit his thick eyebrows and managed to steal the little thunder that was passing between the formal young man and his daughter. "I suppose we do. To metaphorically stop the hand that will slap another's cheek." He stood between the two young people, separating them with more than just his filled-out, middle-aged girth. He wore a musky scent under an outdated caftan. "Are we to be punishers or forgivers? What part does knowledge play, especially that which informs our evolved culture? Spontaneity, surely, is still socially conditioned."

"'Trust in the Lord with all thine heart; and lean not unto thine own understanding,'" Sebastián said.

Erica felt a little giddy and then a whole lot worse. After the video, it was like zapping from the fun of a sports channel to the tedium of a religious debate. She still hadn't slept and she hadn't eaten properly in two days, either, just grabbed a couple of vegetable somosas at the Fair. There was something about her father and boyfriend sparring chummily that ushered her into what felt like the anteroom of a panic attack. She turned and walked its menacing void into the kitchen.

"Hi, Mum. What can I get you?" She couldn't face a drink anymore, but moving bottles gave her something to do.

"Nothing for me, thank you, dear. He's such a nice boy. He doesn't drink at all?"

"Not. A. Drop."

"So responsible. And smart. Oh, how I wish you'd met him before."

Erica felt grim. Grim and exasperated. Not even things being exactly how they should be could keep the tone of lament from her mother's discourse for long. The two of them had grown apart almost from the day of their return to Spain from Morocco, and recent years had seen María become increasingly humourless and hypercritical of her daughter.

"You don't know how I suffered having to watch you go through one disastrous man after another."

"I'll just take my boyfriend his holy tonic, then, shall I?"

"There's no need to be like that, dear," scolded her mother.

Erica felt a sense of self return as she swung, like a mood, back onto the living room stage.

Her father was, as the script demanded, holding forth, and her boyfriend listening respectfully without ceding on the principles which were such a protagonist in their own relationship. Politics, immigration, religion. A volatile brew, yet they seemed to be steering an amicable enough course through it all.

"People talk of a conquest, but there is almost no evidence of resistance to the Muslim invaders who arrived from the year 711 onwards. And what most people don't realize is how squalid existence was back then. The people governed by the Visigoths were primitive and illiterate and their settlements were crude and filthy, much like the rest of Europe. They probably welcomed the new rulers."

"That was then, Alfonso," said Sebastián.

"Two hundred years later, the Caliphate of Abd Al-Rahman III, and what have we got? The arid waste of Al-Andalus has been transformed by irrigation systems brought by the Syrians. Oranges and lemons, bananas, aubergines, peaches and plums, pomegranates. The capital of Cordoba has paving, public baths, street lighting, for God's sake! The rich have gardens with fountains. There is harmonic architecture, poetry, *libraries*: Burke says more than seventy of them in Cordoba. The Moors, as people insist on calling them, brought learning to our ignorant land."

"Fair enough, but that's history. We don't need them now. Now they just bring their poverty and their families."

"Hashish to sell on street corners," said Erica.

"But without them, Europe would have just wallowed indefinitely in the Dark Ages. When Toledo fell to the Christian armies in 1105, they found libraries containing all the major Greek and Roman texts, translated into Arabic, which had been lost to them centuries before. Only thus were the great classics recovered, and philosophy, not to mention Arabic contributions to mathematics, geometry, medicine, optics, botany, music, navigation, algebra... without all this, where would your cars and washing machines have come from? Computing, industry, and the international law that now bars the people of northern Africa from seeking refuge in our country. When we owe them such a historical debt."

We owe them fuck all, Erica wanted to say. Instead, she left them to it and switched the television on to check for the news.

"Spain is a Catholic country," she heard her boyfriend say. "It was Christian before the Moors. And now there are Arabs coming here who want a Jihad. We've seen the terrorism. We've had the bombs."

"Spain for the Spanish," she piped up. "Build the walls higher. Electrocute them."

María brought in a massive salad. "Plates and knives and forks, Erica," said her mother.

"There!" Sebastián pointed at her.

Erica felt accused, angry and guilty, thinking that he was attacking her for not being a good, obedient daughter and wife-to-be, for not having set the dinner table, but he was pointing past her at the TV. It was showing the advert for Asturias that she had seen earlier in the day.

"Covadonga," said Sebastián. "Where King Pelayo's victory initiated the Reconquest. Thanks to him, Spain is a Christian country today, with Christian morals."

"That first battle was an ignominious slaughter by all accounts," said her father. "Pelayo trapped the Muslim troops in a narrow gorge and massacred them with boulders and arrows."

The two men sat down at the table with their drinks.

"Well, the Moors never took Asturias. And it doesn't seem to have done the Asturians any harm at all." Sebastián felt vindicated by the uplifting images and music that streamed from the promotional video.

"Prawns," announced María. "And lemon chicken with rice. Lamb cutlets for Alfonso."

"Not just for me, darling. María thinks they're not right for a summer night, Sebastián, but I say they're always good."

Erica plonked down the rice and sat down next to Sebastián to tackle a bottle of white wine with a corkscrew. She popped it open and poured three large glasses.

"You don't mind if Erica has a drink, then, Sebastián?" said María. "Just a drop for me, dear."

"Gosh, darling, I forgot to ask. Is it alright?"

Sebastián actually turned in his seat to address María. "I think women's rights in this country are extremely important. Gender equality is the law. And a Christian law, too, in my opinion," directing his latter opinion towards Alfonso.

"Muslims don't let women drive, do they?" said María.

"Or drink wine," said Erica.

"Only in Saudi Arabia and one or two other countries," said Alfonso. "You could have driven in Morocco, María."

"Not with the way they drive, goodness! And the way they make women cover their beauty. Those awful things they have to wear."

"Just imagine," Erica said.

"It's just not right," said her mother.

"Female genital mutilation," said Erica.

"Sebastián, have some salad," said María.

"Islam," Alfonso resumed, "is an intellectual faith. It abhors superstition. Is it true, Sebastián, that the Pope offered indulgencies to the faithful who followed Catholic World Youth Day on Twitter? Indulgencies, let us be clear, being time off from purgatory. When Al-Andalus was surging forward in science, the Church was selling remissions from purgatory for large sums of money."

"Dad." Erica silently cursed him for deliberately leading Sebastián out of his depth.

"And what is it happens to unbaptized infants now that the Vatican has so generously allowed that they might no longer be sent to limbo?"

"As long as they are not born out of wedlock, they may attain a state of grace," Sebastián said, spearing a piece of avocado with his fork.

"So does the dog from next door still come into the garden and shit there?" Erica asked.

"We will go out after dinner," said her father. "And I will challenge you to find one."

"Not at the dinner table," María reprimanded them.

"The fact is," said Alfonso, sensing victory through persistence and home territory, "that the seven hundred years of Muslim rule in Hispania were marked by tolerance and peaceful coexistence with Christians and Jews. Come the Catholic regime in 1492 and come the expulsions. Not just Muslims, but also the Jews whose banking skills had made commerce prosper."

"Oh, leave the poor boy alone, Alfonso. Do tell us about your job, Sebastián. You must have quite some stories to tell."

Sebastián was finding it quite hard to concentrate. Just dipping his prawns in the mayonnaise was enough to handle. The only story he had to tell was the one he was hoping would very soon be forgotten.

"I just feel," he said, "that we're not ready for another invasion. We're too different. We shouldn't try and live there and they shouldn't come here. Time was when a boy from Galicia, making a new home in Madrid, would open the door for an old lady because she reminded him of his grandmother. Looked like her. You don't get that anymore."

Alfonso made a brief clearing of the throat and, preparing his next sally, looked up to find the eyes of his spouse fixed coldly upon him.

"Respect," he reined himself in. "Respect in social mores and their ritual is a sign of a civilized society. And one boy at this table demonstrated respectful understanding of the symbolism in Arabic culture *singlehandedly*." Content with his bon mot, which he made patently clear by slipping off a sandal and raising it high above his head, he chuckled and served himself some more rice. "You're not eating, Erica. Have you tried the cutlets?"

Her plate of salad and prawns had barely diminished, but her glass was ready for another refill.

"They're delicious," Sebastián said.

"My father is being provocative," she told him. "He knows full well that I don't eat lamb."

"But you eat meat."

She started on the salad. She wasn't going to let Alfonso control her eating, as had happened in Morocco. Why her father had to push and keep pushing on a dangerous course that was likely to tip over into a family spat would have been beyond comprehension if she wasn't so accustomed to it. It was the behaviour of a bully with an obsession for challenge, no matter how inappropriate. Her mother appeared placid and unaffected. Erica wondered if she had withdrawn inwardly, thankful for the respite of not being the target tonight of Alfonso's imperiousness.

"She had a pet sheep. Did she tell you?" said Alfonso.

Sebastián looked at her, but didn't stop chewing his cutlet.

"It wasn't a pet," she met his eyes.

"She called it—what was it called?"

An expectant pause grew into an uncomfortable silence.

"Billy Jean!" Alfonso pretended to have forgotten and just remembered.

"Happy anniversary, Mum," Erica raised her glass of wine.

"Happy anniversary," Sebastián added his water glass.

"Thank you, dear," said María.

Alfonso clinked glasses and lent across to kiss his wife's cheek and whisper something in her ear.

"Does the feast of Eid al-Kabir mean anything to you, Sebastián?" Alfonso continued. "No? Well, what about the Biblical story of Ibrahim's temptation by the Devil, after Allah had ordered him to sacrifice his son, Ishmael? 'Don't do it,' said the Devil. But Ibrahim obeyed his God, and was about to slit his son's throat when at the last moment Allah presented him with a lamb instead. Well, in Morocco, as in many Islamic countries, Muslims remember Allah's servant with the sacrifice of a lamb. It's well looked after until the day of the feast and then, when the Imam tells people over the loudspeakers that it's okay to make the sacrifice, the family elder makes a single cut in the animal's jugular." Alfonso passed his knife across his throat. "Bismillah Allahu Akbar. I'm afraid we upset Erica," he returned to cutting up his chop.

"For some reason, Erica was obliged to watch," she told her boyfriend.

"It was insensitive, Alfonso," said María.

"A child needs to learn," he said.

"Apparently there are a lot of unpleasant surprises that it's important we watch. And we learn alright." Erica stared at him.

She wasn't going to play her father's game and escalate this, but she wasn't going to let him think he could get away with whatever he liked. The horror of being held there by her father with her arms pinned, seeing the blood spurt from Billie Jean's throat, sobbing and screwing up her eyes until he was empty, the sight later of him hanging in the open window, skinned and somehow obscene, had been permanently fused in her teenage memory with being forced to witness the rape of her best friend.

"What about you and Sebastián?" María said, raising her wedding ring tentatively into the light.

"Oh, Mum."

"We haven't—have we?" Sebastián looked at her.

"Can we talk about something else?" Erica sighed.

"Well, tell us something nice, then. And do take that off, dear," said her mother, looking at her daughter's headgear.

Erica took off the beret that had been concealing her total baldness, placing it in her lap, and went back to her prawn salad. "Is there anything wrong?" she asked, before putting a forkful of rocket in her mouth. The eyes on her were full of reproach that could not be spoken. Unless one was a mother, of course.

"I sometimes wonder where we went wrong," said María.

Erica laughed, coughing into the salad.

"It was a sacrifice required for her job, María. What Erica does is highly important," said Sebastián. "She wouldn't have done it if she didn't have to."

"It reminds me of poor Juana after her chemotherapy."

"Thanks, Mum."

"Times and the fashion always change," said Alfonso. "Nowadays, it's quite standard among modern lesbians, but go back to the days of the Civil War and its aftermath and a shaven head was a sign of shame and defeat. It was a common punishment meted out by Franco's forces to the women of the losing Republicans. The humiliation was often combined with having to drink a pint of castor oil."

"I was just going to ask what there was for afters," said Erica.

"Oh, I nearly forgot!" María exclaimed unnecessarily.

"So how *is* your job going, Sebastián?" asked Alfonso, sitting back.

"I'll help you, Mum."

Before following her mother into the kitchen, Erica placed the beret on the head of a large teddy bear that had once been hers and which now sat on a teak cabinet between a silver tea service and a potpourri. She thought it looked thoroughly pleased with its trim new cap.

"Such a nice young man," María sighed. "He's so respectful to you."

"And why shouldn't he be?" asked Erica.

"And a steady job. You might not think so now, but it's important, you know."

"Actually, I do."

"How many's that you've had?"

"You tell me. I'm sure you've been counting."

"You used to be such a sweet little girl," María pushed a glass bowl of strawberries into her daughter's hands and looked up into her eyes expectantly, as if to give her a chance to revert back to that desired condition.

"I want a divorce. I mean, an abortion," Erica said, putting the bowl down.

"Oh! What *do* you mean?"

"An abortion. I'm pregnant and I don't want to go through with it."

"Oh really! But what does Sebastián say? Perhaps he wouldn't mind. If you got married..."

"It's me that minds, mother. Sebastián mustn't know. He'd be horrified. It might make him break off our relationship. Abortion is like murder to him and a child conceived out of wedlock would be illegitimate in the eyes of his God. For him, it would always be a bastard."

"But he's a modern Catholic, isn't he? You live together, even though you're not married."

"He fucks me on a Saturday night and goes to beg forgiveness and do penance for it on a Sunday morning."

"Don't use that language in this house." Her mother's appalled expression was transmitted to her hands, which shook as she got spoons out of a drawer.

"It's true. I asked him once what he went to confession for. He was quite matter-of-fact about it."

"You very clearly don't know what you want," Erica's mother decided. "Divorce, when you're unmarried. Abortion. None of it makes any sense. You're confused," María smiled at her daughter in pity.

"I'm not confused. I'm in a fix. I want an abortion. Will you help?"

"Of course not. It's quite illegal, anyway. You're police. You uphold the law."

"That law wasn't passed, mother, although it's as if they had. They still make it damned difficult for you. You have to go private."

"Is there anything wrong with it? How many weeks are you? It doesn't show. What does the doctor say?"

"I don't know. I haven't been. I just want to be free if it."

"Well, that's just plain selfishness. I don't want to hear another word about it. How sure are you?"

"Ninety-nine per cent. Tests for positive don't lie."

"Well, you'll have to take it in your stride. Anyway, this just isn't the time or the place. Do let's not have any unpleasantness. Take the strawberries through, will you, dear?"

"Erica told me, Sebastián," said María in a silly, child-like voice, "that you are quite a *foodie*, is that right?"

"What have you got for us, María?" he asked.

"Something very simple, with a twist," she said. "Strawberries. And here's the twist." María took a tall pepper mill from the centre of the table and ground fresh green pepper over the plump, red fruit. "And cream."

Sebastián loved them. Erica didn't. She could tell that her father, guardedly silent, wasn't impressed with the taste, either, and just for once she felt a tinge of sympathy for him.

They took coffee in the garden, where the heat seemed only to increase as the night deepened. At one point, Erica said she would go and wash up. To her mother's protests that that was what a dishwasher was for, she said, just the glasses then, just in case.

In the kitchen she checked the mobile, which had a message not from Zoe but from Olga, suggesting they meet at a tea house before the Fair the next day. *Sure, thanks!* she replied. She darkened the screen and, although she wasn't doing anything she shouldn't, listened carefully to make sure that the other three were all out there talking together in the garden.

Her mother was partly right. The new ruling on abortion, finally made law after a protracted passage through Congress, made it legal to terminate a pregnancy but not on the national health service: not unless the life of the mother was in danger or there was severe abnormality in the foetus. Sebastián, she was sure, would propose marriage as a means of saving face socially and she would be left holding the baby.

Whether it was the pregnancy, or Sebastián's insistence on building a relationship with her parents, or the strain of having to suddenly pretend to be another person altogether in her increasingly bizarre job, or the illicit romp with Dani the previous night and her inexplicable recklessness in making and exploding the artefact, all of it compounded exponentially by the number of years that Zeta, Miguel, Osvaldo and Jaco would now spend in prison because of her, Erica knew that something had to break. Why was her decision-making so blind and wayward? If I could, she thought, I would open the front door to Dani right now, suck him and fuck him in the hallway and then get rid of him, close the door and go and carry on as normal. Take a tray of mint chocolates and iced shots of *digestif* out to the garden in the sultry night, and sit prettily on the grass to mask the rich, spicy smell beneath her light, white dress.

The first time Erica's parents met Sebastián, María had quizzed him about her daughter's housekeeping.

"She never folds her clothes," he said.

It was so underhand, and Erica was so caught by surprise, that she didn't even glare at him. "Not everyone's a Virgo, you know," she said.

"I'm a Christian," said Sebastián.

Erica had burst out laughing and then stopped when she saw the look on his face.

"You're serious," she said.

The question was, had she made a serious mistake in choosing him? Initially, Sebastián's severity—combined with his extra tallness—had been a turn-on. But five months on, the conscientious respect that he was still bringing to their bed was killing the joy in it. He was athletic enough, but his politeness was making her feel unclean. He just didn't get it: get her. She knew that getting what she needed, sexually, was like finding the right combination to the lock on everyday sanity and his inhibition constrained her. It embarrassed her, even disgusted her now: the things she wanted him to do and say to her, and frustrated the hell out of her when, despite her encouragement, he wouldn't. Sex that was genteel was no sex at all.

Maybe she should go back to Dani: but she didn't want that, either. Dani offered nothing and expected nothing. She had imagined that they would share thoughts about police work and support each other, but Dani hadn't cared a jot about the job, other than as a secure, well-paid number with benefits, and he hadn't cared about her other than as a good screw who made unbeatable coffee. With him it was just crudity without an attempt at relationship at all and a filthy, shambolic flat to go with it. He might ask where the sugar or the bottle opener was, but he pretty much ignored her otherwise. When he wasn't slobbed out snoring on the sofa, he was watching TV or crouched over a laptop, his conversation truncated to grunts. What was laid-back at first, without any companionship or any real feeling had rapidly degenerated to sordid and boring.

She had been grateful that he was so easy to despise. She remembered the evening she told him to his face and at length what a foul pig he was and, just for once, he had heard her out. He had looked at her in a way that wasn't just merely lustful or suspicious. He was actually paying attention, she thought. When she had finished saying her piece, there was a hint of a frown or vague surprise on his face and he had straightened his back. His meaty lower lip, the one she liked to bite, hung down in concentration and for a while he was totally silent and still. Then he farted. Farted and harrumphed, rolling himself off the mattress on the floor and padding to the bathroom for a glass of water.

No, Dani was unthinkable. So what kind of man *was* right for her? Did such a man even exist? Or was it her? Was she right for a relationship?

She returned to the garden to find them talking again about Sebastián's feat of intercepting Carol Sinclair's shoe before it hit the murdering bin Zayed in the gob. It no longer seemed so cool to her.

"It was a significant intervention," Alfonso was saying. "Had the man been struck by the shoe, the humiliation in his own country would have been incalculable. I don't think you need be concerned now about saying the wrong thing to him afterwards. You'd have been removed from duty directly."

"What did you say?" Erica asked.

"I'm not at liberty," he told her.

"That bad, eh?" she joked, before acknowledging: "Of course, sorry."

Sebastián's job was subject to the same official constraints as her own. She had reminded him about it only recently. She was intensely curious, though. What could he have said to Al Walid to make him fear for his job after saving the man's face? Did he request elucidation of Sinclair's question? Or reprove the Saudi royal in some way? She would be so proud if that were true.

"Sebastián was telling us what your team did this week," her father said. "How you rescued those poor women, the ones who were slaves. It's the kind of act your mother and I always hoped you might be part of when you joined the police."

Erica waited for the sarcastic sting in the tail, but it didn't come. They were all waiting for her to say something.

"So much has happened this week," she said.

It was María who was first to her feet, putting an arm round her pale-faced daughter's shoulder. "Take her home, Sebastián. She's exhausted, the poor girl."

He even pulled across her seatbelt to fasten it for her, while she sat listlessly in the passenger seat. I probably look like a blow-up doll, she thought. I hope the neighbours are watching. They waved goodbye and were soon moving smoothly along the quiet avenue. Her parents' leafy district with its prim, well-to-do air, its obliging watermelon vendor on the corner, people returning home from evening sports activities in regulation peak caps, their towels and paddle rackets in shoulder bags, a retiree in a pink shirt walking a dog, trees on a high verge standing stiffly to attention as they drove past, was just the kind of neighbourhood that Sebastián aspired to. Quite legitimately, she thought. Any other day, she would have found the area tedious, but right now she found it comforting. She didn't even mind Sebastián's driving like an old man. She leant back and let the shadows pass in procession over their slow and easy progress.

• • • •

MERCIFULLY, ERICA'S conviction that everything was at a breaking point wasn't borne out. The next day, then another, then a whole week, passed quietly and unremarkably by. Her tension slackened to give her a breathing space and then slackened some more. She started getting regular sleep. Her scorched skin had peeled but only superficially, like the sunburn she generally claimed it was, and she was looking forward to being hugged again by her staid but stalwart boyfriend.

Sebastián had regular chauffeuring duties at the Ministry and Erica's almost daily get-togethers with Zoe and Olga allowed her to monitor the girl and send back reassuring reports about her welfare. Even Pastori was mollified. Zoe had been going home to her parents' house to get clean clothes and sleep. She wouldn't respond to her mother's questions, but she did eat a little. She still repeated a wish to die like an empty mantra and wrote what she called "the poetry of pain" in a notebook that she kept private, but that was as far as it went.

There was hope against hope that she might even agree to attend her birthday party, now less than a week away, although nobody in the family dared bring the subject up, knowing that it coincided with the final day of the Field of Light summer camp that the girl was set on attending. Would the police agent do her best? She most certainly would, Pastori told them. Saturday August fifteenth, a National Holiday, was already marked in red on her calendar. It was also the day the Chief was due back from his family vacation on the Costa Brava.

Erica's hair began to grow back. Zoe loved to run her hands over her head. "Like moss on a bowling ball," she said.

The wilder recent events appeared in Erica's memory, the more unlikely they seemed, to the point of losing their solidity and taking on an anecdotal quality. Could all that really have happened? More believable and real were the days that the girls spent together in the shade of trees in El Retiro, the city's central park, often in supposedly meditative silence. For Erica, it was a welcome time-out from anxiety and the summer's roasting heat. She directed uncharitable thoughts at South American families making noisy picnics, while the other girls sought a higher reality on a contemplative plane. Olga, she of the ever-ready smile, claimed to glide and soar. What she never did, Erica noted, was pay. The teenager was expected to fork out every time they took a taxi, ate together, had drinks, whatever, and she clearly couldn't care less. Zoe Iris had turned out to be, almost to her guardian's disappointment, untroublesome, and rather dull.

Erica hadn't managed to enrol on the Summer Camp herself, her probing queries—"You know, this camp thing? I was wondering about the criteria of the programme"—being always somehow deflected by Olga, whose affability towards the new girl had cooled off somewhat once it became clear that she wasn't going to prove as charitable as Zoe. If Zoe's father, the wealthy Sr. Urquizo, was making a contribution to the police's tracking and caretaking of his kid, it certainly hadn't trickled down to Officer Sánchez's operational budget. Pastori told her that the Chief had ordered that it should be as close to zero as possible without endangering the successful outcome of the assignment.

When she wasn't with the girls, as long as she kept filing reports and Zoe wasn't up to any nonsense, which she wasn't, Erica had the rest of the day off, sometimes entire days at a time. Even if she didn't see much of Sebastián, she had time to interview and hire a cleaner to keep the flat spick-and-span and even get a plumber in to fix the water heater, which had been stuck on the boiling hot winter setting, obliging them to disconnect it. These sweltering summer nights, Erica was more than happy with cold showers, but it plainly bothered Sebastián.

Only her most pressing issue, the one in her belly, was proving intractable. A phone call to her mother was met with another flat refusal to help. She had talked with her father, María said, and they were both agreed that it was for the best. It was her chance to be a woman.

Olga's claims that she knew a nurse who knew a doctor who knew a clinic were followed by fervent pronouncements on a woman's eternal right to choose what to do with her own body, but never somehow produced the hoped-for contact. Even less helpful was Olga's suggestion that they all attend a "Blessing of the Womb" by a visiting shaman, followed by a session on Biodynamic Craneosacral Energy, in preparation for which Olga offered to give her what she called "The Teaching." From the way she said it, it was clear that this was a magnanimous gesture of the highest order. Carina's fear was unreal, she said. Reality is transformed. Olga waited expectantly before being obliged to interpret Carina's unresponsiveness as a deficiency. Carina needed to evolve more to receive The Teaching and would be treated to a session of Reiki instead.

Erica regretted mentioning her pregnancy to the girls, even if it did kind of go along with her victim persona. It was far too intimate, perhaps the one irreducibly genuine thing about her. She felt she had cheapened herself by confiding in them. She hadn't approached a doctor because she didn't know one that she could trust. Her GP, Dr Prieto, had never shown her the slightest sympathy and to go to the police medical centre was tantamount to walking into the mess canteen and shouting: "Hey everyone, it's me, Officer Sánchez, and I am looking for a doctor to kill my healthy, unborn baby."

In the end, she couldn't leave it a moment longer and went to see her regular doctor.

"When was your last period?" said Dr Prieto.

"Six weeks and five days."

"We'll do a blood test tomorrow morning and then an ultrasound. Let's take a look at you."

"I don't want it." Erica stayed put in the chair.

"I'll pretend I didn't hear that," the doctor said.

"So you're not going to help?"

"I'm going to examine you. Shall we?"

As she concluded the examination, the doctor said, "Do you think you could pee for me, Erica?"

"I already did the test. The result's over there in my bag."

The pregnancy test stick was hidden inside a box of redundant tampons. She had thought of disposing of the evidence, but the policewoman in her wanted to be able to put her hands on it.

"Can you pee? Yes or no?"

Erica, under the woman's severe gaze, and feeling at a very unfair disadvantage, lying as she was on her back with her legs wide open, decided it was time to be cooperative.

"Okay," she said.

When they were sitting down again, Dr Prieto asked to see the original pregnancy test and compared it with the new one.

"Have you experienced any serious shock recently? Physically?"

"I blew myself up," Erica remembered. "Hence the odd hairdo."

"What happened?"

"I was working. A controlled explosion. Well, not very controlled."

The doctor observed her warily. "Well, you're not pregnant. Like I said, we'll run the blood test tomorrow to make sure, but it's a negative." She showed her patient the result of the new test.

"But I tested definitely positive. I did it five times. You've got the last one there."

There it was, next to the doctor's fingertips, with the tell-tale double stripe.

"It's unusual, but it does happen. It's called a false-positive. If the physical trauma was such that it caused a recent pregnancy loss, the fertilized egg previously attached to the uterine lining can leave behind a biochemical reaction that suggests that it's still there."

She had soaked her shocked body in the cold bath at Jaco's apartment with the stink of petrol in her nose and thought nothing of the blood, like pink smoke, turning the water opaque.

"Happy now? Give this chit to the lab nurse tomorrow, between eight thirty and nine thirty a.m.," said Dr Prieto.

Erica took it and nodded. She no longer had anything to say. She got up and collected her things to leave.

"Be careful what you ask for," said the doctor.

• • • •

"IT JUST SEEMS A BIT weird that you're both going to be there and I'm not?" Erica, back in her Carina persona, told Olga that afternoon.

Zoe would soon be going to the Field of Light Summer Camp, where Olga was to be one of the course leaders, and Erica was making a last ditch attempt to get in. To keep an eye on her ward for just a little longer and, after graduation on the last day, see Zoe on her way to the birthday party that her family so adamantly desired to celebrate with her. Today was August ninth and Zoe would be fifteen on the fifteenth, the day that the Camp and Erica's assignment were due to end. She was more than ready to sign off on her undercover duties and act like a real cop again.

Carina had dropped so many subtle hints about wanting to do the Camp—and Olga had always managed to fob her off one way or another—that it was time to resort to a more direct approach.

"But you don't even know the programme."

"So tell me?"

"The programme is that there is no programme," said Olga, as if to end the matter.

"If you'll be there, that's good enough for me. Are there spaces left on it?"

"Carina, it's very late. And anyway, it's not as easy as that. You need to be advocated by a sponsor."

"*You* sponsor her. You sponsored me," urged Zoe. "I want her to come."

"I can only sponsor one person. That's how it works. And it's expensive. Two thousand two hundred each," Olga looked at Carina.

"Uff!" Would Pastori and the Chief stump up for that? Erica didn't need to ask. Her expense account wouldn't even cover the taxi there.

"What if I sponsor Cari? And I pay for her. My family will pay," said Zoe.

Now that's probably true, Erica thought. "Zoe?" She made big eyes at the girl.

Olga didn't seem the least surprised at Zoe's ability to offer what for many people would be two month's pay as if it were the price of a cinema ticket. "You *are* under twenty-one?" she asked finally.

"Twenty," promised Carina.

"They will check, you know. Fifteen to twenty is the intake age limit."

"No problem. But Zoe's fourteen, right?"

"Technically, it's permitted. She turns fifteen during the course of the event."

"Really?" Carina smiled at Zoe, who looked embarrassed.

"So it's OK," Zoe said.

"Well," Olga seemed to be running out of excuses. "Carina hasn't had The Teaching yet."

"Let's do it," Carina smiled.

Whatever nonsense it took to get her inside the Camp.

"Yes!" said Zoe. "We'll be together!"

"I'll have to check the planetary alignments for the right day. I'll call you," Olga sighed.

Monday, 10th August

"IT WAS A FALSE ALARM, Mum. I don't want you to tell Sebastián, OK?"

"I'm very sorry to hear it."

It was the following afternoon and Erica was staring at the word "Negative" on the lab report of her blood test. She thanked her mother noncommittally, enquired about her father's sciatica which was bothering him, and hung up. She wasn't sure what to do with herself. She couldn't comprehend the absence of euphoria, of cathartic relief at not being pregnant, but put it down to anticlimax. The other notification lying on the kitchen table was from UPS, telling Sebastián that a delivery would be attempted again tomorrow. A smart new suitcase or some gadget from Esquire magazine, she guessed. Sebastián liked that kind of thing and never asked her whether she thought it was a good buy or not. But that was alright. Everything was alright, or nearly so. There was just this numbness.

Perhaps now was a good moment to bring her inveterately cussed nature into line and make sure she hung onto her police job. If she could just get through this last week of babysitting Zoe Iris, she would be back in uniform and on patrols, restored to a regular existence and normal contact with colleagues. A social life, sports activities, studying exams for detective. Maybe she would even find detective work interesting. She thought it probably would. And if she broke it off with Sebastián, which was not altogether unlikely, she knew she'd ultimately be doing them both a favour. I'm just not made of the conventional stuff that he really needs, she cogitated, doodling on the lab report.

He needs a nice wifey who won't take the piss out of him or get drunk, who's happy to move to the suburbs and learn recipes. Have his babies.

That night, she snuggled up to him on the sofa with uncharacteristic wistfulness and they enjoyed watching a movie together, a brainless action movie in which helicopters crashed and hunky men saw things through to the end. She paused the DVD halfway through to make him a mint tea in the Moroccan silver pot that her father had insisted on giving them, and when the film ended, they went silently satisfied to bed.

She let Sebastián answer the door when the buzzer went early the next morning, while she remained stretched out on the black sheets of their bed, arching her spine in a memory of darkness, her hands making round movements on the silk, her mind wondering nothing, nothing at all. She felt a lot better. When Sebastián didn't come back to bed, she got reluctantly up and found him in their living room, where an open box displayed a singularly handsome pair of brown shoes.

"Wow," she said. "Having regrets?" He should have been looking pleased. He hadn't even taken them out of the box. "Hey, it's your money."

"They're not mine. I didn't order them, I mean."

"No? Where did they come from, then? My family?" Her heart sank.

He shook his head. "I don't think so."

"They're beautiful. No. No, don't tell me..."

Al Walid. It had to be.

"I don't know what to think. I mean, I don't know. Who else could it be? Paying me off, or back, one way or another. Letting me know that he knows where I live. And what my shoe size is."

"Don't be so paranoid. Really. Generosity in Saudi Arabia isn't a suspicious practice like it is here. It's a social obligation. For someone in his position, it's probably the least he could do, even if he didn't want to."

That same afternoon, Sebastián Elcano was called away from his coffee break to the Minister for Education, Culture and Sport's private office. On being admitted, he looked around in vain for Francisco Villalba but found himself instead standing alone before Jaime de Abascal, Subsecretary to the Ministry of the Presidency, held in the silence which those in power use to remind underlings of their servitude and defencelessness.

Sebastián prepared himself for an official dressing-down and possibly worse. Unfortunately, he was compounding his original faux pas by sporting the reminder of it. The respectful distance that he stood from the oversized desk paraded the hand-tooled shoes in full view. Of the softest Milan leather and a perfect fit on his long, broad feet, they shone like beacons of his impropriety, a sin unforgivable in government service.

The Subsecretary lifted his stare to Sebastián's eyes and pointed to a seat.

"Your clumsiness in Valencia was regrettable, but you have a sound record and your loyalty's not in question. This shouldn't be beyond you."

He pushed a slim dossier across the desk with two fingertips.

Uncomprehending, Sebastián opened it at a single page of instructions, a data summary, a declaration of legal powers, a glossy prospectus, an engineering report with photographs, a fold-out map, and two sealed envelopes, one marked 1,250 € for expenses and the other addressed to the mayor of a town he'd never heard of.

"I know what you're thinking: you're just a driver. And it's true. But we can't spare anyone else right now and so for the purposes of this duty you will be perceived as a staff officer. You were given training in standard protocol, I take it, prior to Valencia."

"Basic training, sir, yes."

"Well, then. All you have to do is hand over the communication to the mayor and bring back the response, if any. No more and no less. So that you know, central Government is allowing the Chinese limited mining activity in a theoretically protected area. It won't be pretty and it will radically alter the environs of one village. The rest is in the file. Asturias will kick up a hell of a fuss, of course. You've seen their campaign, I suppose?"

Who hadn't? Sebastián thought. The Asturian government's costly drive to promote tourism to the northern Spanish principality meant that it was everywhere: TV, billboards, YouTube, magazines and internet newsfeeds, you name it. Images of solid, honest-looking country folk, wood smoke rising from their endearing stone cottages; helicopter video footage of high lakes and majestic peaks cutting to close-ups of eagles and deer and heavy, brown cattle on the green mountainside; crumbly blue cheese at a fair and cider being shared between friends; cliff walks and sandy shores... the very image of natural Spain at its best-kept and proudest.

"You shouldn't expect the village to protest, however. You will stay overnight as a mark of respect and return the following morning, but the news should be delivered at the outset, understood?"

"Yes, sir. Will I be going on my own?"

"On your own, yes. And Elcano," Abascal held the edge of the desk with both hands as he leaned forward a little. "They're a little set in their ways. On first contact, you will be well advised to salute the Virgin of the Snows, their patroness. They will be looking forward to celebrating her fiesta, which is due just after you arrive, and they should be encouraged to do so, no matter what. It will be the last time that they do. It's a damn shame, but there you have it. Financial compensation is not on the table and should not be brought up. The Chinese have no use for the village. They will be setting up their own housing and supplies. Bear in mind that you are the bearer of unwelcome news, so don't smile. Accept their hospitality, but don't presume upon it or engage socially with the village or its councillors in any sense that is not strictly necessary. Decline any invitation to celebrate the fiestas or hunt, for example. In fact, that's an official instruction. You're not to take photographs, either. You're going there out of respect as a government official representing the Presidency, not a tourist. Well? Feel up to it? You should know that it's going to mean the death of this village to all extents and purposes."

"I think so, sir. Go there, deliver the documents, observe the common courtesies but maintain the distance of formal discretion, and return the following day."

"You forgot to salute the Virgin." Jaime de Abascal raised a finger and Sebastián was suddenly reminded of Saint Pancras making the same gesture in the plastic figures that were so common in shops when he was a boy, back in the days of the peseta. The raised forefinger which shopkeepers would ring with a twenty-five-peseta coin which had a hole in the middle.

"I'll remember, sir."

He read the page in the file that declared the powers delegated to him. It couldn't have been clearer.

LEGAL AUTHORITY IS HELD: NONE
BUDGET AUTHORITY IS HELD: NONE
DECISION AUTHORITY IS HELD: NONE

"Make sure you do. As soon as the commission has been carried out, you will report back to me in person."

The Subsecretary pulled open a drawer and took out a long tube of stiff cardboard, of the kind used to hold rolled-up posters. "Give this to the Captain of the Civil Guard. They have a small barracks there. It's one of these."

He turned in his chair to look up at the twin portraits on the wall behind him of the old king and his son, the new monarch, and held the pose for several respectful seconds before returning to Sebastián a glare mixed with rare emotion.

The interview was at an end. Sebastián left the room with his arms full, a straightforward and unpleasant errand to run that had nothing whatsoever to do with his normal job, and not a little perturbation on his mind.

• • • •

"I AM BEING PUT IN MY place."

He was vexed! Erica retracted her legs beneath her on the sofa.

"It's in the middle of nowhere."

He stood looking out through the sliding glass doors to their high-rise terrace. Not that one could make out anything of the city past the end of the terrace wall. Below in the tedious built-up symmetry of north-central Madrid was concentrated power: embassies and corporate head offices. Not that far away was the bank that Erica had assaulted. There he stood, tall as a glass of water, which was as much he ever drank, hands behind his suited back, rocking on his soft leather shoes.

"There isn't even a hotel."

Erica struggled to contain her amusement. This was so unlike him. "What was the name of the place again?"

"Miga."

"Not very big, then." Miga was a crumb in Spanish.

"Population of forty-three. What I don't understand is *why*?"

"Maybe they don't have enough sex. Maybe the sushi bars are disappointing."

"It's like having to climb up to a mountain cottage to knock on the door of a soldier's family and inform them of their son's death."

"Or their daughter's." He still hadn't told her what it was all about.

Sebastián turned round to his girlfriend, who fairly shone in the centre of the high-ceilinged, understated room. Why she sometimes looked spectacular and other times a calamity was beyond him.

"When you prate, I mean, uphold good old traditional values, it's precisely this kind of place that you're talking about. Now you have a chance to go. And those mountains!"

"It's hardly a holiday. Are you going out like that?"

Her tanned, oval face was sparkling with silver glitter again and her hair was smooth like blonde suede. She tugged on the hem of her pale yellow top, which was embroidered with a tree whose roots seemed to sprout from her bare midriff before it branched luxuriantly out over each breast. The outfit was completed by loose cotton pants tied just below the knee.

"I think you like it."

"It's... I just mean, you look so elegant when you dress normally."

"Maybe it's because I *am* elegant," she said. "And right now, I'm in my working clothes, just like you. And you never change. Boring in, boring out. Whereas I am going to slip into normal-girlfriend and well-mannered-neighbour self for dinner and it will be just another disguise, like Young Person for the Pope was, like Strict Orthodox Muslim was, like Spiritually Lost Ecoperson is. What if the real me turned out to surprise you?"

"I'm not sure I like surprises."

He sat down in an armchair and picked up his brief to scan through it once more. He had most certainly disapproved of her infiltration of the Pope's multitudinous Mass for Catholic Youth at an airfield, and her little less than jubilant report on an isolated orgy that took place in the midst of it.

A wave of affection rolled over her desire to tease him. So he was a bit of a stick-in-the-mud and a career man. So he liked to prove his worth and be rewarded for a job well done. That wasn't so terrible. That was Sebastián, and it made him kind of mature and boyish at the same time. On the sofa, Erica wriggled a little. She rested a spangled sandal on their Balinese table and the wave rolled back to reveal the teaser in her again.

"For a Roman, to be sent away from Rome was to be banished from the world," she imitated the voiceover for a melodramatic documentary. "He was ripped from the mother breast and cast out among wolves."

"I don't mind going, Erica. It will make a refreshing change. Mountain air, good cooking and all that. You're right, I'm obsessing and it's affecting my judgement. But they don't do things for no reason in the service and yes, to be sent out of Madrid for even a day is death to senior civil servants, unless it's a trip to London, of course, or Paris with shopping time. And I'm a nobody. Just a driver who got his hopes up because a gay Minister once made promising overtures to him. It's too convoluted is what I'm saying. I just don't get it. Why not send someone from Industry and Tourism? I'm attached to Education, Culture and Sport."

"Who's gay? Never mind," Erica corrected herself. "I'm hungry. Tell me about it over dinner. I'm going to get ready."

"Keep it on," he said, standing behind her as she wiped off the glitter in the bathroom.

"A good undercover girl like me? No way." She threw away the cotton wool and rinsed the alcohol off her cheeks with cold water. "Seb, whatever it is, it was some bigwig politico who appointed you with it, right?"

"Yes. Jaime de Abascal coordinates the presidency with its ministers directly."

"Well that's good, isn't it? It means they're talking to you. It sounds like: accept this with good grace, do the job diligently, come back—and we'll see. You know. Handle it properly and maybe we'll reinstate you in the junior staff ranking."

"But this man advises the President himself. If you want to slap someone down and find out if he's ever going to be useful, or just be forever a bloody chauffeur, a gofer, there are lesser people and much simpler ways to do it."

"Maybe a gay Minister put in a word for you."

Changed into a calf-length white cotton dress and the dangly earrings he had given her for her birthday, Erica drove them swiftly and deftly to the restaurant and dropped the keys into her boyfriend's hand before striding to the door. She chose steamed asparagus as starters for them both and leaned over the table to whisper.

"So what's the mission, Supermessenger? Secret?"

"To add insult to injury, it is, yes, along with the protocol. No internal need-to-know, no press, no public enquiry, and I'm to report directly to the Subsecretary."

The nature of their jobs would have made conversation sterile and dead long ago if they had observed the complete confidentiality required of them. For the sake of their relationship and their sanity, they had agreed from early on to rely on each other's professional discretion as police officer and government employee.

"I am to tell the village that a Chinese consortium has been awarded mining rights in the municipality and that works are set to commence next week. Nine days from now."

Sebastián sipped his water. Erica bit on a cracker topped with soft cheese and waited for the bombshell.

He shook his head. "That's it," he said.

"That can't be secret."

"At the site they want to do this, above the village, there's an ancient, disused mine. Like one imagines an old mine to be, with an entrance and shafts going down into it. It was Roman, originally. This spot, in a high valley, in pristine mountains and virgin forest, will be ruined, along with the village's hunting grounds and livelihood. I think the government's done a deal with Asturias Tourism in order to keep it under wraps."

"That's got to be it. Everyone knows how protective the Asturians are of their mountains. It's all idyllic picture book stuff. And with their campaign in full swing: it would destroy that. There has to be money involved. A lot of money. The deal must already be done."

"No compensation going to the village, though, apparently."

"They're just little people, Seb. They don't count."

"What's it got to do with the President's Office, though? Like I said, why not send someone from Industry, which also covers Tourism? In fact, if they can circumvent the law without even going through the motions of holding a public enquiry, why not just phone the village and post them the official letter?"

"It's obvious, isn't it? They want to placate the village so that it's kept quiet. Not everyone gets a courtesy visit from the Ministry for La Moncloa. As far as they know, you will be the personal emissary of the president. And there must be some sweetener in the envelope you have for them. Job creation. Revival of the local economy. Maybe something else you're not to know about."

Sebastián looked unconvinced. He pulled up a photo on his iPhone and showed it to her. "This is one that already exists in Galicia."

"Is that a mine? But it's horrendous. God."

The image was in shockingly high definition. It showed a huge gouge taken out of a valley, swirled round by muddy tracks for works vehicles and in-filled with what looked like either a pool of iridescent blue-green liquid or a giant, irregular lens reflecting the sky. A single, parked truck told of the vast scale of the operation.

"Directly down the mountainside from the proposed site is a major fresh water reservoir. What you're looking at in the picture is liquid mud and it's that weird colour because it's cyanide. They use cyanide to extract the ore. They say these basins are contained and treatable to leave behind non-toxic waste. But just look at it."

"Environment is allowing this to go ahead?" Erica made a face.

"It just seems wrong," Sebastián said.

"What are they going to mine, anyway?"

"Gold," he said.

Gold? she mouthed. "I didn't know there was any. I thought the mines were exhausted."

"The Chinese are pretty sure of it."

"The Chinese. So we're going to invite foreigners in to destroy our natural heritage and take our gold."

"I know."

"My undercover persona's ecology-in-action friends would have a field day with this," she appeared to think it over. "And if the press were to hear about the gold..."

"That's unthinkable."

Good grief, she had never seen him look so shocked.

"Sweetheart, I wasn't being serious." She put her hand on his. "We're not disloyal."

"No, we're not." He leaned back to allow the waiter to put down a grilled trout. "It wouldn't do any good, anyway. The Area of Outstanding Natural Beauty has been reassessed as semi-industrial, so the whole thing's legal. You know what they say: if it wasn't for the Chinese, there wouldn't be any investment at all in this country. But I don't like it."

"Nor do I. When do you leave?"

"On Thursday. We're not going to be seeing each other much. Before this cropped up, I was already scheduled tomorrow for some twenty-four-hour shindig in Aranjuez, and on Wednesday night I said I'd sleep over at my mother's."

"Is there something wrong?"

"No, no. It's her saint's day. I said I'd take her to a show and stay over after supper. You're invited, of course."

It was an easy out. Erica didn't hit it off with Seb's mother and she couldn't abide the theatre outings the woman liked so much. She felt pretty comfortable with the way things were turning out. She wasn't pregnant and she probably wasn't going to have to attend the teenage Summer Camp. Olga had discovered that the stars were not propitious to give her The Teaching until the day before it started, which left precious little time for her application to be processed.

"I'd like a white wine," she told the waiter.

Tuesday, 11th August

AS THE PLANETS FINALLY consented to line themselves up at least tolerably tidily, the venue Olga chose for Carina's initiation was the living room of an empty apartment that she had a key to. They would meet Zoe outside the Summer Camp before it started the following morning. Meanwhile, she was going to hang out in a cooperative-run former tobacco factory, where African boys played music and smoked dope in the cellar alcoves. "Last chance for three days," she had said.

"Did Zoe mean last chance for boys, or joints?" asked Erica as Olga lowered the shutters of the living room, and then realized that it was rather a sassy thing for Carina to say.

"Zoe's a virgin," Olga replied. "Help me with the table and chairs."

"Of course. But she can still like boys..."

They cleared a space in the room, shifting furniture into the hallway. Olga also insisted on removing the TV and all other electrical items, which consisted of a DVD player, a lamp and a battery-driven clock. They would interfere with and even nullify The Teaching, she said. She positioned two straight-backed chairs facing each other in the centre of the room, separated by about a metre, and told Carina to use the toilet and drink some water. Carina did as she was told.

When she came back from the kitchen, Olga was waiting for her on one of the chairs. Erica went and sat on the chair opposite her.

"Close your eyes," said Olga.

For the first two minutes, the two women sat there without speaking, without the tick of a clock, with just the faint sounds of passing traffic in the street four floors below them.

"Don't smile," Olga said.

More silence.

"Who are you?"

"Carina Delgado Ruíz."

"How old are you?"

"Twenty."

"Who are you?"

Erica's defence mechanisms came online. Was this an interrogation?

"Keep your eyes closed."

"Sorry."

"Answer yes or no. Are you satisfied with yourself, Carina Delgado Ruíz? With your life?"

"No."

"Does that produce an element of fear in you right now, however small?"

"Yes." Erica wished she had asked how long the session was going to last. Her heartbeat was faster than she would have liked.

"There is something in your mind. Look at it carefully. The question is: is it something new?"

"No."

"It isn't, is it? Fear never tries anything new, unless it has no choice. There's a challenge, and whenever there's a challenge fear resorts to the tried and tested. To the past, which is thought. Can you rid yourself of it now by force of will?"

"No."

"No. As long as fear is there to drive it, thought is self-reinforcing. But it's just a recording, Carina, a loop of circuitry in the brain that is triggered over and over. It's the response of a machine. Is that what you are? A machine?"

"No," she said emphatically.

"Prove it to me. Do something radically new and break out of that loop of fear, of thought."

Erica gave a visible shudder.

"Describe your life now."

She sighed. "Complicated." A look of distaste took over her face. "Crap."

"The mind fights awareness. If life is crap, it says, the last thing I want is to be more aware of it."

"With good reason."

"And so we become thought-addicts, because thinking can only be about the future or the past. But it is never still, never at peace. It always has to solve something. Having no clue what the present is, it tries to solve that, too. It tries to calm a pool of still water by agitating a hand in it. No peace there, either. We do not feel at home in the interpreted world and so we develop defences and an attack capability. We think possessions will defend us but it is we who defend them. Thought is mechanical and so that is exactly what our daily round becomes. That is what our experience becomes, and our experience is everything that we are. And so we become mechanical. We are always at the orders of this machine, this thinking mind, which though immeasurably useful, an extraordinarily complex and powerful tool, is still only a machine: one which we have left in charge of our living present. It's very good at information and ideas, but no good at all at processing them in terms of anything but itself. We cannot think what cannot be thought. The thinking brain cannot think outside its own box. It cannot know what else there might be beyond itself and it ends up suspicious and hostile towards the prospect, because it feels its controlling power may be diminished, or something even worse. 'Me or chaos,' says the thinking mind. And thus it becomes a closed loop, a closed society. Like masochists who should know better, we fall back on the strategic laziness of the this mind, where the default setting is automatic pilot. We are not whole and we know it, but the fragment we have become has no answer to itself. We are closed off from unimagined experience and greater life.

"And thus does all life fall flat.

"But we hate being the fragment. We hate being ashamed or frightened of the content of thought. We hate the boredom of it. And then pride and resentment, unwelcome guests, creep in and make themselves at home in our lives.

"Daily existence becomes a burden and experience is empty. You have truly become no more than a machine when you do no more than run and rerun past recordings. When you never experience anything truly fresh and new.

"Why do you do what you do? What is the point? Do you even care? Do you care about your life?"

Under the dullness of Erica's closed eyes swam a featureless anxiety. She regressed briefly to the chair in the beauty salon, where she had felt so choked and confused. But here she had no button to press, no blast to burst her chains.

"We know when we are just that fragment. We know that it's not enough, and we suspect that we should do something about it. In fact, we long to go beyond it, but we don't know how, because we who have become thought can't think beyond thought. No wonder there is so much mindless TV, so much porn culture, so many bars."

Yes, Erica, nodded. A drink would be a very good idea right now.

"The medium and the structure of thought is language. Words, Cari, divisive words. Words have a lot to answer for. They make ideas that we kill and are killed for. Our poor thinking mind has nothing more subtle than words at its disposal to perceive all that there is, and obviously that's impossible. However, and these are words of my mouth, words got us into this evolutionary mess and words will have to get us out of it. Poetry is anarchic. It is irreverent. It points past itself. To what?

"What is that which cannot be spoken? What is beyond words? How would I find out? I will need the courage to do this here and now, because accepting more thought at this point is like an alcoholic aiming to go dry by having one last drink.

"I am going to give gentle rest to the overwrought machine. Because I want my life back." Olga spoke with soft determination.

"The fragment which is thinking activity has taken over and occupied consciousness to the exclusion of all else. To all intents and purposes, I have become the fragment and the fragment is me. Thinking cannot just *be*, it has to be about something, with predicate and object, and that means power play. Consequently, activity in the material world becomes predicated on a world of other people and objects to control, manipulate and generally exploit.

"The thinking tool analyzes the past to project the future, and deletes the living present from your life. It demands that you store up possessions to protect you, but the more you have, the more you have to lose. It demands that you change and become a better person, but how can you be what you are not?

"We cling to poor compensations, which is all we have. We have a car and a husband and some nice shoes. We have the past—personal memory, culture, country—and we have a future of fearful hope. We have no life.

"But we do have fear. Fear of now, fear of more of the same, the past continued into the future with no prospect of change. This past and future are the projections of a busy little corner in our brains, which then sprouts ideas in our minds that we feel obliged to believe and obey. Hopes and aspirations which enslave us. But the past and future don't exist, except as a semantic background to our lives. Only now is.

"You are not what you think. You create a fiction you call identity, but there's nothing there."

There was a pause in Olga's flow and Erica listened with perverse scepticism for the rustle of paper, in case the other woman was reading from prepared notes, or from a book.

"We can bear pain. Pain is easy. What we can't bear is meaninglessness. And when a mind knows it must break out to find freedom, the left hemisphere of the brain where the thinking happens becomes insufficient unto itself and shuts up. The right hemisphere, open to the infinity of all there is, comes online and something beautiful happens.

"To be sensitive, open, wondering, here in the living present, simply requires the thinking mind to step back from centre stage. The chatter must cease so that we can listen: listen with all that we are, our whole being. The right hemisphere does not and cannot force its way into your consciousness because it does not act or decide. It is simply there.

"The living now is always simply there. And awareness of that is what we are here for. We know it through the faculty and dimension of meaning. To be fully aware, with your whole being, to be completely, quietly, sensitively, sensibly aware of this now, is to be free of the thinking mind's endless attempts to analyze the past and control the future. Control is a unfunny joke. Will you give it up? Do you have the courage to be here? To be yourself without running away? It is the source of life. It is your birthright. But you need to do it. Will you face up to it? Will you do that? Do you have the passion to claim it?

"What do you want, Carina? What do you choose?"

Erica waited for several seconds, until she was sure that they had come to the end and silence had settled on the room, before opening her eyes on Olga's radiant countenance.

"Nothing," she said. "Nothing. But thanks, anyway. It was very good." She stood up and found her bag on a corner table. "See you tomorrow, I guess. And Zoe. Say hi from me."

She closed the door on Olga's huge, brown eyes. Erica wondered if what they expressed was simple disappointment at the failure of her Teaching to have any effect whatsoever, or whether Olga was realizing that she'd have to put back all the furniture on her own.

Out on the street, Erica felt utterly disoriented, as if there was a script to follow but she had forgotten it. She asked a passer-by the way to the Metro and called Pastori to explain that she'd need two thousand two hundred euros to get into the Camp and watch over Zoe, and it was likely too late anyway.

"*Now* you tell me. Well, I don't suppose it matters. She'll be supervised and off the streets. Just make sure to be there when she gets out. Get her home safely and the slate's wiped clean."

Erica wasn't sure she wanted any slates wiped clean. All she knew was that she didn't want to go home to an empty flat. Between Ministry duties and his mother's, Sebastián would be away for the next two days and nights. Erica sometimes wished his love-of-family might rub off on her and sometimes she hoped it wouldn't. He was so complete and she was so deficient, so erratic. Such a mess. She didn't need any Teaching to know that. There was nothing she really had to offer him, which made missing him all the more guiltily perverse. Of course, when he got back, there was a remote possibility that she would be incarcerated in the Field of Light head-fuck camp, listening to more of Olga's New Age twaddle. A bus stopped alongside her and Erica got on it, for no better reason than it meant a decision, without having a clear idea of where it was going or where she would get off.

Later, much later, after dark, her cleavage glistening in the city heat, she entered their apartment and walked carefully down the hallway, as if by stumbling she might wake someone in the empty rooms. Four different men had attempted to chat her up during the hours that she had occupied the same, high stool in an almost respectable bar, and all four had withdrawn defeated by her unresponsiveness. Even the barman steered clear of her as he served other customers. Her thinking mind had gone into abeyance, but nothing had stepped in to take its place, no profundity, nothing. She was an inexplicable blank. When she knocked back the last tequila shot, she wasn't even drunk, and yet had the barman asked her to authorize two thousand euros on her Mastercard, she wouldn't have hesitated or cared.

Back home, sitting on her own toilet, the alcohol caught up with her.

Her mind? Herself? What was that? What will you give me for it, Olga? Sod all. She felt stupid and wrong and nothing more, nothing else. In her giddy mind waited a tight-lipped detractor, wanting to tell her just what it thought. Where was her grip? Where was her professional fucking focus? She had exploded an artefact that could have seriously hurt or killed someone and the blame had gone on innocent fools who were now going to spend the best years of their young lives in prison. Her mauve mobile was blinking. Try as she might, nothing occurred to her in response to the three messages from her boyfriend. She couldn't pretend she hadn't received them, as her private messages were forwarded and anonymously retrievable on her working phone. But they held no interest for her. I am no good: no good for you. When she plugged in the device to charge overnight on the bedside table, the screen illuminated a fat grey # and large blue numbers, which shone out in blatant provocation. One call to Pastori and give them both the satisfaction of her resignation. Yell at her. Make threats. What she really wanted was a SWAT team to come and remove her. She would shout and swear when they broke in, struggle like an animal, challenge them to demonstrate what committed police work really was, make them kick her, slam her against a cell wall, brutish and bloody, but love me, love me.

Wednesday, 12th August

SHE WAS DISTURBED DURING the night, perhaps by sirens. The third time she woke, she had overslept. It was gone nine and she was going to miss the rendezvous with the girls outside the Summer Camp. She couldn't even hurry there as the venue was a building or series of buildings on the outskirts of the city beyond a ring of motorway, where it was a good half hour's walk from the outlying Metro station, and Dani—Sebastián, she meant—had taken the car to go to Asturias. If she took a taxi, it would be spotted and struck off her expenses claim along with any other item that wasn't unequivocally justified.

Erica's dirty hangover was not made any better by waking to an oddly unrecognizable apartment. The cushions on the sofa were plumped up and symmetrical. Why was everywhere so neat? Even the kitchen. She checked inside the dishwasher. Not even their breakfast things from the previous morning. In the spare room, her clothes lay stacked and ironed, like the elves had been there. Then she remembered about the cleaner. The one she herself had hired to come twice a week. Right. She had been too pissed last night to notice the difference.

She showered and took a toiletries bag back to the bedroom, where she grabbed a few clothes from the wardrobe. Next to some colourful summer dresses, a navy police uniform hung incongruously, increasingly estranged from whoever she was. Just to make sure, she pulled out the bottom draw to check that her badge was still there. It was, together with a holster clipped over a heavy revolver and a pair of handcuffs attached to a leather belt. She shook away heavy thoughts and finished packing an overnight bag on the off chance that she might be admitted to the Camp. She tugged on a floral top and a pair of white hotpants, and shoved a folded printout of a map marked with the location into a back pocket.

When she finally reached the distant Metro station, the walk from there led her past modest apartment blocks and shops selling paint and awnings, past looks from garage mechanics, a closed furniture shop and a store yard for prefabricated swimming pools until the buildings came to an end and then there were just vacant lots, marked off by a sagging chain-link fence and overgrown with scrub and tough grass that the relentless summer had threshed into yellow stalks.

It was nearly noon and Erica wished she had brought more than a small bottle of water, so warm already that it tasted sweet. The blazing sun pinched the back of her neck like a mean child and she picked up her step. The road was now no more than a dusty thoroughfare for vans and skip trucks, one of which hooted at her as it thundered by. She took a right turn. The unused road she crunched turned into a gritty track before passing under a motorway flyover, where Ron's Crew graffiti and bits of decaying trash were the only sign that the place was still part of inhabited Madrid. Erica wondered why well-to-do parents would pay a substantial fee to bring their delicate youngsters to such a rough, deserted edge of the city and leave them here for three days. Probably because they led lives too busy to check on the details, she decided. If it cost them enough, it had to be alright. She stopped to breathe in the dark, rank air under the rumbling concrete and unfolded the route map. She was quite close. She had her failings, but a sense of direction wasn't one of them. It took her out into the sun again and through a zone of cleared wasteland cordoned off by more metal fencing, after which an old road and a pavement of kinds resumed, crumbled and cracked by weeds and lined by a long length of broken wall and nondescript, red brick façades. They ended at the litter-strewn backyard to a still impressive precinct of buildings set in a square formation, like an old school or a high-walled patrician's residence.

It stood out as a strong and still viable edifice in this ruin of an area. The road widened to what might once have been a broad turning circle for horse-drawn coaches and a main entrance of balustraded steps going up to a set of doors with peeling blue paint. There were even a few tall trees that lent shade and dignity to the nine or ten cars parked opposite. Standing out like an importunate visitor amongst the expensive black vehicles was an old Citroen 2CV, and next to that stood Olga, saying "Hola? Hola?" into her mobile. The rest of the scene was a mere haze in the glaring sun.

Olga didn't even return her greeting and launched instead into a tirade against the management of the course, who had flatly refused her entry at the door, despite having told her back in March that her philosophy meshed perfectly with the ethos of the Camp and assured her of the three morning sessions.

"Zoe?" asked Erica.

"Waltzed straight in. They have to pay me two hundred and fifty euros a day for the three days. They won't even answer the phone."

"Do you have the contract?"

Olga gave her a little "oh-aren't-we-clever?" smile which Erica took to mean that the agreement had been a verbal one. "And they promised I would meet J."

"Who's J?"

When Olga told her, Erica gave an involuntary laugh. "That's so improbable." She just couldn't imagine the ageing star at such a shabby site.

"Why do you think it's so expensive?"

"So why not advertise it with his name on the publicity?"

"It's not that kind of course. It's not about egos. You still don't get that."

It was true that there hadn't been any publicity. Just a static website homepage with no contact details. "So why are you so keen to meet him?"

"The spirit is free but the body has to eat. I need a break. I'm skint. I'm positive we'd understand each other. Are you going try to get in? I'll come with you."

Olga's striking looks and free-spiritedness probably would make an impression on the man, Erica thought. "No. If they see you with me, they won't let either of us in."

"Talk to them. Say you signed up especially to have me and that they have to let me take the mornings."

Erica put on her best mature teenager air, which she hadn't bothered with for Olga, and walked across the sandy forecourt and up the steps. She pressed an old round button next to the high doors and waited. There was a security camera pointing down at her. Maybe it had been deliberately left decrepit on the outside and was amazing, mind-blowing, on the inside, she thought.

"Who is it?"

A round grating in the door, somewhat lower than head height, had been swivelled half open so that an irritable male voice could be heard.

"I'm Carina Delgado. I'm a bit late."

"This is private property. What's your business?"

"I'm here for the Field of Light Camp. I'm just a bit late. Carina Delgado Ruíz."

"Wait."

Carina looked sweet and anxious for the camera.

"What do you want?" A different voice this time. A woman's.

Carina explained again. "Is this the right address?"

"I have your name but the money hasn't come through. Come back later."

"This afternoon?"

"Or tomorrow. It's up to you. Okay?"

"Is there a number I can call?"

"No."

She wandered back over to Olga and the shade of the trees.

"That makes two of us," she said.

Olga gave her a flat look. She got out her mobile again, one of the cheap outdated ones with no internet capability, and tried the same number.

"Shall we go?" Erica asked hopefully. The prospect of walking back the same way under the same sun, lugging the overnight bag, was too much. She had set out dehydrated from the hangover as it was. Olga hung up and stamped the ground before going to the car.

On the way back into town, Olga remonstrated with one and sometimes both hands off the wheel of the straining Citroen, which she had in the wrong gear, at the injustice and disrespect with which she had been treated.

"I needed that money for a flight to Ibiza," she said. "I have a job offer for a month."

"Let me help," Erica said. "There's something I need to do. Lend me your car for the rest of the day and I'll give you thirty euros. I'll look after it with my life, I promise."

"I need at least fifty."

Fuck it, Erica thought. "Alright, fifty. But in that case I want it until Saturday. Fifty a day: that's a hundred and fifty. Then I'll come and find you and we can go pick up Zoe."

"I'm not interested in Zoe anymore. But OK. Have you got the money? Can you drive?"

Well, how your tune has changed, thought Erica. But the deal was worth it to get some wheels. To be there waiting outside Saturday lunchtime and—hopefully, cross fingers, touch wood— drive Zoe home to Mummy and Daddy. In the meantime, she might have to make more than one return trip to the Camp's old buildings. She could have waited round until Pastori got a supply car to her, but Officer Sánchez had no real desire to involve anyone else. She also had a throat like a scouring pad.

"I can drive," she said.

Not content with the hundred and fifty euros, Olga insisted on a photocopy of Carina's ID. She was still staring at it as she handed over the car keys, confounded, Erica was certain, to discover proof that Carina really was only twenty years old. They parted company at Oporto Metro station and arranged to meet at the same spot in three days' time, August fifteenth, day of the all-important birthday party.

Erica felt a different person now that she had a car, even if it had the dynamism of a supermarket trolley and no air conditioning. In any case, leaving the windows open helped vent a lingering smell of incense. She drove down the ramp at their apartment block and into the underground parking space left vacant by Sebastián's BMW. After calling a thoroughly uninterested Pastori to keep her in the picture and drinking a pint of pineapple juice straight from the carton in the kitchen, she sat back on the sofa and listened to her heartbeat, nostrils drawing in the cooled air, until her eyes closed in gratitude.

"Fuck!" Erica grabbed her mobile to check the time. It was half past two. Only an hour had passed since she fell asleep. "Thank God for that," she breathed out. There was a message from Sebastián, which was probably what had woken her. All was well and he missed her. "Make a joke," she implored the phone. If he wouldn't, she would. "Careful with the Asturian girls," she replied. "They will fatten you up and eat you." Then she remembered that he was in Madrid still, working, before going to his mother's, and not leaving for the assignment until the next day. I'm losing track of you, she thought.

She decided to return to the Camp venue much later, in the early evening, when it would be cooler but still light, a plan which gave her time to clear her head and do her aching body a favour.

It was a work-out at the police gym, a bout of judo with her old instructor and a power shower, her second of the day, which did it. She felt a bit more like her old self again. If not fighting fit, she was still lithe and strong. What made her feel even better was seeing and greeting a number of uniformed colleagues as she passed through the corridors. Very soon, she would be putting her own navy blue back on again and she anticipated even now the relief from role-playing. She should never have volunteered for undercover work. It had gotten to her, making her feel more than ever a misfit and a pariah.

When, in the late hours of the afternoon, she was turned away from the door at the lonely building for a second time, the old place looking not unlike an abandoned Civil Guard barracks, it didn't bother her in the least. It meant a free evening and another night in her own bed. She called her friend Marta, who suggested they go see a comedy movie. When they came out of the Renoir, they went for tapas, still laughing.

They found an old tiled bar that hadn't been turned into a franchise and were served small glasses of beer, the head creaming down the side, just like it should.

"So what's he like, your boyfriend?"

" Nice," Erica said. "Do you want some anchovies?"

"Nice?" asked her friend.

"Yes. A bit serious." She popped the stone of an olive out of her mouth and carried on chewing.

"Are you happy?"

She wrinkled her nose. "I think you have to give it time."

"Like hell."

"I take it you disagree."

"You have no idea. How long have you two been going?"

Erica could have kept the evasiveness up indefinitely, but what was the point?

"Nearly six months. But together? Really together? Never. Satisfied?"

"Good. The truth. Now you can have the anchovies. And don't look so glum."

Erica smiled and reached over to squeeze her friend's arm. "What about you? Still with Victor?"

"He wears me out." A meaningful look said that this wasn't a bad thing.

"Really?"

"Really." The two girls leaned their heads further in to talk some more.

By the time she reached home that night, she was resigned, but not unhappily so, to an inevitable break with Sebastián. On the night bus, she had invited any hidden feelings and voices to make themselves known: to object, to speak up if she was making a mistake, and none had come. That he hadn't messaged a reply to her earlier attempt at humour came as a relief. Cheer up, girl, you're moving on, she told herself. My God, I was nearly a mum. She was already looking forward to being plain and simple PC Sánchez and the predictability that went with it. When she looked past her reflection in the bus window, it was to the cautionary image of her own making as the bus passed by the still pockmarked and blackened wall of the bank she had assaulted. She was sorry to see a tree missing, the unintended collateral damage of her enthusiasm, but she noted the regret without feeling it. Calmness was already filling her like a rising well and she rode the rest of the way home upon a swell of certitude.

Seb had swung by the apartment during the day—his attaché case was gone, and some shirts—but there was no note. She walked through all the rooms, light and shadowy, in the well-ordered flat. She wouldn't have a place like this again, but then again, she had never felt comfortable in it. It had always been too masculine for her liking, too tidy, and presumptuously big. Soon she could and would assume her natural level in some cheap rental. Go back to leaving knickers and other feminine debris lying around. She checked the mobile. There was nothing from Pastori, or either of the girls, and her mother knew not to call when Erica was working. Everyone was leaving her in peace tonight.

Thursday, 13th August

SEBASTIÁN HAD BEEN pleased to see his mother, but he was even more pleased to be on his way. She had become needier since his father had died and her fussing over him, insisting on making him his boyhood favourite of French toast for breakfast, nearly made him late leaving. At the last moment, when he was already in the car, she hurried out to give him a gentleman's umbrella that had been his father's. "I do wish you'd take a coat. Asturias is not green for nothing, you know," she said.

He cruised for two hours through an inert landscape of forgettable monotony on the northbound A-6 before interrupting his journey for an energy drink and a toilet break. He stopped at a petrol station and took off his suit jacket, folding it carefully onto the backseat of the BMW. When he went into the cafeteria next to the petrol station, there was one other customer, who was talking to the waitress about the news story on the TV. Sebastián seated himself at the bar next to a display of key rings on the theme of skulls and the waitress unstuck herself from the chubby guy to come and take his order. The Pope's image came on the TV and Sebastián felt piety and pride straighten his spine, reminding him of the greater mission of us all.

The girl brought his drink and stood back in a slouch, chewing her gum, giving him a sullen checking-out.

"Is there a church near here?" he asked.

Her random eye movement betrayed an inner disquiet. Had he said that? Did he mean something else by it? In the end, she decided she hadn't heard. She put a finger in her mouth to bite on the nail instead, while keeping the corner of a darting eye on him.

Sebastián picked up his mobile and car keys and went to the gents. Within seconds he was joined at the adjacent urinal by the other man. He was so much shorter that Sebastián could see his head turning.

"Do you need a friend?" the man asked.

The physical discomfort from interrupting his stream was such that Sebastián didn't and couldn't wait for change from the perversely sluggish girl. In no time at all he was out in the car and back on the road, unrefreshed and grimfaced. He emptied the rest of his bladder in a lay-by picnic area where he shouldn't have and then sent Erica a routine message by way of restoring a due sense of correctness to his expedition.

The road and landscape resumed their unrelieved desolateness. He turned off the radio and prayed. Sebastián's sense of humour was undeveloped but his faith was steadfast and he soon found reason to thank the queer incident for awakening in him inner purpose and the resolve of responsibility. He found some chewing gum that Erica kept under the dashboard and before long he was imitating the waitress in the cafeteria and her unflattering facial expressions. It made him feel a whole lot better.

• • • •

ERICA WOKE WITH HER police head on. She even packed her revolver and handcuffs, rolling them up inside a towel and placing it in the bottom of a plastic travel bag that she had picked out for its trendy nineteen seventies throwback design. She had seen male colleagues at the police gym with them and made a mental note not to date them, but for Carina's image it was just the thing.

After a session on the exercise bike that Sebastián had put in one of the two unused guest rooms, a shower and coffee, she brought her report sheet up to date and was sending a message to Pastori on the police mobile when a recorded voice call came in on it from someone on her private contact list.

It was Raquel, inviting them both to evening sushi cocktails. How fashionable and boring of you, Erica smiled. But why not ask Sebastián? He's your friend. I'm the erratic drunk, remember? The event was to be in "a progressive ambience," which could only mean more sculpted beards and beatific smiles marking their owners out as artistic and special. How kind of you, she texted back. I'll check with Seb to see if we can make it.

She messaged Pastori that she would attempt to gain access to the Camp for the final two days and, failing that, had a vehicle in which to take the girl to her parents when she came out.

As she finished the message, another call came in.

"Hi, Mum."

"Your mother can't sleep."

"Hallo, father. Have you tried giving her earplugs so she can't hear you droning on all night?"

"Very amusing, Erica. I think she's worried about you."

Why? she thought. Because I'm not pregnant anymore? Because I might not want to be? Wait until she hears I'm leaving Sebastián.

"Tell her I'm doing just fine. I was just a bit tired the other night, that's all."

"I'm glad to hear it." He paused and Erica could hear muffled words in the background. "Sebastián makes a very favourable impression on us both," he said.

Maybe the three of you can go on holiday together. "I'll be sure to tell him that. I have to go."

"You must come again soon," Alfonso said.

"Yes, sir. Love to mum. Byeee."

And see you at Christmas. Perhaps. On balance, she preferred Raquel and Antonio's sushi cocktails, whatever they were. If it meant swallowing live clams in vermouth, hell, she could do that. Hold her nose and down it would go.

She picked up her bag and Olga's car keys and decided on the floppy hat. As she left the apartment, the air conditioning clicked off. It was Thursday, then. The maid didn't come to clean on a Thursday, or Sebastián would have programmed the air con to stay on. He was nothing if not considerate, she thought, and hated herself instantly for thinking it.

• • • •

HIS STEADY PROGRESS north took him past León. When he emerged from a long tunnel to a vista of distant, flint-grey mountains, the already lighter highway traffic slowed its hurrying, as if relaxing in collective relief. Sebastián put on a CD of Alejandro Sanz. After a few songs, the female voice of his satnav interrupted the CD, advising him, in a tone bordering on dulcet, to prepare to turn off.

The country road she directed him onto was only just wide enough to permit two-way traffic, but the open valley allowed him to see so far ahead that he was able to drive at comfortable speed along the long straights and curves.

"After two hundred metres, turn left."

He came to a T-junction.

"Turn left."

With infinite patience and ease, she guided him thus along minor and main roads. What she didn't know was the names of the villages.

"Turn right."

"For La Cabaña," he told her, reading the sign.

They passed beneath La Cabaña without a sight of the village or knowing for sure whether it existed. The countryside came on, bend after bend and ever more dense, the BMW handling a little heavily on the tighter turns. Outside the car registered 29°C, but inside the air conditioning blew true to specifications. Sebastián, as always, proceeded smoothly and composedly. He was getting a little hungry. He was making good time on a tank that showed half full still, only it was gone two p.m. and his chances of finding a hostelry in these increasingly remote hills seemed slim. He licked his lips to taste some salt. The sun dazzled turn by turn. The shadows were thin and dry. It had been a while since he had crossed into Asturias and longer since he had seen more than two buildings together.

The tarmac road cut a line around a hill before starting to climb. It passed through a forest of beech unnoticed by a driver who was concentrating on the road and aware of nothing more than steel safety barriers, monotonous banks of rocky earth and the foliage of spindly trees, all of which obscured the world beyond. Brambly hedgerows shouldered closer in as the road wound up and up, and then all of a sudden there was a rapid glimpse, and another, of a broad valley way below to his right. There was nowhere to pull off, so he stopped the car in the middle of a straight length of road, leaving two wheels on the white line of the kerb and the car half hidden in the shadow of the tall trees.

He got out and looked down at his feet. He had become defiantly enamoured of his exquisite new shoes and dared not risk them getting scuffed. In the end, he stepped very gingerly down into the undergrowth, over a couple of fallen branches and through ferns, crunching pine cones underfoot but never somehow approaching a point where the view was going to open up to him. The immense valley was there, shimmering beyond a mass of tree trunks and far away there were hazy peaks, but the interminable woods presented a barrier to getting any closer. He felt distinctly out of place in his city clothes and unnerved, in the hot, sweaty, buzzing nowhere, by the absence of another human being. It felt wrong to be stopped here all alone, on the hillside, for no good reason.

Sebastián retraced his steps to the car where he wiped his shoes with a soft cloth and sipped on a bottle of water. He strapped himself back into the driver's seat and consulted the interactive online map. According to the screen itinerary, there were just 48 km to go.

"Continue straight on," the navigating voice admonished him gently.

A minor detour in the hope of finding at least a sandwich took him to a settlement that was more semi-industrial than agricultural. There was not a soul to be seen, just houses made of breeze blocks, ill-kept yards, warehouses, rutted tracks and barbed wire fences. A sign pointing to the "Bear's Pathway" invited the visitor to tread through hoof-marked mud before dealing with a padlocked gate. Sebastián was glad the ugly place didn't seem to have a name to remember it by. If Asturias existed as he hoped to find it, the welcoming idyll so benignly promised by the publicity, then he was still in transit to it.

When he was a little less than five kilometres short of his destination, his female satnav companion decided that it was time he worked the rest out for himself.

"At the next safe turning point, turn round and drive back," she said.

"What did I miss?" he said to her. "What did *you* miss?"

She remained silent. He drove on for some way, the steep, twisting descent leaving him no other option. A little stone bridge took him past the roaring torrent of a stream in a wooded gully that was engulfed in shadow, before the narrow road levelled off and straightened. Half a kilometre down this stretch was the entrance to a field. It gave him just enough room to back the car in and put it round with a four-point turn. As he passed over the brief bridge, the cascade hollered again and the road started to wind back up.

"At the next safe turning point, turn round and drive back."

This time he had a longer way to go and always climbing, to find a spot to turn. The engine of the black city car exhibited signs of labouring for the first time. On the way back down he drove slowly, looking out for a road sign, maybe a worn, wooden one semi-obscured by foliage that would point him up a lane, or just a track. He looked in vain.

"At the next safe turning point, turn round and drive back."

The BMW mounted the same cramped entry to the field and he put the handbrake on, sweating from nervousness. He had been entrusted with a simple commission and here he was unable even to find the village. He brought up the itinerary on his mobile. A continuous blue line describing the route came to an end on this side of the gully—the wrong side, if the unforthcoming satnav were to be believed—and blue dots then led off at a tangent, indicating a track or a path which meandered for three or four kilometres before petering out. Miga didn't show up as a name or identifiable settlement on the map. The dossier that Jaime de Abascal had given him didn't even include a telephone number to contact. He really was on his own.

He got out of the car and walked up into the field, which lay fallow and sloped up the hillside. The access ramp turned left immediately inside the field and a furrowed track ran parallel with the road as far as a muddy corner, where it angled right and upwards to follow what must be the contours of the gully. On the basis that there was no other visible road or track at all, and seeing as the car was pointing that way, he decided to chance his luck. He advanced warily, in first gear most of the time, for fear of scraping or disabling the car. He turned off the air con and lowered the windows, the better to hear his way forward. As he reached the top of the steepening field, the stream gushing noisily but unseen off to his left, the ruts in the track deepened and a stony clunk from beneath the car caused him to swallow. Sebastián slowed to a crawl and the radiator fan came on. The BMW's front wheel drive heaved the car over a hump, dragging the undercarriage heavily, before levelling off and he turned to pass over the stream on a crossing made from concrete slabs. From here on, the farm track was even but narrower, and tough, desiccated vegetation threatened to scratch the paintwork. By now, he was quite sure he had made a mistake, but at least the going was easier and he changed to second gear, dry grasses hissing and creaking under the vehicle. Nearly two kilometres later, he came to a wide metal gate preceded by a cattle grid. On the other side of the gate stood two men. One was tall and thin and his hollow cheeks had the effect of turning his eyes askew. The other, who carried a shotgun and a leather satchel over his shoulder, looked hard and patient at the same time.

Sebastián got out, leaving the engine running, and nearly slipped on the shiny round bars of the cattle grid. "I'm looking for a village called Miga," he called out, holding onto the car with his right hand. "I went the wrong way."

The men made no reply. One aimed a steady look both at and past him, as if expecting another car to arrive; the other, who might have been looking anywhere, flexed his head back, as though he had dropped off to sleep, and then recovered himself.

"Can you tell me where to find Miga?" Sebastián tried again. "I'm on government business," he added somewhat pathetically. He wondered whether these country people spoke only the autochthonous Asturian tongue called Bable and didn't know any Spanish.

"The Government," said the hunter. "Have you got the papers?"

Why hadn't he kept his mouth shut? Now he was going to have to humour them. He obviously couldn't insist on a straight answer and theirs was the only prospect of help for miles around.

Sebastián made his way round the back of the car to open the boot and take out his accreditation from the attaché case. He clonked back over the cattle grid to the gate and held it up for the men to peer at.

"May I?" said the swarthy man with the gun, taking it from Sebastián's hand and scrutinizing it for several, long seconds, before handing it back. "You can't take the automobile, sir," he said, moving to unlatch and swing the gate open. "You have to walk. Polo will carry your luggage."

"So this is the right way?" Sebastián asked, but Polo was already going to collect his Samsonite suitcase, leather attaché case, tablet, folded suit jacket, clean ironed shirt on a hanger, cardboard poster tube and umbrella.

With misgivings if not resignation, he left the car locked up behind the gate and turned up the path in the company of two strangers who were aware that he was perturbed, who said little or nothing, and who had relieved him of all his belongings, including the official papers. Instead of asking the questions beating at the door of his need to know, he attempted to ingratiate himself with his walking companions and found his small talk repaid in the coin of silence. The only information that he managed to elicit was that they had been shooting partridges.

The path turned steep and stony. He offered to relieve Polo of at least the attaché case, but Polo shied away from him. He knew his duty and he wasn't about to release his multiple load to anybody. The way they had to negotiate was well-maintained, if challenging. Where rock protruded from the ground, channels had been cut across for storm run-off, but not even a high-clearance four-wheel drive could have made it along here and they would probably have been better off on mules. At least the man with the gun had been telling the truth about it being impassable for vehicles, but Sebastián's anxiety wouldn't leave him, not even when he spoke the Lord's Prayer to himself. He felt both fit and strong and helpless at the same time. They trudged on, often in single file, with him at the back.

After what was already a considerable hike, the brow of a low hill opened up to a vision that caused him to stop in his tracks. Thick with trees, a snug, steep-sided river valley presented a patchwork in shades of green for miles ahead, all of it bound by mountain. The forest had been cleared only partly, by the river, to make way for arable land. It otherwise spread like a green fur over the body of the craggy mountain, covering heights and reaching into deep creases as far as a suggestive swelling at the valley's end, a mound dense with leaf itself. He wanted to stand and stare, but the other men had already gone on into the forest and so he went after them, an after-image remaining in his mind of a self-contained, breathing world, populated by ancient trees. It was like he imagined Eden to be.

The men descended in a steady, rhythmic pace down what was now a gentler slope and a softer path through oak and birch. They had already gone so far that Sebastián knew that doubling back to the BMW to resume his search for the village was no longer a realistic option. The stream he had crossed might as well have been the Rubicon. He might still have the car keys and the ability to trek back, but if he was going to lose possession of the confidential documents then he might as well vanish from trace and make a home in a cave. He seriously doubted that he could count on the cooperation of the two country men, whose single-mindedness in escorting him into this fast wilderness had bent the back of his resistance with each step that they had taken from the abandoned car. If Sebastián had faith in the goodness of a world ruled over by his God, that world was Madrid, or at least that milieu of the capital to which he belonged, where the streets were cleaned at night and policed by day, where he could get a coffee served in a matter of seconds, the spoon rattling into the saucer, and where attitudes for or against the establishment were an establishment themselves, as unthreatening and predictable as the Metro, which took you just about anywhere in half an hour. Here, he didn't know what he was walking into. His composure masked the hopeful compliance of a captive and he was ashamed to admit that he would gladly settle for coming to no harm and something to fill his belly.

As they rounded a great oak, there appeared unannounced a pair of low stone houses. They left the houses behind and woods still dominated the scene but at a white post the path widened to become a dirt street and suddenly they were in the village proper. Three straggly hens waddled quickly away, expressing indignation that no one had told them to expect a visitor and they hadn't been given a moment to preen their feathers. No other people yet, but more stone dwellings, a grain store and a weather-eaten cross where the street divided and they branched towards the right. Polo, who led the way, hitched up about his bony person all of Sebastián's travel things—spare suit and sensitive government papers, hair oil and clean underwear, shoe polish, mobile charger, toothbrush, umbrella and all—and sang out a clanging sound that made a distant dog bark, then another. Polo and the other man, known as Pepe, waited for Sebastián to come between the two of them and thus he walked, breathing more freely, tucking a crumpled white shirt back into his trousers and smoothing back his hair, into Miga.

• • • •

ERICA PARKED OLGA'S Citroen opposite the Camp building in a large gap between two SUVs, wishing it was always so easy to park in the capital. She got out and looked over at the brute square of the edifice, baking already in the morning sun. Locking the car door, she lifted the bag to her shoulder and decided on a jaunty approach and a big smile. Carina positively skipped across what once had been a street and up the steps. This time, after she had buzzed the button, a watery eye lingered on her from behind the grille in the door.

"Carina Delgado. Please check."

"Give me your ID," said the same male voice as before.

She obediently handed over the plastic card that proved her false identity and age and the grating fell shut. Almost immediately, it opened again.

"You should have been here yesterday," a different, foreign accent said.

"I was. I came twice."

The door opened inwards and in the shadow of a cloister stood a woman with a clipboard, her blonde hair tied in a bun. Next to her was a security guard in his forties.

"Come in."

The door was bolted behind her and they stood in the cool shadow of a high cloister. The columns were not rounded to make pleasing, ecclesiastical arches and formed instead functional rectangles, while beyond them was not the garden one might expect but an empty arena of packed sand, giving the facility an almost military aspect.

"I paid. A sponsor paid for me."

"Yes, we know that. Sign here and here."

Carina Delgado put her name to two closely typed pages that were quickly removed from sight.

"Mobile." The woman held out a long-fingered hand.

"I need it. I have to call my family."

"Or you can leave now."

Carina gave it up.

"Another?"

Carina shook her head.

"If you haven't called already, it's too late now. No mobiles. You'll get your so-called possessions back when you leave."

She sounded Scandinavian, maybe, or Dutch. Erica could differentiate Arabic accents, but northern Europe wasn't her area of linguistic expertise.

"My bag," Carina protested as the guard carried it off in the opposite direction.

"You missed Day One. There is a great deal you'd better learn very quickly. There is no 'my', there is no 'bag', there is no 'Carina Delgado.' Come with me."

Erica followed her through the light and shadows of the wide cloister, kicking herself for not knowing the ground rules at the Camp. But then again, she wasn't aware that they had been published or made available. It didn't look as if she was going to be allowed to keep a change of clothes, or even her basic toiletries. She would just have to trust them not to go through her belongings or she would be all kinds of trouble. On no account was she supposed to take her firearm on the assignment.

The clipboard woman handed her over to a young monitor, who led her downstairs to a damp cellar that might have been medieval. The ceiling was oppressively low, but that hadn't prevented them from erecting bunks in there. The two of them were alone and Erica was starting to wonder where the other Camp participants were.

"You're here," the girl tapped the upper bed with her hand without having to reach up. "Put these on." She took a sports vest and shorts and a pair of flip flops from the folded sheet on the bunk and handed them to her. Erica took a deep breath and sighed. She turned round to take off what she had on and put on the synthetic kit. The girl gathered up her things and put them in a shrink-wrap bag.

"How many other boys and girls are there?" she asked.

"You're not allowed to ask questions," the girl said.

"Pardon?"

"Not without permission. You're going to be late for Meditation Seven."

Erica allowed herself to be ushered up a different flight of steps to a narrow corridor. They went past a room emanating a curdled breakfast smell and kept going until they found themselves blocked by a queue of young people wearing the same unbecoming clothes.

The monitor turned round to face her. "No talking, no touching, no eye contact," she said. "Repeat."

"No talking, no touching, no eye contact," said Carina.

"Good. Now you may be no one and nothing."

On that promising note, the expressionless girl made her way past the line of girls and boys, leaving the newcomer on the end.

Erica was unimpressed. She could see which way this was going and she doubted her patience to see it out and still be there holding Zoe's hand when they awarded the certificates and told them how far they had advanced in the spiritual boot camp.

The set-up wasn't a new idea, but it worked. You stripped spoiled rich kids of their iPhones and designer fashion and isolated them. A rule of silence so that they had no chance to bond or influence each other with attitudinizing. Then, once you'd given them a taste of army-like discipline so that they felt they were having a real hard time of it, you'd mix in the pseudo-self-transformation crap so that they felt that the radical regime was true and right and special, just like they themselves were, and so worth every cent their parents had paid for it. Kind of the bad cop, good cop routine extrapolated onto a theatre of supposed self-realization. Any old claptrap would do as long as it was delivered with a straight face. For three days, you kept kids in a state of shock, fed them carrots and chamomile tea and baloney, then sent them home to Mummy and Daddy and laughed all the way to the bank.

She might be wrong, of course. Anything was possible. Beer might go out of fashion. Pigs might fly.

A shrill whistle sounded and an older, male monitor at her back commanded the line to move forward up a dog-legged stairway. At the top the steps, they shuffled out into a blinding sun in the vast sandy arena bounded by the cloisters, where the whistling increased in pitch. Erica felt her arm grabbed and she was pulled, half cooperating, half not, in harried steps to a spot where she was pushed down and released. During a brief interval of silence, there was time just enough for her to look around and see as many as fifty lonely teenagers spaced out more or less equidistantly from each other. More girls than boys. And there was Zoe, five participants away, kneeling with her hands behind her back like some hostage ready for beheading. One of her neighbours, a boy with long hair, bore an expression of amused defiance. The others looked anxious.

A roll of thunder passed over their heads like a spinning demon, causing several youngsters to cringe and duck. It was, Erica realized, a clever sound effect, probably produced by speakers placed at strategic points.

"You are shit. You are nothing."

Whoa, thought Erica.

The words spat out electrically over the same speakers as the sonic boom, coming at each isolated camper from all sides.

"You? Who are you? You is a fiction. You created you, and now you are ridiculous enough to believe in it. You do not know who you are."

It was Olga's language in a mise-en-scène that, depending on how Erica blinked, was either a rock star stadium presided by an evangelical psychiatrist, or a heavy duty detention centre where the commandant was telling them why they had no chance. Either way, the disembodied male voice was warped to a spiteful severity by a cheap PA system. The visible presence of its authority was manifested in four sturdy men, positioned at each corner of the sunlit quadrangle on raised wooden platforms from where they could survey the proceedings. It was a woman, though, who walked slowly through the dispersed attendees, looking for what? A smirk? A sign of weakness?

"Which of you has the courage?" crackled the loudspeaker. "Which of you will break through? Because to know the truth, to know the real you behind all posturing and thought, you must break through and break out. The inner resistance must give way, and the ego must die. Verily, you must die in order to be born anew. But can you kick out the cuckoo imposter in the nest of your conscious being? Can you fuck. You're letting ego put up the same old blocks, the same old arguments, hoodwink you with its immature chatter."

The woman left a mark with yellow chalk on a boy's shoulder and moved silently on.

Erica guessed that the venue had once been a military school. She could imagine horses and soldiers parading on the compact sand of this Field of Mars to the sound of stiff drums. The open gallery of cloisters made up three sides of the square courtyard, while the fourth was simply a towering façade of brick. High up on the wall was a carved crest that she couldn't make out with a small window on either side, otherwise it was solid and unrelieved. The kind of wall that one could stand people up against and execute by firing squad.

"Are you resisting? You are resisting. Go beyond. Beyond the self. Give up the body. Give up the self."

A terrible crash of rocks made them all flinch. Big rocks, offloaded from a heavy duty dumper, thumped into the sand at the far end of the courtyard. Their cracking together echoed around the cloisters like rifle fire.

"Who are the Six?" the distorted megaphonic voice demanded. "Stand up. The Yellow Six."

One by one, those who the woman had marked with yellow chalk got to their feet. The last to stand was Zoe.

"The six must choose a partner. The rule of silence remains."

Erica waited, the passive victim of inevitability, until Zoe's eyes settled on her in sudden recognition and the girl came over. Under the heavy eyebrows, her eyes smiled more than Erica found right.

"Having a nice time?" Erica asked.

"Shhhhhhhh!!" A ubiquitous hushing made clear the imposition of silence was not to be trifled with, the more so as it came not from the reverberating speakers around the arena, but from the other girls and boys. Erica had missed induction and the first day of Camp, but all the same she was shocked by the collective acquiescence of the young people. Zoe shook her head in a way that could have meant one of two things. Either she couldn't express to Carina how important all this was to her, or Carina wasn't with the program and really needed to get with it. Erica looked at the boy with the long hair and the sardonic expression. He showed her his tongue and looked away.

"Face your partners," ordered the tannoy.

Erica stood and squinted in the sun, which was now overhead and beating down. Zoe was shorter and dumpier than she remembered. Otherwise, for a girl supposed to be mixed up and conflicted by authority figures, she seemed quite unperturbed.

The woman returned, walking nonchalantly through those seated or crouching to the twelve youngsters who were standing in pairs. Draped over her arm she carried what looked like dark grey bags or sacks and she handed out one each to the six individuals stigmatized with her chalk. When Zoe received hers, she held it up. The thing was floppy, open at one end, with no handle or drawstring and made of smooth, hard-wearing cotton. It was a hood. The woman sashayed out of the arena.

"One of you must wear it. Let the Six decide," pronounced the voice.

Zoe considered the hood in her hands for some while, much longer than the others who made their choice almost immediately. Her deliberating look said that she was weighing up a decision of grave responsibility. Then she took a step forward and raised her arms high to bring the hood down over her partner's head.

A whistle blew and the six unsighted ones were left out on their own, as all the non-players were waved off the court and into the shade of the cloisters. Their six sighted partners were directed to the far end to stand with their backs against the high wall. Two monitors arranged them so that they were a couple of body lengths apart, before leaving them there in a narrow shadow at the sand's edge. At the opposite end of the court lay the pile of rough-hewn rocks, dusty and white.

The hollow darkness inside the closed hood had heated up in seconds. Erica told herself that it was a game, that she was the adult among the teenagers and could tear it off whenever she wanted, but if the intention was to challenge the participants, they had inadvertently found her out. After a long minute inside, she was flushed and sweating and ready to panic into asphyxiation. Her mind raced like an alarmed wasp.

"Six slaves for six masters."

The voice gave her something to hold onto, something to hate. In that moment, Erica decided to make a stand and defy the persecutor. Whatever the perverse game was, whoever or whatever she was fighting, didn't matter. It was now a personal affair. She closed her mouth and breathed through her nose, slowing her rapid, shallow breathing to a manageable agitation, tightening her lips together, waiting for the next move, the next play.

Her ears pricked up at a slithering sound. Behind her, two men were running past the young masters and mistresses backed up against the long wall, leaving twin parallel lines in the sand with iron bars. One line ran just in front of the teenagers' feet, the other was a couple of metres distant. They might have represented a road, or two frontiers to cross.

The two men with the bars then ran back the same way, leap-frogging each other for fun, and stopping to draw seven perpendicular lines between the two parallels, so that each sighted player now had a large rectangle in front of them. A game was about to begin.

"Masters, your slave must bring five stones to your drop zone. You may direct them but not use their name, should you know it. The last master and slave to complete five stones don't get to eat or shower today. The last slave will remain alone in the centre of the court until midnight. On my whistle. One, two, three!"

The chaos of confusion that ensued as masters shouted out instructions to their hooded puppets changed the atmosphere entirely. As the six blind mice ran back and forth, left and right, lost in a maze of contradictory yelling, holding out their arms, the general merriment that it produced among the spectators met with no reprimand this time and soon the pent-up nervousness and anxiety of the boys and girls was expressed in boisterous hilarity, to the exasperation of at least one of the slaves, who ripped off her hood and ran crying into the wings.

"The slave who broke the rules," barked the Voice. "Put her in The Pit."

Two staff led the girl away. "No!" she cried, but she was as weak as a doll to their grip. She disappeared, taking the crowd's laughter with her.

The campers turned their attention back to the patio and watched with interest as, one by one, the wandering slaves eventually found their way to the rocks and felt around, trying for a light one, only there were no light ones. Erica was the first to get one in her arms and start treading back with it. Not only was she now extremely focussed, she also enjoyed an advantage in knowing Zoe's voice as she called out "to the right, to the left." She had chased the demon of claustrophobia from the hood, but breathing was still seriously difficult and the stone very nearly too much for her. She got to within feet of Zoe's "Here, here, here, here," and would probably have dropped it anyway even if Zoe hadn't told her to.

"Now go back and get another one. Come on."

Yes, mistress, Erica thought, panting. She swallowed drily and started the long, uncertain walk back like a woman in the desert, blinded by the sun and wind. The summer heat was now extreme and it soon became clear to those watching which of the five slaves remaining was going to fail. One small girl was simply too weak to transport the stones. Unable to lift one, she tried rolling it in the sand, or toppling it over rather, as all the rocks were irregular and anything but round, but she got hers no more than a few turns and in the wrong direction before the exertion became too much for her and she had to rest. One of the boys, meanwhile, a large, podgy youth with a singularly determined attitude, was starting to outpace them all. He wobbled up to deliver a second rock to his mistress, to the undisguised envy of the girl next to her whose weakling slave was floundering still with a first stone so that she had nothing but empty sand to the other five's one rock each. When the tubby boy had just a few steps left to go, she called out: "Over here, boy, you're nearly there. Good-looking, to me, to me!"

His true mistress was either too slow or too shocked to react. The boy staggered over and dropped his load at the feet of the other girl. "Well done! We're winning. Keep going."

He turned round and plodded off.

"That's not fair! That's cheating!" the boy's mistress protested.

The other girl ignored her. "Listen to my voice, boy," she told him. "Think of a clock. Walk towards two o'clock. Good, good. Now eleven o'clock."

"Don't listen to her! She's not me. Bitch!"

"Bitch, yourself," returned the girl, who had just applied the first rule of survival strategy.

The spectators, who even in the shade had already started to tire with the heat and incipient boredom, saw and heard exactly what had gone on. They perked up. This was now girl-against-girl. They started shouting from the echo chambers of the cloisters, taking sides. It was going to be all against all. This was gladiatorial.

Any lost citizen walking by outside in the weed-grown precinct of decaying buildings, anyone able to bear the dirty sun and forty degrees of city heat, would have heard pyrotechnics of youthful enthusiasm that simply didn't belong there at all, didn't add up. Youngsters who minutes before had been downcast, kneeling in the sand, proceeded to scream at the slaves as they wandered aimlessly, stumbled and staggered with their loads, walked straight into each other and fell like drunks, or simply sat and did nothing, until howls of execration got them to their feet again and then they waited, listening for the voice of their mistress or master to tell them which way to go.

Dragging down into her lungs the overheated condensation of her breath, Erica stopped where she was and listened to them chanting and clapping. Her feet were getting burnt by the sun. Children should be strangled at birth, she thought. *Fuck you, fuck you, and fuck you,* she addressed the three cloisters in turn, mouthing it silently with her lips since her vocal chords had stuck together like congealed spaghetti.

As the stones arrived one by one in their laborious progress, a staff member went to change a number hung on the wall above the slave-owner's head, so that the boys and girls watching knew exactly what the score was. Thanks to the first bitch's cheating, imitated with less success by the other masters, the losing master-slave pairing was by no means clear. The heavy boy continued moving stones as if born to the trade, apparently unable to count to five, or uncaring. Erica may have been fitter and considerably stronger than the teenagers, but Zoe's voice would sometimes falter in the mêlée or simply not be heard at all, and she spent long, lost periods getting and going nowhere.

The pace slowed. With the broiling weight of the sun so unforgiving, picking up a stone was like lifting a monstrous brick from an oven. The crowd's fervour grew hoarse and thin in dry throats as the heat forced even the cloisters into submission. The anonymous slaves could now teeter a few steps forward and release their load without being verbally set on from all sides. Disorientation and dehydration were sapping the five blind mice, but whatever their motivation may have been, whether trepidation, conformity, defiance, confusion, pride, or the simple desire to get it over with and come out of the dark blaze, the slaves kept on going. The pile of rocks diminished. They were down to the very last few.

Zoe had four sitting in front of her, like ugly giant eggs, as did the two boys to her left. The two girls on her right had four and three respectively. Thanks to big boy's appetite for punishment, his twin mistresses, the rightful and the usurper, had as good a chance of filling their quota and therefore their bellies, as well as getting a cold shower, as the others. The contest was going down to the wire, which was going to be barbed for the unlucky loser.

The first to reach the finish line was Erica. Once her suffocating fear had gone, her greater stamina and strength had only been outperformed by the insane doggedness of the slave the crowd called Fatty, but he had had twice as many rocks to fetch, of course. She had picked over the final rocks, semi-embedded in the stiff sand, for the smallest of them, which still weighed a good twenty kilos, but was going to be her fifth and last. Forty metres of radiated pain later, she walked directly at Zoe as if she were able, at the end, to see through the thick bag over her eyes. She marched forward and was almost face-to-face with Zoe when the girl moved over to the far side of her dropping zone, at its limit with the next Mistress and called, "To the left, to the left." Erica stopped and turned, aiming at Zoe's voice. She pushed herself forwards to be granted blessed relief of the dense weight, "Yes, yes, yes!" guiding her all the way to: "Drop it."

She was about to pull off the sweating mop of a thing about her face when the score keeper said, "Four stones. Go back for another."

"That was five," she croaked. "Five."

"You missed the drop zone. There are four. Go back for another."

Dizziness took hold of Erica's consciousness. If she had chosen that moment to free herself of the clogging hood, she would have seen that the rock had fallen just inside the catchment area of the girl next to Zoe, completing her tally of five. Erica turned and wandered erratically. A strangled sound escaped her. She no longer knew where she should be heading and her legs were failing her. By the time the tubby boy struggled the last ten metres with his tenth rock, large and pointed, which he held like some Obelix about to toss a menhir into the Romans, she was lost and out of the game. Two staff members went over to take off Erica's hood where she half sat, half lay, and give her some water. In the blurry, blinding sunlight she could see shifting bodies as the Campers were led off. She was helped up and led to the centre of the square, where a rudimentary pavilion had been set up, made of four poles holding up a square of canvas. While open on all sides, it provided shelter, at least, from the overhead sun.

"You have to stay here. You're a failure."

Seeing that she didn't have the strength or even a voice with which to oppose them, they left her there under the tent, lying flat on her back. There was a litre of water which she drank half of, getting up on one elbow, and coughing violently, before sinking back again, her head swimming in a semi-conscious delirium.

Time passed and then some more. As she slowly returned to herself, Erica found herself amazed at what she had permitted to be done to her. She noted with pale irony how flimsy her self-image as an effective police agent had proved once again. But maybe participation in the madness *was* her job. Unless she was going to get up and walk out on Zoe—and she wasn't now sure that she should—it meant sticking it out with her for two days. Presumably, the level of physical punishment would stop short of causing serious harm, if the Camp—whatever and whoever the Camp was—intended to return Madrid's pampered rich kids to their parents intact and not be prosecuted all the way to prison. Who *was* the Camp run by? Right now, there was no sign of anyone. The courtyard and cloisters were empty and she could hear nothing and no one. What would happen if she went walkabout? She stood up as best she could under the low roof of the open tent and stepped out into the Field of Light.

The speakers crackled deafeningly alive.

"Stop! The failure must go back to her meditation."

Erica unbent her spine in the same fierce sun that had been her scourge for nearly an hour's insanity and considered her assessment confirmed. The Camp had a game plan based on a kind of psychosocial totalitarianism and to continue she must comply. Not a nice game. She backed into her open-sided cell and sat on the sand with her arms around her knees. She drank the last two inches of warm water in the bottle—it was fast becoming her drink of choice this summer—and began, as instructed, a meditation.

If she could locate and lay her hands on the mobile to call Pastori without being seen or heard, which seemed unlikely, what would she say? If she told the Detective Inspector her assessment of the Camp and what had happened that day, it was very possible that Pastori would find the whole thing positively entertaining and ask if she had anything important to report. To express concern about the integrity of the Camp without any specific evidence that Zoe's safety was compromised would meet with little sympathy. It would simply furnish an invitation to her superior officer to remind Sánchez that she was supposed to be the protector, not the protected.

Right, meditation over, she decided.

After that, her concentration drifted between thoughts about where the car was parked, her mother's sleepless nights, clean underwear, the whereabouts of water, Sebastián's respectful chumminess with her father, possibly even with a gay politician, the shockwave of the explosion at the bank, Zoe's family address, the correct time, gazpacho and olives, her inability to form a healthy relationship, the uneaten oranges back at the flat, getting another job, another apartment, but what, and where would she move? Disjointed thoughts that jumbled and turned, competing for her attention like drowsy flies. Lunchtime came and went and the pointless minutes of the afternoon tugged at her with their hooks. Deprived of food, her isolation became lonely. The monotony was broken only once, by a crow that flapped down to check out her tent. She let it totter nearer with its beady eye before blaring out a roar that it reacted to lackadaisically, flapping away.

"Hi, I brought you some melon."

Erica woke with a start and backed instinctively away from Zoe's face, which shone in the light of the lamp she was carrying. It was dark and it was still hot, but Erica shivered. There was movement all around her in the enclosed arena, little lights swaying and crisscrossing and small footfalls across the sand.

"And some Aquarius."

"The lemonade. Please." She glugged back the drink. How long had she been asleep? Why did Zoe look so happy? Before she could ask, they were joined by two of the Camp's team of monitors, a boy and a girl.

"Would you like anything else?" asked the boy.

"More lemonade. And a sandwich," Erica said. "Tuna and tomato."

"OK," he said brightly and went off, leaving his colleague, who was about Erica's age, to sit down and make herself comfy with the two girls.

"What are your feelings right now?" she asked Erica.

"Can I go first?" asked Zoe.

"Sure."

"Angry, excited, pitying," said the teenager. "Getting Carina to miss with the last rock made me realize how pathetic some people are. Someone that wants to die is free because you're not attached to the world. I am now so honest and that's so exciting. I wanted Carina to lose and suffer because I hate her. And it feels so good to say that. I've been wanting to for so long. She's this good-looking, interesting woman in a young person's environment and it's so phoney. She seems more like thirty than twenty. She's got a boyfriend because she's always checking her mobile, but she never talks about him."

"Carina?" asked the Camp monitor.

Before she had succumbed to heat exhaustion and boredom late that afternoon and fallen into a heavy slumber, Erica had had a lot of time to think about game plans. In order to have a chance of bringing her own to a successful conclusion, which meant walking to the waiting car the day after tomorrow with a Zoe ready to go home, she had to win the game they played at the Camp by playing along with it. What she hadn't bargained for was finding the fourteen-year-old so hostile to her. How was she to play this one?

She most certainly couldn't afford to alienate her ward to the point of enmity, but brattishness like Zoe's wasn't going to let itself be placated, either. She pushed away the plate of melon cubes that she had been eating, the ones Zoe had brought her.

"Nobody really wants to die."

"Oh, but I really do," Zoe smiled. "That's what you've never understood. That's what no one understands. Death is my country."

"From which no traveller returns," Erica said.

"You missed the afternoon Truth Evacuation. We've been working on our feelings," the Camp girl said. "What about yours?"

"I have them and I don't have them," Erica said. "They might just as well be different ones, so it's like: what do they matter?"

"What have you learned today?"

"Life is suffering," she said.

"Pain is the White Door," said the girl. "Beyond lies deliverance. You might say that we are the angels of death."

"Catharsis," said Zoe.

The White Door, thought Erica. I wondered when we were going to come to that. She looked around the quadrangle at the flames of lamplight that formed a twinkling network under the night sky. At every lamp, three people were sat quietly, like themselves, gently talking. It was so implausible after the day's divisive offensive. Each pair of campers was accompanied by a monitor, which meant there was a considerable contingent of trained staff. Until now, Erica had figured the 2,200 euros that Zoe had paid for her multiplied by at least fifty participants in a venue that couldn't possibly charge more than five hundred a day added up to easy money for whoever had the ambition to get away with it. It came as a surprise to see so many actives on the Camp payroll. They could easily not have bothered with these labour-intensive love-ins or hate-ins.

A little bell, carried by a girl smelling of patchouli, tinkled as she ran past them on bare feet.

"Change and move on," said the girl, taking Zoe's hand and disappearing with her.

Erica could hardly believe her luck. She popped another melon cube in her mouth.

The actors revolved around her and another Camper-Monitor pairing took their place.

"Oliver here told us in his last intervention that he thought all words to be deceptive in the context of the collective conspiracy. He wishes to contribute non-verbally."

Oliver waited patiently for the monitor to finish and then began an odd dance that involved his arms mostly. Erica was content to be nonplussed. The Camp's Bad-cop-Good-cop cycle was in full nice-nice mode and the longer it went on the better. As if to prove the point, her sandwich was delivered by the cheerful youth who had gone for it. Tuna and tomato. It came with another cold drink. There was even a serviette.

"I thought the losers didn't get to eat," she said, to which he simply shrugged and smiled some more.

She wished to high heaven the lemonade had been a beer and was drinking it back like it was one, still watching the whirling Oliver, when the surrealism of the day made a bid for fame. The star, the household name that Olga had said was going to be there suddenly was, looming out of nowhere in all his impossible celebrity so that she nearly ejected the lemonade from a full mouth. He took her hands in his and then put his own together in a praying motion, like a Hindu, before going to dance with Oliver, who was by now in full flow.

After which, Carina was excluded again for no more obvious reason than she was included before. As the night wore on, she assumed the senselessness of her captivity. From her tent in the centre of the pitiless arena, in the time-owning heat, she would look out to the glimmerings in the void where the triads of young heads were talking and nodding. She would see them all stand and move on once more, all changing places except for one, who was the hub around which the ballroom rotated, gently sharing under the polluted sky.

Behold the slave, Erica spoke to them from her mind. Behold the loser. She is beautiful.

• • • •

AS IF TO COMPENSATE for his inferior physical stature, the mayor held himself stiffly upright to receive the holder of rank in the national government's highest office. Standing in the front parlour of his house, where the native pungency of the wooded settlement mixed with furniture polish, he nodded a brief introductory bow.

"Osvaldo Beltrán, at your service. And Juan Leger," he turned to present a naturally smiling man of about thirty. "Who, as I'm sure you're aware, enjoys our complete confidence and is detailed to be of personal assistance to you during your stay. You come alone, sir?"

The question was at once deferential and quizzical. It had been some while since they had been entrusted with the honour and this gentleman was unfamiliar. The man's small, round face stared in anticipation.

"Sebastián Elcano Domínguez," he shook both the other men's hands, without smiling. "Ministry of the Presidency of the Nation. I am to deliver this into your hands." He took the official communiqué from the front compartment of his briefcase and passed it to the civic leader of Miga.

"Please make yourself comfortable," said the mayor, indicating padded, armless chairs in nineteenth century style. "What will you have to drink? Have you eaten?"

"Water, please. Maybe I might eat something later."

Sebastián sat and the man called Juan left them alone. Even though there was brilliant sunshine outside, the room's small, high window let little of it in and Osvaldo Beltrán read the notification by the light of a standard lamp, which shone unappealingly on his balding pate.

Sebastián stared down at a threadbare crimson carpet on the otherwise bare earthenware floor. He was about to say, I will answer any questions to the best of my ability, when the first one caught him out completely.

"Why has the Minister not come?" The mayor's look was one of incomprehension.

Because you're so insignificant you don't even feature on the map. I shouldn't be here myself. This would have been so much more neatly dealt with by registered letter.

Sebastián set aside the impertinent answers his mind pressed on him and said, "I'm afraid he was otherwise engaged." He could have added: "And sends his regrets." But there was no need to elaborate on the pretence, especially as he had no idea which Minister the man could possibly have had in mind.

"Would you excuse me?" Mayor Beltrán stood up and his visitor rose with him.

"Of course." As he watched him leave the room, Sebastián remembered, with an onset of guilt for his unspoken impudence, that he had just served the man with a death sentence for his village.

Less than a minute later, Beltrán returned with Juan Leger, expressing a desire for the distinction of their guest's company at dinner that evening and commending him into the latter's good hands.

Juan's bright smile was a relief after the awkward formality preceding it. "Bet you've never seen a village as pretty as this," he said, as he led Sebastián out and across the square.

"I haven't really seen anything yet."

"You'll see. Come with me."

The village square, struggling to reach two storeys, was dominated by the copious trees which rose up at its rear, overhanging their branches which rested here and there on the roofs. The sagging plaster-and-timber exteriors were clearly of residences, outside which plain wooden chairs or benches had been set. Red peppers, and even washing, were strung out to dry in the sun. There were no shops that Sebastián could see, or any place that might have served as a bar for the local inhabitants. One building, whose national flag at the entrance marked it out as municipal premises, presumably the Village Hall, was of heavy stone blocks, and to its side was an even smaller square, more like a recessed patio. There were no habitués of the plaza, there to pass the time, nor any others inquisitive to see the stranger. The initial excitement caused by his arrival had given way to a reserve or shyness that had cleared the thoroughfare of Miga's people, save a woman who walked quickly past with a scarf pulled over her face and a small boy playing ball. When the football he was trying to scoop up into his arms escaped him and rolled out towards the two men, Sebastián went to intercept the ball and kick it back, but instead of waiting for it, the boy ran off down a darkened alley.

"Señor Leger," began Sebastián.

"Juan," he insisted. "Everyone calls me Juan. All our guests," he paused. "Without exception."

"Juan, I need to make a phone call and I can't get a signal. Do you know where's good to get a connection?"

"Oh, we don't have that," laughed Juan Leger. "Did you bring a pair of boots?"

He was looking down at their visitor's supple Italian footwear. Only the small area of the square by the Village Hall was paved in stone and they now found themselves on the bend of a sandy street, peopled by a variety pack of higgledy-piggledy houses. Ahead of them, the street straightened and rose, offering more of the same hard-packed sand.

"Why would I need them?"

Juan shrugged. "So that I can show you around properly."

"I'm not going to be able to do much, I'm afraid." Sebastián remembered Jaime de Abascal's explicit instruction to him, as the bearer of ill tidings, not to fraternize with the village. No sociability, no hunting (as if he would), or photos.

"Of course you will!" Juan branched off to the right and they climbed up steps past a terraced vegetable plot, going about as far as they could go within the trees and still be in the village. He pushed open the oak door of a cottage and sat Sebastián at a rude wooden table in front of a pitcher of water, a metal cup and a chunk of bread as big as his fist, while he greeted a woman who was dressed to Sebastián's eyes like a peasant in a history book. Juan wasn't much different, he noted, in his worn leather waistcoat and heavy trousers. The woman made a fuss of them both, welcoming the visitor as if he was long overdue and asking if he would have a salad to go with the stew. He said "yes" to everything. His hunger, suppressed for the duration of his meeting with the mayor, and encouraged by Juan's enthusiastic acclamation of Josefa's cooking, rose up in him like a wolf. The smell coming from the kitchen in the wooden house mingled with rich summer scents welling in through its open window to swell an appetite he hadn't known in months.

And yet not even that imperative could distract him from what met his eyes. He couldn't be sure whether Juan had brought him here for the food or the view. The table was pushed against the window, from where he had the clearest sight of forest hugging the mountainside all the way down the sinewy valley, its river twinkling below. He fought back the temptation to take a photo with his mobile. Juan saw him, as might be expected, to be somewhat tired and lost in thought. He clapped a hand on the visitor's shoulder and told him he would be back to show him to his lodgings. Sebastián nodded his assent and, when he had gone, drank down a draught of fresh, cool water.

After a second dishful of venison stew, tearing apart the bread that kept arriving at his table, and refilling his metal mug with water, he felt that he was getting into this place. Honey bees examined the lupins in the garden and a soft wind played among the branches of a willow. On an old sack in a rusty wheelbarrow, a scrawny marmalade cat lay curled in the sun.

When Josefa carried in a tureen of stewed fruit, he allowed himself to relax for the first time, stretching out and breathing in the sweet air. He sniffed at before declining the bottle of aromatic liqueur that she finally set at his elbow with a tall shot glass and made space instead for a pot of black coffee. When she brought out a towering milky cake, his protests were only outdone in vehemence by the hostess when he got out his wallet and asked what he owed. She waved her arms and sent him away, firmly admonished, but chuckling, down the steps.

His now heavier frame was grateful for the soft landing from the last high step onto the dirt street. The sun shone straight into his eyes and he squinted at what proved to be Juan, who was approaching carrying what looked like gardening clothes.

"Have you eaten?" he asked.

"Very well," Sebastián replied.

"We'll go to your accommodation. Have a rest and then we'll go for a little walk. These should fit you," he held up a pair of ancient boots.

A walk. Well that came under the heading of respectfully accepting hospitality, he thought. He would take the walk, paying courteous attention, and thank the man for his trouble. He undressed in his room, or suite of rooms, rather, as it had a separate sitting area, and was relieved to see that the WC had a proper seat, rather than the hole in the ground at Josefa's. He had lain back on the creaky bed and closed his eyes for what seemed like only seconds when there came a hammering on the door.

"Mr Sebastián."

"Just a minute," he called, dragging himself upright and belching. So much for the siesta. Courtesy and forbearance then, he told himself. He opened the door a crack and confirmed with Juan that he should change into the clothes and boots the man had brought. He splashed water into his face, dried it carefully off, and left his unusable mobile charging on the bedside table.

"Where are we going?" He had to hurry to keep pace with Juan as the man danced down a path descending from the lower reaches of the village.

"To the river." Juan moved from shadow to shadow, his feet knowing every stone and turn.

Sebastián watched where he was going, while his darted glances absorbed scenes of the dense woodland that they passed by. The shadiness was warm with the resin of trees. He couldn't lag behind or he would lose his man, but he was surprisingly comfortable in the old boots and was soon jogging down the stones in quick succession, rolling up his shirt sleeves as he went. Juan moved in a rhythm of the terrain's making, playful and practised, and following him was like a game. Sebastián could hear the river below breaking and pouring over rocks. He peered over a lip of open ground, hoping to spy it, but they weren't quite there yet. In that brief pause Juan was lost to view, but with only one path to follow there was no chance of going astray. Sebastián all but ran down a gentler slope which levelled out to a flat dirt path leading through poplars, quivering in the sunlight. The tall trees gave way to an open glade at the river's edge, where Juan had unpacked fishing rods and was sitting among a patch of ferns, taking his boots off. Further up the gorge, the river tumbled unevenly. Here, where it was broader, a group of stubborn trees stood engrossed in its steady, quiet streaming and the current spooled at clumps of reeds. The riverbank offered places of peaceful shade onto deepish water, where one might easily swim.

"Come," said Juan, going back into the vegetation and dragging some green netting off what proved to be an old wooden boat. It was quite bulky, but made for no more than one rower and a couple of passengers. "You pull, I'll push." Juan stashed the fishing equipment inside and positioned himself at the stern, while from the front Sebastián strained on a rope. It was cumbersome and heavy, and Sebastián knew that he wasn't helping much at all. Juan said nothing and heaved the boat to the river's edge before calling, "Move away, move away," and giving it a shove so that the boat was lodged halfway down the bank, with its bow bobbing in the water.

"In you get, Mr Sebastián."

Fishing wasn't hunting, Sebastián decided. He dragged himself up over and into the boat. It was not the most elegant manoeuvre. He half fell in, holding on to both sides to stop it from overbalancing, only to find himself moving forward as Juan slid the boat into the water. Sebastián watched Juan's boots come tumbling came over the side, promptly followed by Juan, who wasted no time in picking up the two oars stashed below the benched seats, inserting them in the rowlocks and pulling out into the placid stream. Once they were out in the open water, he let the river take over and float them slowly but surely downstream, an occasional caress of dipped oars being all that was needed to keep them on course, missing a clump of vegetation tangled around a fallen branch and steering through the first of the river bends. Sebastián, at a gesture from Juan, repositioned his behind for better equilibrium in the centre of the wooden strut that served as a seat. They drifted along, silent onlookers in a rare idyll. Sebastián sat upright to take in the scene. He did not want even to breathe deeply lest the spell be broken. Soothing forest sounds conspired with the river's dark to displace time in the late afternoon's heat. A bird's low, looping call was answered by another's warbling. As they floated downstream, the men were comfortably shaded by a panoply of trees which populated the steep hillside all the way down from a clear blue skyline to the water's edge, where they sank their roots into the mud. A new turn in the river revealed a narrow shore where a small, creamy-white aquatic bird was feeding in the grass. Juan shipped the oars so that they glided by, carefully observed by an eye set in bark-coloured plumage.

"Sandpiper," said Juan, when they had passed out of startling range.

Sebastián felt a modicum of annoyance that he was once again denied the benefit of an internet connection, since he had gone to the trouble of downloading onto his mobile an app for birdwatching in Asturias, which identified each individual by its call or song. He had been hoping to use it and return to Madrid with a number of them ticked off. Instead, he contented himself with a passive role as passenger and digesting his formidable lunch, yet even he recognized the next bird, which he spotted over the shoulder of his softly rowing guide. He held up a hand to request stillness and Juan raised the oars out of the water. Part of the bank had been washed away by the river in flood and there, on an exposed root in the earth wall, perched a kingfisher. Juan didn't so much as turn his head but waited motionlessly for it to come by. Seconds later, the kingfisher dashed into the water and came out with a little fish flashing silver in the sun, adding glitz to the bird's turquoise and orange flight. Juan pulled again and they moved on.

As bend gave way to bend and the river's narrative developed, Sebastián sat and let it all come on to him. In doing so, he found that his eagerness to note and record everything, his concern not to miss anything, gave way to an undifferentiated consciousness of all that surrounded him. The dense greens and tans of the forest and riverbank became a comfort to his soul's eye, as changing and unchanging as the dark water sliding beneath the boat, minute by shadowy minute.

During one of their interminable waits outside important addresses, one of the other Ministry drivers had once showed Sebastián a videogame of a jungle in which the player-protagonist was the sole survivor of an airplane crash. In the game, the player was set upon by wild animals and had the treacherous, inhospitable jungle itself to contend with. He had accepted the cartoon representation at face value, having no more sense of the language of nature than any other city dweller, but he wouldn't ever again. Here he heard and saw and felt and smelled an inexorable paradise of hunter and hunted, predator and victim, shelter and trap, where all that was living perpetuated itself in unintentionally violent equilibrium.

With each turn, the river conveyed the little boat a little further into the wilderness that Sebastián had looked out onto from Josefa's cottage window. If little Miga was the closest he had ever come to life in the woods, it was still a human habitation, run and ruled by human law and feelings. This was different. It was the deep, living valley itself. A fascination, humble and proud, silenced his mind and his tongue.

Juan, who had kept similarly quiet all this time, now offered the rower's seat to Sebastián, who accepted, grateful for the chance to break his reverie, stretch his limbs and flip the view round by a hundred and eighty degrees. The oars were heavier than he expected. The only other time he had played the wherryman was on a pleasure boat in the park in Madrid; this was more solid and real, like the world he was discovering. When he overcompensated a little, lifting the blades higher than was necessary, river water ran down the oars, wetting his arms to the elbow.

"Up here."

From the stern, Juan pointed to where an arm of the river branched off.

"Bring her round."

The boat reacted more slowly than a car, but he had the measure of it and took them neatly up the turning, where they were out of the flow of the river's current.

"That's it. That's enough." Juan waved his arms and they let the wooden boat coast towards the bank, where it was brought to a halt by tall grasses in the water. Juan took hold of one of oars and used it as a pole to push them off the grass and under a tree. Throwing the mooring rope over a heavy branch, he tied up and announced cheerily:

"We're going to fish fish! Here."

He tossed over a small metal object from a knapsack. Thinking it was a box of live bait, Sebastián fumbled and nearly dropped Juan's hipflask. He uncapped it, wet his lips and passed it back.

"Is there any water?" he asked.

"Yes, sir," Juan produced a more substantial flask and waited while his ward drank down the ice cold water, before supplying him with a rod and getting ready himself.

They were stationed over a broad, transparent pool. Juan spun his line in an arc and it popped into the water a fair distance from the boat. Sebastián got half as far with his own, but was satisfied not to have tangled the line up in the tree over their heads.

"Do you do this a lot, Juan?" he asked.

"Always. I like the mountain as well, of course, but I always come back to the river. I listen. I learn. Look over there."

He lowered his rod and passed Sebastián a pair of binoculars. They were compact but powerful. Sebastián followed the line of Juan's outstretched finger to a glistening patch, patterned and blue-black. Zooming out a little, he realized that it was the oily fur of a mammal, its head bobbing in the deep green water. It was an otter.

"We're taking her supper," said Sebastián.

"There's enough for everybody," Juan said.

"Nice binoculars."

"They were a present. No, hang on to them until you go."

If only they could see this, Sebastián reflected, thinking of Erica and his friends back in Madrid. He felt a measure of resentment at the official prohibition to take any photos during his visit. What harm would it do to demonstrate a genuine interest? Not that he could message the images to anyone from here.

"So what do you do if you need to make a phone call?"

"We don't need anything here," was the simple reply.

"But sometimes you need to contact, I don't know, an authority."

"For that we have the priest," said Juan.

Sebastián didn't know what to make of the man's answer. He sat motionless for a goodly while, his mind flooded with thoughts of purity and suffering, power and ignorance, spiritual authority, guilt and the law: a turbulence in which his rod caught nothing.

The sun had already dipped behind the mountain when Juan called an end to fishing time. He had three trout and a carp to the visitor's none, but insisted that it was a shared catch. He took the boat back out into the river and fifty metres upstream to a mooring post, where there were wooden steps going up the bank.

Sebastián clambered out onto dry land and Juan passed him out the fishing things. He was just wondering how they were going to get back to the village when the figure of a man appeared above them. It was the dark, intense man who had walked him to the village with the tall, awkward one. Juan greeted Pepe by his name and they climbed up to a narrow path, where two saddled horses waited, a grey and a tan, munching on the greenery.

"Who's on gate duty?"

"El Polo. With Ubaldo."

"Who's going to put the lights up?"

"My father-in-law. He has the tall ladder."

"Very good. Till later, then. Let's go." Juan swept himself onto the large horse and Pepe stood by the grey to keep her still for the gentleman.

Sebastián hadn't mounted a horse before, but he put a toe into a stirrup and managed to hitch himself up until he was sitting astride the mare, who raised her head in surprise. This was an unknown person on her back. They moved off at a trot, which Sebastián found distinctly uncomfortable until the terrain slowed them to a walking pace, followed by a strenuous climb, an effort for the horses, which had to push hard with their hind legs in order to scamper up. Sebastián clung on, flattening himself forward against the sturdy neck by grabbing the mane. A last, long jolting trot (the horse recognized she had a novice and bounced him unmercifully in the saddle) brought them into Miga in the early evening, where it was still light.

Sebastián dismounted and handed the reins to Juan, standing unsteadily in the street, hoping the shaking in his legs didn't show. A salty smell of firewood smoke came from somewhere, as if defying the summer's fierceness: someone was cooking, and just knowing that there was a pot on someone's hearth was a comfort to him and a promise. It made the return to this quirky hamlet, unknown to any map, existing only in the memory of its mountains and limited governmental documents, feel like a homecoming. The village into which they now walked had never known a motorized vehicle, never known anything but its people and their animals. It was the sounds of their lives that made the place: a whistle and a call, a hammering on metal, children running, the bray of a donkey, the contented clucking of hens which wandered free, all joined to the silent voices of the trees which watched over the settlement, forgot nothing and lent it shelter. As he and Juan clomped up the dirt street with their catch and the late sun steadied itself to say farewell to the village's ever-present wildness, a bell sounded in the church tower and Sebastián's fascination drained away. The purpose of his presence there tolled unhappily and regret sank into his boots, which were cumbersome and caked in fresh mud.

They passed by an old woman who was sitting on her doorstop, shelling beans, letting the white legumes drop into the lap of her loose skirt. She had a deformed nose and mouth that made her face look frighteningly like a root.

"Buenas tardes, Francisca," said Juan.

"Buenas tardes, gentlemen," Francisca returned.

Her greeting was dutiful but genuine and Sebastián felt not a little ashamed to be treated with such graciousness. He was by rights the most unwelcome of intruders and yet he perceived nothing more than primitive curiosity in the beady eyes that stared out from windows in the tumbledown cottages, each of which seemed to have a personality of its own.

Further down the street, there was knot of villagers from which exclamations of hilarity arose and a woman's cry of alarm. A pig's squeal caused them to laugh even more. Juan hesitated, putting his hand on Sebastián's arm, before continuing. As they drew near, one of the men stood back so that they could see a middle-aged woman, clad in a ragged red dress, being held by three people who were attempting to sit her on the back of a massive black pig. The pig was hemmed in but wouldn't keep still. In the end, the woman slithered straight off and the pig bolted away up the street.

"Dirty pig!" called a girl.

"Let's drag the red," shouted a youth.

"Leave me alone!" the woman mewled from the ground where she lay, although they were all standing back from her. "I will curse you."

"Mad cow."

"Stupid cow."

"Witch."

Juan tried to guide the village's guest past the commotion, but the woman caught sight of the tall stranger and started to let out a pitiful wailing.

"Oh, sir, you sir, help them, save them. You can do it, for the love of God, save my boys, save my children—"

"Shut up." A man stood over her with his fist raised and she cowered, whimpering.

Sebastián guessed that the dire news which he had delivered to Mayor Beltrán was now common knowledge. It made sense for any news to spread like a rash in such a tiny place as this. He was grateful that the man had cut short her complaint. He couldn't save the mad woman's family, or anyone else.

Back at his private quarters, Sebastián Elcano Esq. found a note requesting the pleasure of his presence at dinner by invitation of the Mayor. As long as he was here, he would belong to the village, it seemed. One way or another, he would simply have to accept the seclusion and its society. His mobile was fully charged, but with no signal it remained inoperable. It was somewhat glumly that he recalled Juan's fobbing off of such a superfluous trapping as a phone. He stripped down to his underpants to cool off and lay back on the bed, waiting for the light of day to flicker out and dinner hour to creep up. Would the evening be straightforward, or tense and heated? Could he engage with the local dignitaries and not be found out as an ignoramus?

He had already made the acquaintance of more than one of them, including the priest and starting with Commander of the Civil Guard, whose antiquated gun had halted his progress into the village. Captain Luís Echevarría had held out his rifle barrel rather longer than was appropriate, the fault of a nervous pride, before shouldering it and saluting stiffly. He had then swivelled aside and stamped down his foot, permitting Sebastián to continue forward to the Mayor, who had doffed his hat and actually clicked his heels before ushering the visitor to his private residence. Sebastián's briefcase was returned to him, while his luggage disappeared to these clean but spartan rooms. It had all been very gracious and proper.

He washed and dressed with sombre thoughtfulness for what was an occasion of consequence. The dated lodgings, formal and musty, seemed to accord with his mood. He pinned cufflinks in the clean, white shirt that the gawky villager, known as El Polo, had conveyed from the car without suffering it a speck of dirt or a crease, and straightened his tie, which was dark grey with a pale pink fleur-de-lis motif. In that complete silence that city dwellers find so unsettling on being removed to the rural world, he donned his suit jacket and considered himself in a tall mirror that was tarnished with age. However inadequate he might be as the government's supposed envoy, Sebastián told himself, the moment had come to prove worthy of the trust placed in him. Miga's worthies would have had time to digest the import of the government's ruling on the mine and they were entitled to be angry. He would simply have to take any expressions of resentment on the chin.

He needn't have worried. When he entered the vaulted stone hall, they actually stood to be introduced by the mayor. There were his young-looking, dark-haired wife, Miriam, Captain Echevarría, Don Vicente, Don Alonso and his wife, Angela, Doctor Pereira, Father Raimundo and Juan, whose unfailing smile and handshake were reassuringly warm and firm. He himself was presented as Don Sebastián Elcano, Officer of the Presidency of the Nation.

A cordial tone was set from the beginning by Don Alfonso, who took it upon himself to dispense cider. This meant decanting it in the requisite Asturian fashion, holding the bottle at shoulder height to let a golden stream fall into a glass held low, which was passed round and drunk straight off while the brew was still airily alive. Sebastián smiled and accepted his share with thanks. To refuse all alcohol would have smacked off aloofness. He trusted to the stomach medication he had taken in his room to protect him from the worst effects of the booze that night. Mayor Beltrán gestured his guests to an elegant table set with platters of aperitifs and tall candles in silver holders. Sebastián found himself standing next to Miriam and aware of her scent taking precedence over the pungent blue cheese in his mouth when she asked him how he liked their village. He swallowed the rest of the morsel without chewing it.

"It's beautiful. Like no other I have ever seen," he said truthfully.

"Do try the chicken liver," she lifted the plate for him.

"Very kind," he said. "I am fortunate to be dined on the very best of Spanish cuisine: the Asturian."

"We don't know any other," said Mayor Beltrán's wife.

"And this, Don Sebastián," the mayor arrived from behind them carrying a plate of delicately carved cured meat. "You will only find here in Miga."

All the eyes in the room were on him as he took a piece. It was not unlike cured beef loin with a hint of sweetness. He would have tried some more but the plate was already disappearing round the table so that nobody would be missed out.

"Well, now you are one of us," Don Vicente said. "Our village is your village. Do take a seat and we can all be at table together."

The others had remained silent while the old man spoke and they now arranged themselves around the table. Sebastián was placed opposite Don Alonso who filled all the nearby glasses with deep red wine. Even the sample of cider was far more alcohol than Sebastián knew how to tolerate, but on this particular occasion he knew that he was just going to have to take his medicine. Father Raimundo said grace in one of its shorter forms and two tureens were hurried across the room by serving ladies. It was trout bouillabaisse, fresh that day from the river, Juan told everyone, sending his fishing mate a broad wink.

"Thank you, Don Sebastián," smiled Miriam, elbowing Don Alonso's wife next to her, who gasped, holding her hand to her mouth in a gesture of fear or titillation.

Sebastián raised his glass and cleared his throat. "Health to you all," he pronounced.

"To all, health, health," the table clinked glasses.

"Do you ride often, sir?" enquired Don Vicente.

"It's not a hobby of mine. I'm more of a car man, myself." Sebastián was fairly certain that his riding ability hadn't gone unremarked.

"A lot of people have automobiles these days, isn't that so?" continued the elderly gentleman.

Sebastián stepped over the flippant reply in his mind and restricted himself to confirming that the cities had never been more transited by vehicles.

"Is it safe?"

"Sometimes I wonder, when my fiancée drives," he gave up his soup bowl only for it to be replaced with a huge plate weighed down with half a kilo of prime beef steak. Appetite had never been short in him, but what with the late lunch at Doña Josefa's and the fuggy heat trapped in the low-ceilinged hall, he resorted to another gulp of wine to keep his stomach open.

"Your fiancée drives? A woman?" Captain Echevarría's incredulity was such that he had put down his spoon.

"She thinks she's better than me. Of course, there are airbags these days."

"The bottle is with you, Doctor," Juan observed and it was passed down the table to him.

"Who are these Evas?" he heard old Don Vicente ask Mayor Beltrán.

"The women in Madrid are very beautiful, they say," commented the wife of Don Alonso. Unfortunately, the same could not be said of the woman who had directed the comment at their guest of honour. Sebastián's wine-drugged consciousness struggled to find an acceptable rejoinder. He had a very hard time of it not to divert his gaze to the dark-haired woman sitting next to her. He could feel her eyes on him.

"Not as natural as the Asturian ladies," he managed in the end.

"To which parish do you belong?" asked the priest. Whether it was because he spoke very softly, or in spite of it, the careful silence kept by the gathering held a hint of tension while they waited for the response.

"I attend the Basilica of Saint Michael, Reverend Father," he said.

"Aah." The clergyman didn't look up from his meal, but the expression of approval was so patent that the table relaxed with visible relief.

"I hope to have the honour of hearing Mass here," Sebastián added.

"Our little church is much neglected, I'm afraid," said the priest. Sebastián still waited for an invitation, but none was forthcoming.

"The padre tells us that Madrid won last week," Juan chipped in.

"Who were they playing?" asked Don Alonso.

" Malaga," said the Father Raimundo. "At home."

"Did you see the second goal?" said Sebastián.

"I believe," said Don Alonso, "that you are referring to the television. That does not reach us here. We used to have the radio, but experience proved it to be unnecessary. Harmful, in fact."

It didn't explain how the priest knew what they couldn't, but Sebastián wasn't yet so inebriated as to abandon all his manners to inquisitiveness. All the same, his next question smacked of a certain insolence.

"When were you last in the capital?"

"We do not go to Madrid. Madrid comes to us," said Don Alonso.

Sebastián looked at the man seated opposite him and then around the table. It wasn't the first time that he had the sensation that forks and knives and conversations hovered and hesitated a few milliseconds, before returning to their earlier naturalness.

Dessert was carried in, a pumpkin pie that Sebastián was obliged to welcome and partake of, although etiquette excused him from brandy and liqueurs in favour of a plain coffee. Cigars were passed round the table and accepted by most of the men. Sebastián declined with thanks. Miriam lit a cigarette. The dinner was drawing to a close and Sebastián was looking forward to retiring gracefully.

"We don't want them to eat our dogs," said the doctor to Sebastián from the end of the table.

"I beg your pardon?"

"The Chinese occupying Asturias?" Doctor Pereira fairly shouted. "Communists? Over my dead body."

"Our loyalty is not in question," Mayor Beltrán interrupted, sending the doctor a reprimanding look. "The Minister knows that we serve Spain, as always. Don Sebastián, we will present our duty tomorrow, so that you may deliver it to the authority. If I may be permitted, though: a question. The day after tomorrow is the feast of our patron Lady of the Snows, on which it is our custom to honour the traditions of Miga. Are we to be allowed to celebrate the fiesta? The hunt? It would be—there are no secrets between us here—our last."

"Mr Mayor, the word from the Presidency is that it should go ahead."

"Very good. Ladies and gentlemen, I give you the King," a pleased-looking Mayor Beltrán lifted his brandy glass and the table rose.

"The King!"

"Gentlemen, let us withdraw."

"Are you sure?" Sebastián heard Miriam say to Don Alonso's wife.

"Yes, it's late and I'm tired. You don't mind?"

"No, of course not."

The serving ladies busied themselves around the table, clearing away the last dishes and glasses.

Sebastián had stood up and found his head swimming. "I think it's the Koreans that eat dogs," he said.

"Come, sir," Miriam said, or commanded. "Have you seen the vaults?" she asked as they filed out into a cool, unlit corridor. Sebastián was having trouble coping with unaccustomed drunkenness as he followed her blindly down the stone passageway and then, without warning, down some winding steps. Rarely had he felt less coordinated, lurching into the curved wall as they spiralled down.

When he stepped off at the bottom, the vault turned out to be little more than a crude cellar, illuminated by a weak light. Bottles were racked against the wall and a couple of massive barrels set in the centre of the intimate space had spigots to draw off their contents.

"Can you stand? You're very tall. So why you? So young."

"I don't know what you mean."

"Yes, you do. Do you respect our customs?" She gave his chest a light push with one hand.

"Of course."

He blinked a couple of times to focus on her face and intentions. The confined air was muggy and thin and they both had to breathe a little faster. Miriam lit a candle which flickered and burned low. Sebastián's heart beat wildly.

"I must do penance before the feast of our Lady. Will you do what is necessary?"

"I don't understand."

"Well, you don't have to understand. You have to do what is required." She put one of his hands on her left breast. "Squeeze it."

"But your husband."

"The honour falls to the mayor's wife, once a year. It is a debt. I am fortunate this time to exchange eminence for youth and strength. The other one. Harder. Put your hands where you want."

The light summer dress was alive with her. She turned and left him groping. Going to one of the great oak barrels, she stretched herself forward over its curve and put her hands through a pair of leather loops on the other side, so that she was lifted right off the floor. The delicate dress had ridden up and her satin briefs were the colour of butterscotch.

"Take the switch. Use it on me."

He looked round in a kind of panic until his eyes settled on a black-handled whip with short tails hanging on a stone column.

"Do it. Take my knickers off. What are you waiting for, you bastard? That's it. Fucking hurry. Now punish me. Ow! Ow, shit!"

He felt demented. Her shouts were drowned by a silent howling in his head. The red weals across her buttocks were so blatant that he thought he could read a message in them. And he knew what he wanted that message to be.

"Now have me."

He buried himself in her.

Devotion, he already knew. This was zeal.

Friday, 14th August

BEFORE BREAKFAST WAS over the next day, Erica was in The Pit.

The night of sharing under the stars had eventually come to a close and the campers had gone late and sleepily to their cots, ready for a long rest, but their slumber was shattered after just three hours by the massed monitors who passed through the dormitories slamming metal bars against the sides of the bunks in a terrible, clanging din. They screamed at the boys and girls to get themselves back to the sandy amphitheatre, where they were ordered to strip in the pre-dawn gloom to a horrible wailing from all sides: the loudspeakers had come back to life as grotesque, deafening sirens. They penned the campers into a naked huddle at the centre of the arena, from which Erica's tent had long since been dismantled. The monitors rolled out heavy yellow hoses and sluiced cold water, first as a spray and then as buffeting jets, which a few kids, such as the robust boy who had carried so many rocks, were able to withstand for a short while by turning their backs and hunkering down. Most were unceremoniously spun round or forced backwards, or simply knocked over flat like bowling pins to acquire thick patches of sand over scoured skin. The hosing was derisively effortless, industrial or military in its impact. Even in the hot August night, the coldness of the water was shocking.

"Go back to your bunks, get dressed, stand by your bunks, you worthless maggots," the speakers' distorted taunting shouted in their ears and two men on horseback charged into the arena, riding round, corralling them, herding them back indoors.

It was all over in less than twenty minutes.

Many of the youngsters were sobbing and shivering or worse still, downcast and silent, standing by their bunks with hands behind their backs, their eyes averted. Even the log-haired boy who Erica had down as the Camp's rebel looked defeated.

Her own mind was sober and clear. She was sure that the camp organizers wouldn't dare to cross certain boundaries, but equally, she was in no doubt that Zoe would be going away from here with additional and premeditated trauma to complicate her already disturbed young emotional being. For the first time, she wondered how, if push came to shove, she could extricate the girl. It was by no means obvious. To all intents and purposes, the camp was as secure as a detention centre. In a little more than twenty-four hours, the young people would be released to the arms of their hopefully loving, probably impatient, competitively dressed mother and fathers, and she guessed that even the most obstreperous and contrary of these children was already homesick enough to appreciate parents they had made it their business to detest. For the meantime, though, they would have no contact with the outside world, and the systematic vanquishing of the individual ego that Olga had so devoutly advocated was leaving them bereft of any capacity to fight back, or even resist. Erica, who had had quite enough of the charade already, marshalled these practical thoughts into a principle of readiness.

When they were told, under the rule of silence, to occupy seats in the refectory and were given an apple each and a mini-carton of pineapple juice, it was the absence of a decent cup of coffee that ultimately decided her that it was time to test the camp's regime.

"Do you think this is normal?" she asked the long-haired boy who was sitting opposite her. His mop of hair looked far better roughed up, she thought. The day before, he had been all ironic smiles and defiance, but now he looked simply scared. "I mean, being abused in the name of spiritual enlightenment?"

"Silence," a monitor slapped the legs of her chair with a rubber truncheon and a surprisingly nasty tremor passed through her body.

"I want a coffee," she declared loudly.

"Take her to The Pit," ordered a voice and she was dragged out of her plastic chair.

"See you later, I guess," she told the staring youth, who had not touched his juice or his apple and followed her out of the room with his eyes.

She was trussed in a harness and hauled up by a rope over the round opening of what had once been the compound's well. As she turned slowly on the rope, one of the cheap flip-flops hanging from her feet fell off and disappeared down its dark maw. A monitor pushed a bottle of water into her hand and she was lowered down the brick shaft for three uncomfortable minutes until her feet found the floor. When the release of tension in the rope allowed her movement, she felt confident enough to yell, "Where's my fucking coffee?" She listened but there was no response, just a tiny gleam of light way above her and the probability of tedium. But no panic, or even anxiety. After surviving being hooded, this new incarceration held no fear for her. She found the fallen flip-flop and put it back on.

Thankfully, the girl who had run crying yesterday from the Trial of the Rocks, as Erica now thought of it, wasn't still held down here. She couldn't have stood the whimpering of a teenager in such a cramped space. And the girl's release did at least suggest that the Camp was aware of the legal limits of its dubious activities. Sooner or later, her punishment would presumably be deemed sufficient and she, too, would be hauled out of the hole. In the meantime, she had an opportunity to analyze the situation at the Camp and weigh up the options open to her. Rather than sit on the ground, which bore a hint of urine, she placed her back against the dank wall and bent her knees, pressing her feet up against the wall on the other side.

One. Reasoning with the camp's directors to negotiate an early exit for Zoe and herself was obviously not on the cards. And she had no police ID to back up any such demand.

Two. A wishful fancy of leading a revolt by the young campers, Spartacus-style, was as romantic and worthless as a coin tossed down the well shaft.

Three. Her primary objective, then, had to be getting to her mobile to call in a squad and put an end to the sadistic nonsense.

Four. In the same overnight bag as the mobile, she was well aware, loaded and wrapped in a towel, was her service revolver. Pastori would take a delight in having her kicked out of the force for unjustifiable use of a firearm, but that didn't prevent Erica's mind returning compulsively to the thought of the dense metal object. An unanswerable weapon, waiting patiently in some dark, locked room. Sending out a faint signal to her mind. Here I am, Erica. Come and find me. Come and find me.

But Erica wasn't listening. She had slumped helplessly asleep. The well shaft had switched from vertical to horizontal and in the tunnel it had become, Erica walked.

She advanced towards a disk of light at the end of the tunnel. It expanded and split into a symmetrical pattern of white diamonds. The arrangement displayed for several seconds and vanished. She kept moving and the circle of light reappeared. It expanded of a sudden and pink and green petals unfolded within the white ring, petals that split and changed to blue and yellow, as if someone had played a piano chord in a preordained dance. They stopped and white squares came out of black squares out of white squares out of black, until their turn was over and geometrical stars arose, orange-and-gold, followed by a multi-form capriciousness of shapes. They stayed long enough for her to see and note them, like models on a catwalk, then left for others to take their place.

The kaleidoscopic show, for her eyes only, transformed itself pleasingly and effortlessly, time and again, out of nowhere. It was a dream and she knew she was in a dream, staying with it because she chose to.

The circle was a wheel and she was its spoke. It turned clockwise and she turned with it, hands and feet stretched out against the cardboard wall of the tube in order to hold herself in place and not fall. When it stopped revolving, it left her upright and the light blinked once. A shadowiness restored depth and gravity to the horizontal cylinder and Erica found herself in the dripping emptiness of a Parisian sewer.

She started walking quickly, her black high heels echoing, kicking cushions out of the way, Moroccan cushions, which became more plentiful the further she proceeded down the tunnel. Even within the dream, she felt justifiably offended by the incongruity of the cushions in the roman noir setting, all the more so since they were mounting up, soft and embroidered, blocking her way, in such a great mound that she had to scramble up and climb over them close to the brick ceiling, before seeing that there was a way ahead and past them down the lamp-lit sewer, where the tunnel's straight line stretched out indefinitely into darkness. She could easily have rolled over the top of the pillows to slide down the other side of the piled heap, but something stopped her.

Something, she was sure, was hidden beneath the cushion mound. That's why they were there. She started flinging them away, with both arms, with concentrated intent, making a dent that became a crater, shoving and kicking a way down, throwing out the cushions that fell back on her, hearing her father's mocking intonation, hearing not the voice, just its mocking manner, until she got through them all and found it.

A birthday present from the gods. She ran her hand over the smooth, bright red, carbon fibre chassis of a Formula One Ferrari. Her footwear had changed from the high heels to a more practical pair of leather shoes, worn down by long usage so that her feet would connect intimately with the pedals. She slipped inside the cockpit and sat there for a few seconds, eyes closed, getting a feel for it. When she opened her eyes, the tiresome cushions had gone. The way forward was clear. In the silent air of expectancy, an owl flew over her shoulder and flapped off into the unknown future. She sat, nicely balanced, in the driver's seat, seatbelt fastened and ready. There was just her and the car, a straight and narrow tunnel, bricks glistening in the underground stillness, and an older man she didn't know sitting next to her as co-pilot. She immediately pressed the button starter to get away from him and the car warped ahead with immense G-force acceleration. Speeding along the one-way track, unexpected side-tunnels appeared, but she dared not look left or right in case the man was still there and she recognized him. She could only go faster, faster, squeezing both thumbs into the intuitive buttons on the steering wheel so that the car raced madly, red-shifting to blue as it did so, to escape velocity.

She was yanked out the dream by a rough pull on the harness, which was fastened to the rope at her back. She was too groggy to shout up the well and simply sat there, getting her bearings again. Out of the gloom appeared a plastic supermarket bag tied to a cord. She guessed correctly that she was being provided with a form of lunch and undid the bag to find a roll filled with cheese and tomato, a bruised peach and a small carton of pineapple juice. She wished she had pencil and paper to send back a suitable message of appreciation. Instead, she tugged on the cord as if it were the cistern chain of an old WC and watched as it was pulled up.

Another hour passed, and another. Echoes reached her in the empty place whenever the speakers in the arena were cranked up, but she could not make out the words. Erica stood up and stretched her limbs, prepared to wait it out. She was fairly certain that the punishment hole, however disagreeable and pointless, was preferable to being subject to any of the camp activities designed for the last day, and her thoughts returned to Zoe.

Like everyone else, she hadn't taken the girl's maudlin pose seriously, or the self-dramatic declarations about wanting to die. But there was something dark in that girl. How could anyone tell what went on inside a fourteen year-old's mind? We forget what it's like to be a teenager, she thought. No sooner do we get past adolescence than the hormonal memory cuts out and a forgetting gene kicks in. She suspected that Zoe, in some dismal condition of her mind, really did want to die, yet when she examined her feelings towards the girl, beyond a sense of professional responsibility, all she found was the indifference that commonly indicates a personal dislike. Or was it boredom? She had been down in the well a long time now. It was clammy and she was feeling cramps in her belly. She knew she wasn't forgotten, but a part of her was proposing to doubt it. She was going to have to add to the smell of pee and squatted down to relieve her bladder.

After which she refused to sit and soil herself, and so it was that, an unknown time later, but much too long, a tensing on the harness raised her torso upright from the hunched position, partly jammed against the wall, where she was standing on her dignity. She was too tired to do anything but hang in the air and be lifted, turning slowly, as her particular confinement receded. When she was led back through the cloisters, which retained a concentrated heat like a clay oven, her legs threatened to buckle beneath her.

Just before they brought her back into the great patio, indistinct under a darkening evening sky, they marched her past a heavy wooden door, left half open. It connected via a passageway to another door, painted white, which was closed hurriedly, but not before she had seen a naked boy inside, with a gag in his mouth, being buggered from behind by a bearded man she hadn't seen before. Erica was driven out into the open arena and propelled by pushing and poking to the far side. A monitor pointed to the sand where she was to kneel along with the others. The sense of degradation that she had brought up from the Pit and the shocking reality she had just glimpsed were only augmented by the scene around her. The boys and girls strewn around the sand showed every sign of exhaustion and defeat, except for when the famous personage, dressed in loose white clothing, approached one of them and then they would straighten their backs and bend their head forward. Hoping for reward, thought Erica, or a reprieve. There was more than one bad smell. A low, rhythmic murmur churned out like a mantra by the overhead speakers was briefly eclipsed by the double boom of a gong and then those who had the will or the strength edged forwards on their knees towards an opening in the cloister wall. Before the opening, a curved white line drawn in the sand denoted a limit. Beyond it lay the doors that Erica had seen through.

Erica spotted Zoe near the front of the hopefuls and moved towards her as effectively as her stiff knees and thigh muscles would allow. The gong sounded again and they all stopped where they were. The woman from the Trial of the Rocks opened wide the heavy-framed wooden door and came towards them in her slow, stately gait. On outstretched arms she bore wreaths of flowers and as she stepped around those youngsters closest to the cloister aperture, the ones who might pass through, she placed the garlands over their heads. At the end of the passage gleamed the White Door.

"Which of you has finally left the ego behind?" Erica heard the woman ask. "Which of you will be free? Of mind and body. Abandoning the past, to a new awakening in maturity. Die to yourself and know the truth."

How they longed to be the one, Erica saw. And when she heard Zoe's voice, pleading with the woman to "Take me, take me," adrenaline charged into her consciousness and motor centres. She was now galvanized, if powerless, ready to rush the woman if she picked Zoe, even if the rescue attempt was futile.

Somewhere not far way, rockets were let off. One raced up above their stadium. Out there, in the real world, people were celebrating a wedding, or a football result, or a firework party on the eve of the Feast of the Ascension, which would be Zoe's birthday. The woman touched the head of another garlanded girl and held out a hand to help her up. The girl stood unsteadily to accompany the woman, with as much poise as she could manage, brushing the sand from her knees with her free hand, and entered the stone passageway. The old door closed behind them.

Minutes later, the gong sounded again, and the young campers, for the most part schoolchildren from well-to-do families, very possibly unruly and spoilt in their own world, even big-headed and mean, were either left far behind on their knees in the murky courtyard, where they had given up hope, or soldiered desperately on like amputees towards the white curve sprayed in the sand, as though by a football referee directing a free kick.

By the fourth gong, Erica succeeded in forcing a way through what was now a dense, kneeling crowd, all festooned with garlands. Zoe was still there. Erica came within a couple of metres of the girl before other bodies blocked the way. The abdominal pain she had experienced in the well twisted inside of her. Erica gritted her teeth. Out of the doorway swept the national star in his cotton whites, long past his prime but revered for all that. He seemed, to Erica's frantic mind at least, to make a beeline for Zoe. The girl laid back her head in supplication as he approached. The man stood before her, above her, as if his presence alone would raise her up off the ground. Then a strange thing happened. The blonde woman Erica remembered from her admission and who still, extraordinarily enough, carried a clipboard, ran across from the wings and whispered urgently in his ear. The silver-haired man bit on a knuckle as he took the words in and looked at his watch.

"You expect me to wait nearly twenty minutes?" he smiled, showing his white teeth, and the scene turned tense. Erica half expected him to slap the woman so hard that her spectacles broke, but instead he bent down to Zoe, looking into her eyes for a few seconds, and spat in her face. Nobody moved. Nobody made a sound. As he returned inside, the clipboard woman signalled to the monitors, who emerged from the shadow of the cloisters and made their menacing presence felt among the flower children.

What Erica needed right now was a paracetamol. It was period pains and, as always, they made her feel useless and ineffective. She felt her crotch as blood came trickling down her thigh and held up a hand smeared with a dark stain.

"What do you want?" The blonde woman was pleased to find someone to taunt.

"I'm bleeding."

"And why would I care about that?" she queried.

Erica had no easy answer to that.

"Let her bleed," said one of the monitors.

"It hurts," Erica said.

Perhaps recognizing a familiar voice, Zoe turned round. Erica met her usual stare of dull apathy, only to see it dissolve into an altogether more lively expression.

"But she's pregnant! Her baby!"

Erica was taken by complete surprise, as much by Zoe's memory as by her evidently genuine concern. Of course, she had told the girl, but she had then forgotten all about it. And she hadn't told anyone apart from her mother when the pregnancy was lost. Whether Erica's shocked look made any difference or not, the blonde organizer acted as if startled for the first time.

"Take her to the doctor. Go on, you idiot!" the woman told the monitor who seconds ago had been just as content as herself to see a menstrual discharge seep from the cropped-haired older girl.

In the cloister, Erica laid on the act, hobbling and bending over in apparent agony.

"This way," said the surly young man.

"No, I have medication. It's in my bag: the one I brought. Quickly! I'm going to lose my baby." She gripped his arm.

"Shit," he looked uncertain. "Shit."

"Please..."

He made a call on a walkie-talkie and when they came to a flight of steps, he helped her down them and along a short corridor to where an older man, who looked like a janitor, waited outside an unmarked door.

"Have you got permission?" the janitor asked.

"Just open it," said the monitor.

The light from a bare bulb showed racks of colourful bags on different levels. There were an awful lot of them. She shuffled in.

"Which one's yours? What's it look like?" The janitor didn't want her in there, but she was already looking.

"This one." The last bag in was on the end of the middle rack. "Do you intend to watch?" She raised two bloody fingers. The monitor took a couple of steps back, but the old man stayed right where he was and carried on looking. She unzipped the black-and-white Adidas hold-all and felt around inside. Her gun, a standard issue compact revolver, was folded inside a towel right at the bottom. It was too well wrapped and she struggled to get at it. The gun had one bullet in the chamber ready to fire, plus eleven more. In common with her fellow officers, she had been trained in its use, but had never had fired one outside the practice range. She felt herself trembling a little. Should she flick off the safety before she took it out the bag, or afterwards?

"What's the medication?" asked the monitor.

"This. It makes me feel a whole lot better. It's real," she said, holding the gun on them. "Move inside. Give me the keys," she told the janitor. "Give me the keys or I'll kill you. Lie on the floor, face down, both of you."

They slowly realized that it was no joke and did as the girl ordered.

"You," she held the muzzle of the gun to the monitor's head. "Who's behind this place?"

"People."

"What people? Give me names."

"I don't know. Somebody important. They don't tell us."

"Not J," she named the ageing star.

"He's nothing. He's just invited for free."

"Why couldn't he take that girl just now?"

"Which girl?"

"Why does he have to wait twenty minutes?"

"It wasn't time."

"Why not? Start talking," she shouted.

"Legally she's under age. Until midnight."

Zoe's birthday. At midnight she would be fifteen and of the age of consent. So they may be shameless, reckless even, but they had some important legal bases covered. Erica wished she had read the forms the clipboard woman had given her to sign.

"If you keep quiet, I won't have to pop you," she told them, receiving a dutiful silence in response.

There was nothing to tie them with so she used her police handcuffs, linking them through a metal rack so that the men could not reach the door and hammer on it. After taking their walkie-talkies, which were short-range communication devices rather than phones, and the janitor's set of keys, she turned off the electric light and locked the door quickly from the outside. Erica checked the other contents of her sports bag. The mauve mobile was there, but there was no signal. Her fake ID was missing, no doubt in the possession of the Camp administration. Not important. More significantly, the key to Olga's car was in a side pocket, and the janitor's set presumably included one to the main public door of the building.

Fight or flight? said her beating heart.

She ought to call in reinforcements, but the mobile said it was five minutes to midnight. Could she risk it? How long would Zoe be toyed with behind the White Door before they raped her? Five minutes? Ten? Less?

Feeling very scared, the bag hitched onto her shoulder and her right hand holding the gun hidden inside it, she walked fast back the same way she had come, through the cloisters, passing one monitor who turned and looked at her in puzzlement, and then she was out in the great sandy square, kicking off the awkward flip-flops and striding across to the kids kneeling behind the sacred white line like so many petitioners hopeful of a blessing at the altar rail. She didn't give the clipboard woman a chance to speak but fired two shots into the air, at which the woman fled.

Erica pulled Zoe to her feet. "Come with me."

"No!"

"You have to come. It's a trick. They're abusing and raping the kids in there. I saw it." She spoke to Zoe but also to the other teenagers, around twenty of them.

"I'm not a child. I want to go through. Is that a real gun?"

Erica was aware of staff members taking up positions behind the cover of the cloisters. She turned the girl's arm behind her back in a judo hold and started propelling her in the direction of the main entrance.

"The rest of you come with us. We're getting out of here," she told them. But they were either too confused and fatigued, or frightened by the girl with the gun, to do anything but stay put.

"Stop it. You're hurting me. Help!" Zoe protested.

Crossing the dark cloister directly to the main door meant passing between two thick pillars, behind which any number of monitors and security might be hidden. She made a slight detour to a low wall between more slender columns, looked beyond it both ways and pushed Zoe's bent arm so that she was obliged to climb over. She lifted her own legs up and over and nearly dropped the revolver when the sports bag fell from her shoulder onto her forearm.

"I don't want to, I don't want to," moaned and screamed Zoe, making it difficult to concentrate as Erica forced her along the broad cloister.

Someone up ahead slipped into a nook a few metres past the entrance door. "We've called the police," said a man's voice as she fumbled with the janitor's keys.

"I am the police."

"All our papers are in order," the voice was infuriatingly calm. "This is illegal abduction."

"Come out and I'll shoot you," Erica said.

After turning a great iron key twice in the lock, the door was still secured by two heavy bolts. She pulled them across and it shifted open a crack, after which she was able to tug the door open with one hand and bundle her prisoner through.

"We're out, Zoe!" She felt the rush of a real possibility of freedom.

"Let me go!"

"Let her go!" echoed other voices. There was a lot of moving around just inside the door that they had exited. "You're not going to get very far."

In another judo move perfected in police training, Erica raised the teenager's arm high behind her back and pulled her backwards on her bare heels, down the steps, keeping a close eye on the door. When she was approximately half the way across the precinct to the cars, she pulled the girl to the ground, held the revolver at arm's length with both hands and fired five loud shots into the ground at mid-distance, aiming carefully away from the entrance in case a ricochet diverted inside. The bullets kicked up dust as in some spaghetti western.

She guessed correctly that they wouldn't risk coming out while she could still shoot at them, but when she took Olga's car keys from the bag, her hand was shaking so much that she dropped them. She cursed, struggling to bend down and retrieve them in the same hand as the gun while still restraining the uncooperative girl with the other.

"Stop struggling. I don't think I can control the gun. Be very careful," she told the girl, who went quiet and still at last. Before Zoe could remember that she wanted to die, Erica got the car open, pushed her inside and locked the door. She ran round and opened the driver's door. Inside, the old car smelled stale from overheated air and Olga's incense but she could have kissed it when it the engine started first time.

"What are you doing? Where are we going?" Zoe's voice was the whine of a child.

"Shut up," said Erica. She drove off and saw flashes of lights in the rear view mirror and shadowy bodies as they left the precinct behind. The Camp's security people were out already and possibly meaning to come after them.

She braked unwillingly when the Citroen's weak headlights picked out a cat dashing across the roadway, then turned right for the motorway underpass. The car shook over the rough ground.

"Why've you got a gun? Take me back!"

"I saw them, Zoe. Once they get you behind the White Door, they do what they want with you. It's vile. There was a man fucking a boy."

"So what? We're all going to die anyway. I think he liked me."

"Who? Oh, Zoe Iris."

"Don't call me Iris. I hate it. But... how did you know that? I didn't tell you that. You're one of them, aren't you? Working for my father. You're a liar, just like all the rest. I hate you! If you take me to my parents' house, I'll kill myself."

"You know what? I have a good mind to do just that, because I really don't care. Only I don't know who the people running the Camp are and what they might do. They will certainly have your address and I can't trust them not to be waiting for us."

My apartment, she thought. Hide the car in the underground car park and then take her up to the flat and call Pastori. Get Sebastián to help if the girl wants to make trouble.

Erica felt the car hit smooth tarmac and put her foot down. When they got onto the long road that led into town, wire-fenced wasteland on either side, a car's headlights appeared in the rear view mirror, but she was a good distance ahead and sure to get into normal midnight traffic soon.

"Are you angry because you lost the baby?"

They passed one car and then another coming the other way. The shuttered workshops sped by and the Citroen swung through a roundabout with a squeal of tyres. Erica had to shove her foot down hard on the old car's brake to stop at a T-junction with a busier road, where they joined a thoroughfare of cars and buses, all of which seemed to have all the time in the world. At a red light Erica found herself opposite a municipal police car. Before she could wind her window down to hail it, its yellow lights twirled and it was honking and whooping up sirens. Erica could see the looks on the faces of the two officers and didn't like what she saw. The driver, who wore a dark beard, swerved across in an attempt to block her, failing to notice a bus travelling over the crossroads. Both vehicles had to pull up sharply to avoid a collision. It left a gap that Erica popped the hippy car through, leaving the police car to manoeuvre laboriously in order to get on her tail.

Fuck. They had police contacts on their side. How many? Who? How high up?

She was never going to outrun the cop car with this amount of traffic and bugger-all acceleration. Somehow she had to dump the stupidly conspicuous 2CV and get Zoe into a safe place unnoticed. Quickly. Erica got off the main road at the first available turn and started weaving through the empty back streets of an industrial estate.

If she called Pastori on her direct line, the DI could pull rank. Hell, she'd phone the Chief when she learned was going on, even if it was the last night of his vacation. But who could she trust? If only she had time to think. Her heart jumped when she saw a vehicle coming towards them. The emergency light on its roof was turned off and it was advancing steadily. Her nervousness remained and even increased when she saw that it was a private security vehicle patrolling the estate, because here was an opportunity. Zoe hadn't said anything for a while and seemed withdrawn. Hopefully she'd stay that way. All the same, Erica said: "Remember the gun, Zoe." She slowed down and waved a hand out of the window and the two cars stopped next to each other.

"Hi, I'm a bit lost," she apologized. Would they think the Camp gear she and the other girl wore to be out of the ordinary? Could the driver see how grubby and even bloody they were? Could he smell the sweaty, pissy stink they gave off?

"Well, where do you want to go?" He had a lazy, unconcerned drawl and a kindly, bespectacled face.

"A friend's house. We're going to do some theatre."

"What's the name of the street?" He smiled, definitely not worried by two girls in a beat-up old car. But he wasn't going to get out, which is what she really wanted.

"Calle Vicálvaro, number seventeen," she said and saw the two of them look at a screen on the dashboard which displayed an online street map. She opened the car door and got out carrying the sports bag. "Can I look?" she asked, peering in through the window. The driver motioned her round to the passenger side and when his partner opened the door, she stepped up into the high vehicle.

"There's no Calle Vicálvaro round here," said the other security man, pointing to the screen.

"Don't move. Don't touch anything." She held the gun against his head. "This is a police HK USP and I've already used it once tonight. Either I kill you, or you give me the car."

The man's face had gone white and it was the driver who spoke. "Anything you want, but don't shoot."

"You shut up. Say one word into your comms to Control and he's dead. Take your colleague's handcuffs and cuff your right wrist to his right wrist.

"We don't want—"

"I said shut up!" she sounded as mad a woman as possible. "Right wrist."

When they were chained together, she took their pocket radios and the guns from their holsters, tossing them onto the backseat. There was a smell of shit. "Get out this side," she ordered and they clambered out clumsily, half helping, half hindering each other. "Come on, come on," she ordered them to the side of the road outside a warehouse for oxygen tanks, where a tubular steel hoop in the pavement gave her the ideal fixed point to attach the two men using their second set of cuffs.

A minute later, she was driving off with Zoe in a high-powered security vehicle, leaving the two men shackled in the dark street with only the unwanted 2CV for company.

But what could she do with the girl? If the police were after them, she daren't go home now, or anywhere else they'd suspect her to go, such as her parents' house, or Dani's. The only anonymous place that she could think of—and which really was a shelter—was the place they took the Muslim girls after the raid. It wasn't a great plan but it was worth trying.

When they arrived at Residencia La Paloma, there was a new Audi taking up the centre's assigned parking space and the rest of the street was bumper to bumper. Erica left the patrol car double-parked and went quickly to the building, where a light was on. She pressed the intercom button. Instead of a guard looking out through the plexi-glass door, a camera which hadn't been there before checked her out.

"Who is it?" asked a female voice.

"It's an emergency," she said in Arabic. "I am the police officer who brought the three women. You haven't seen my face before because I had my head covered. Please."

A buzzer sounded and she pushed the door open.

"I recognized your voice," said a woman whom Erica also recognized, notwithstanding a flattering transformation. Before, she had been indistinguishable from the destitute girls given refuge here, but now she was dressed expensively, wearing what looked like real pearls, as if for a high fashion event. The shelter itself looked as insolvent as always.

"I have a girl in the car outside. I need you to take her in for the night. It's a total emergency." As she spoke, Erica could see the woman looking at her. At her filthy bare feet and blood-streaked legs.

"I'm just leaving, sorry. You'll have to come back the day after tomorrow, it's a public hol—"

"It's a police matter," she insisted. "We'll pick her up in the morning."

The woman looked uneasy. "I will need your police badge and fill in these forms," she said, without taking her eyes off the messy woman's perspiring face. "But I don't have authorization and it's too late. It's gone midnight."

Erica could see the plan dissolving in front of her eyes. The woman was dangling a car key by means of making her point. What was she to do? Unholster the gun and threaten her? Hadn't she done enough of that tonight?

"Never mind," she said looking more closely at the key ring. "Is that your Audi out there? How can you afford that?"

"We have a new benefactor," the woman said defensively.

Erica had no idea that it was Al Walid bin Zayed, fulfilling a personal oath as his honour and Islamic religion obliged, since Sebastián had been too gallant or embarrassed to tell her the full story of what had happened in Valencia, but that didn't stop her mind from visualizing Sebastián's precious shoes for a few confusing seconds before realizing that she was wasting precious time. She hurried out of the centre and back to the private security car. Before she even got there, she could see that Zoe's silhouette was missing. She opened the door. The girl was gone.

She ran the way she guessed Zoe might have chosen and looked up and down the side streets at an intersection. Panic almost made her sob. There were quite a few people out this summer night on the eve of the national August fiesta, but no small figure fleeing in flip-flops. Erica ran back past the car and tried the other way but there was no sign of the girl there, either. She could be hiding in a doorway, or under a parked car, or she might have been out of the car and running from the moment the Residencia's door closed behind the hated Carina.

Erica's head was pounding and her throat was dry. She returned to the security vehicle and took the police mobile out of the hold-all. She plugged it in to charge with a USB lead and connected it with her password. Ignoring the pings of notifications of messages and lost calls, she hit #100. Drops of sweat fell from her forehead. Her lungs were gasping for air.

There was a muffled noise and then Pastori said, "What's going on? Why haven't you called?"

"I couldn't. Listen, my cover's blown and the girl's gone."

"Gone? Where is she?"

She told the Detective Inspector the name of the neighbourhood and probable streets.

"Listen. You'd better come in."

Could she trust Pastori? "I don't know," she said.

"What's the matter with you? Why did you steal a car?"

Christ, thought Erica. How could they know so quickly? They would be onto her in seconds. She started the car up and got moving.

"Officer Sánchez. Answer."

Why did I steal a car? Was Pastori being droll? What about the rest? Why did I discharge a fire arm without just cause or due care? Why did I make threats to kill? Why did I abduct a minor with a deadly weapon? If I was protecting her, why did I then let the girl escape?

By the time Pastori had got round to stacking up the charges and the Police Board had summoned her to answer them, there would be no justification that sounded plausible. She had a horrible feeling that the taunting words of the man at the Camp would come home to haunt her. "All our papers are in order." What if the children who were taken through the White Door were all over fifteen and of legal age of consent? What if one of the papers they had signed confirmed an unequivocal willingness to engage in sexual acts? Legally, the Camp might be untouchable. What if the Camp had other VIPs apart from the famous singer? What if their police contacts went all the way up the ranks to the top?

"Sánchez? I'm bringing you in."

Erica clicked off the mobile and stared ahead at the bright, sleepless city.

She was finished. She had no idea where to go, or what to do. The flat that she had decided to leave really was out-of-bounds now. Pastori would have a car outside watching and waiting for her round the clock. Sebastián wouldn't even notice it. Rightly or wrongly, fairly or unfairly, she missed him and needed him. She used the encrypted police mobile to phone him. Her call jumped straight to his voicemail. She tried calling their flat, but there was no answer there, either. He would be back from his work trip and asleep already. It was nearly half one. Why were there no messages from him?

There was one way of checking for sure where Seb was, though. A GPS fix on his car. It was one of those gimmicks he liked so much and in seconds she had the app downloaded. It took quite a while for it to load and zoom into focus on the screen, but when it did it indicated a location a long way from Madrid. He was still in Asturias. Erica punched the GPS coordinates into the dashboard navigator.

"Call me. Urgent. I'm coming to find you," she messaged as she got moving in the car.

She had no hope, but she did have a place to go. In fact, it could be just what she needed. She might as well leave the city behind and go disappear there forever. In one of those mountain cottages with an open fire, why not? Be a nice wifey for Sebastián. Raise some chickens and bake bread for the market. Erica guffawed.

Minutes later, Detective Inspector Pastori decided that it could all wait until the morning. The missing girl had called her parents from a late night bar and a car was on its way to pick her up and take her home. Sánchez really wasn't cut out for undercover work, but she wasn't a bad cop, and the girl was going to be returned to her family, which was all the Chief wanted.

The car theft was a curious incident, but they'd bury it. She certainly looked forward to hearing how Erica had pulled it off, because it was really rather amusing. In fact, Pastori was almost prepared to congratulate Sánchez on her resourcefulness. Olga Vanderveldt, of all people, had reported a certain Carina Delgado Ruíz for taking her vehicle under false pretences, after giving her three fifty-euro notes that turned out to be counterfeit. When a police patrol had spotted and attempted to detain the stolen vehicle, their car had been outrun by the delapidated Citroen, which Pastori assumed her officer was still moving around in. Sánchez really did deserve her reputation for odd behaviour and neat driving.

Saturday, 15th August

SEBASTIÁN WOKE TO AN unaccustomed headache in his cool, high-ceilinged room, which was dark save for a meagre light that found its way past a wooden shutter. His signal-less mobile told him that it was early morning. It was eerily quiet and yet he sensed movement outside the window. He could see his trousers draped over a chair placed at an escritoire, on which his briefcase rested. He lay there, feeling unwell and shocked. Did that really happen? Could it have? But it had been no drunken dream.

He never drank. Only that could explain what had transpired in the wine vaults. There was that sound again. Sebastián got up and went to the high window. He pulled open its hinged shutters to the new day. The guest room he had been given was an annexe to the village hall at street level and its window, which had no pane of glass in the frame, opened directly onto the small square where he had been met by the mayor the previous afternoon.

As he stood looking out, Sebastián's mind insisted on replaying certain scenes from the previous day, jumping determinedly down into the vault, and he preferred to concentrate on the memory of being escorted there by the two men, Pepe and Polo, more people joining their procession, children shouting, and halting briefly at a church with a tall tower where Sebastián remembered to pay his respects to the patroness of the village, the Virgin of the Snows, dropping down on one knee and crossing himself. They had continued to the square, where Sebastián could see a short man in a bowler hat standing as erect as his tight suit would allow, when suddenly a large-boned Civil Guard had stepped into his path. Sebastián was recalling his fright as the policeman shoved a heavy rifle towards him, when a great black pig, the one that had escaped from the rough-and-tumble with the mad woman, jumped up at the iron grille on the window, making a high-pitched squeal quite at odds with its enormity. As he recoiled, Sebastián could smell the animal's fetid breath. He quickly closed the shutters and his hand found an old ceramic switch, which turned on a dusty electric chandelier in the middle of the ceiling.

The sooner he were gone the better, but he still had to see the mayor to collect the village's official response to take back to Madrid. Mayor Beltrán being the last person Sebastián wanted to see after his sordid fornication with the man's wife. He would shower and present himself for breakfast, he decided, and just take things as they came.

The bedroom, exceedingly large for the one bed and few sticks of furniture it contained, had windowed doors to a similarly huge bathroom with curlicued tiles. There was a small piece of white soap and a pull-out shaving mirror, but no plug for the rectangular basin, so he decided to shave in the shower using the gel he had brought with him. The shower curtain in the bathtub was of a thick polythene that he struggled to pull along its rail and the brass taps were of a kind he had only ever seen in old films and exclusive hotels. He smiled as the pipes gurgled and the overhead shower rose coughed before emitting a light, chill rain of water. The morning was not yet warm and he had never liked showering in cold water. It reminded him of boyhood and hard times. But half a minute later, the back of his hand told him that the water had heated up appreciably and Sebastián stepped into voluminous bathtub. He let the warm, hard water stream down over his face and massaged himself, thinking back to the previous night and wondering, not very sensibly, if he might get a chance to be alone with her again. He dried off the water using both the towels which, like the bed linen, were of cotton worn desperately thin, and padded over the polished brick flooring of the bedroom to his luggage. It was neatly laid out on a low wooden rack and he lifted out of it clean underwear, a shirt and tie, socks and a comb. Before he dressed, he sniffed last night's underpants. They had more than just his smells.

Closing the latch of the door behind him, there being no key, he ventured past a stairwell and across what might have been a lobby into the same broad, low-ceilinged, stone hall where they had held the formal dinner. A single table had been set to one side for breakfast, its starched white tablecloth bearing silver cutlery and an onyx ashtray, but there was no hint of another soul. Behind a high-backed chair, on a shelf, was a stuffed fish he hadn't noticed before. Sebastián walked over to a door in the far corner, trusting his nose to lead him to smells of bread or coffee or people, but he found nothing to relieve him of a sense of desertion. Having no better plan, he went and sat himself at the table.

The moment he was seated, a uniformed waitress appeared out of the woodwork and clonked over the wooden floorboards with a pitcher of coffee in one hand and another of hot milk in the other.

They exchanged good mornings, but he was the only one to smile.

"I'll bring you the bread," she said.

"There's no need," he told her, but she had already turned on her heel and the clonks were changing in frequency as she disappeared across the hall. After the previous night's feast, he wasn't the least hungry. All he really wanted was to know how and when to present himself to the mayor for any reply to the official communiqué before returning to Madrid.

He looked again at the inert mobile he had placed hopefully on the table. There was no signal anywhere here. There hadn't been since he left the car behind in what now seemed another dimension of reality altogether. With no newspaper to read or anything else to occupy him, he felt nervous. He got up and fetched a small stack of leaflets from the end of the stuffed fish's shelf. The top one was a list of proverbs in Bable, the rarely spoken Asturian language, whose sense he could decipher or guess at in Spanish. After the first saying, *Xelu tras de lloviu, ñev'hasta'l llombu*, which translated roughly as "Rain and then frost, in snow you'll be lost," he soon realized that they were exclusively about the weather, with a special obsession with the months of February and April. The next item, a single piece of printed paper, extolled the forests of Asturias and walks through their phantasmagorical scenery, where ferns and lichens grew, fungi and moss. On the other side was an illustration of a prancing, horned figure, its thin, hairy legs jointed like a goat's. This, said a caption, was the ancient spirit of the forest, which one might see there. It was the protector of tree, animal and stranger. Its name was Busgosu.

Here came the waitress again. She bore a tray laden with plates of cured ham and cheese, fried quail's eggs, a pound of butter, plum jam and a basket of toasted bread. She reached into her pinafore and brought out a sealed envelope.

"For you," she said, laying it next to the jam. "Anything else, sir?"

"Do you know where I can make a phone call from?" he said, waggling his phone at her.

"I don't know anything about that," her eyes opened wide, as if he had accused her of something.

"Never mind. Nothing else. Thank you."

He waited for her to withdraw and opened the envelope. It contained a formal note requesting his presence again, this time at a plenipotentiary meeting of the council, at one thirty. Oh well. If it didn't drag on, he would still be home before dark. Meanwhile, it gave him the whole morning to do as he pleased, and he had two commitments demanding his attention.

One was with the Civil Guard, to whom he was charged with delivering the cardboard tube with the poster photograph of the King. They would have His Majesty looking down on them for however long it took them to wind up and leave Miga. The other was at the church, where he hoped to hear Mass, but above all to make confession. It was a pressing need in him, not unlike the bodily symptoms that alert the brain when it is ready to defecate, and right now he was experiencing both.

Before Sebastián went out, he opened up the Ministry dossier in his room. A glossy leaflet proclaiming Asturias as Spain's Green Paradise had been somewhat thoughtlessly included. The Asturian Tourist Board's campaign, which gave such prominence to healthy gastronomy, hospitality, safety and natural beauty, was about to succumb to betrayal by a handful of politicians who treated the country as their private fiefdom. Somewhat incongruously, the leaflet had a photograph of Woody Allen at a conference event, wearing a beret. The next item in the dossier was the delegating text making clear that Sebastián had no authority to act or decide. Then came the envelope containing an exaggerated float for expenses and copies of documents delivered to the mayor: the legal papers adjudicating rights to the Chinese mining concern in the UNESCO Biosphere Reserve, and which promised to have taken under maximum consideration the rare wood of centuries-old yews below the mine; a series of maps; undisguised projections of the mining operations and the aerial photographs of the comparable site in Galicia which Sebastián had shown to Erica.

On their own, the images of the gouged, scoured landscape were horrendous. But they were made even more macabre by reports on the risks of contaminants in the event of accident or leakage: probability graphs and predicted consequences for the local environment based on the technique of cyanidation to extract gold from low grade ore. The process called for a huge pond of aqueous solution of cyanide. To confine the poison liquid to the site was, in the opinion of the surveyor, unrealistic. The best case scenario saw the yew forest reduced to a tenth of its size and the associated eco-system for plant and animal life rendered permanently toxic. The data was extremely candid. No attempt had been made to paint over the facts for the village council: to mitigate the impact of the evidence or the judicial ruling.

If there was no recorded opposition from conservationist groups, it was simply because the scheme had not been announced and they had no knowledge of it. Some deal had obviously, if surprisingly, been struck between the national and the Asturian governments. Even the stringent Cantabrian

Hydrographical Confederation had signed off on the project, notwithstanding the evidence that the cyanide would leach and eventually infiltrate the reservoir below, where salmon and trout were bred, and which provided drinking water for an array of towns and villages.

It wasn't as if any of this was new to him. He had read through it all back home in Madrid. What was different now was being here. He closed his eyes and asked his God for guidance.

Sebastián let himself out of the building. As soon as he set foot in the dirt street, he surrendered to the quaint harmlessness of the place with his first breaths of the mountain air. The silence was almost complete. He wandered the forest hamlet in the early hour, the cardboard tube under one arm, feeling himself a privileged being. The unwelcome intruder's duty, he intuited, was to know this place and to take heed of it. A deep sense of peace rose in him, together with the rich smells of tree and beast. He bid good day to staring cows in their pen and pressed on up a path until he was able to see out over most of the dwellings in their organic labyrinth. Here they were, in the arms of nature. Here was equilibrium. It was proof to Sebastián's mind of a historical rightness that had been lost and forgotten in worldly society. The Moors had never conquered this land—King Pelayo had beaten them back—and in Miga, Sebastián saw the tiny badge, the enduring faithfulness of the old Spain. It was a self-sustaining community, as humble as humble can be, whose well-being relied on an ignorance of the world's triviality and a rooted sense of belonging. Was he to be the last witness of this? Why him? Miriam had asked. Had God brought him here to deliver a death sentence to these simple folk and abandon them to their fate? If you're not on googlemaps, you can't exist: was that it?

He was greeted cordially on the street by a man emerging from a particularly higgledy-piggledy cottage, of whom he asked directions to the Civil Guard barracks. This turned out to be two small houses knocked together and only distinguished from the others by a drooping flag propped up outside and the motif "All For The Homeland" carved and painted into the lintel over the main door. Like every other door he had tried in the village, it was open.

He startled the officer on duty, who scrambled to his feet and saluted. When he enquired, he was told that Captain Echevarría was on an inspection but would be with him directly. The captain presented himself in fact within two minutes, his hair uncombed and one button still undone on his uniform. Would the gentleman do him the honour of stepping into his office? How could he be of service?

Sebastián was prepared for old-fashionedness, but he had to do a double-take at the portrait on the wall behind Echevarría and his intense gaze. Behind the times they may be, but to have preserved the image of Spain's old dictator was beyond the pale. No wonder the Ministry had determined to send the appropriate portrait as its replacement, even if it would only be for the last two weeks or so before the barracks was decommissioned. An astonishing thought crossed Sebastián's mind. Was it possible? But how could he put the question?

"You do know...?" he said, gesturing politely towards the proud, military likeness on the wall.

Echevarría's face clouded over. "Yes, the reverend father brought us the news."

It was forty years ago, thought Sebastián. "Captain Echevarría, the Presidency of the Government of Spain," he spoke factually, employing the language the man would expect for such a moment. "Has authorized me to give into your possession and safekeeping and to display in the loyal Barracks of the Civil Guard this modern image of the nation's highest authority."

The Captain received the long tube and started to unwrap it but his stubby fingers didn't have the nails to get under the strong brown tape.

"López!" he shouted. "Scissors!" he told the officer's alarmed face.

A minute later, he pulled out the poster and unrolled it across the wide desk. His head was trembling as if in disbelief. "Thumbtacks!" he ordered López. "And bring De la Fuente and Soto."

When the handsome print was finally put up, somewhat askew, and not in place of but alongside the portrait of the Generalísimo, Sebastián thought it somehow fitting that it should show not the new young monarch, but the old king, his father, who like the village of Miga was doing what he could to live out his last days in privileged obscurity. The greatest of excitement, however, centred on what appeared to be a hand-written signature in the lower right-hand corner.

"Officers, long live the King!"

"Long live the King!"

"Long live Spain!"

"Long live Spain!"

Sebastián found himself saluted again and his hand gripped. Thus excused, he was relieved to exit the oddly emotional scene and return to the street. A dazzling sun had topped the ridge and he had to shield his eyes from it as he walked past a goat, alone and possibly lost, and two women carrying between them a heavy basket of chopped firewood. Miga was fully awake now. When he paused to let someone jog past, it turned out to be the immense black pig from earlier, which appeared to enjoy the freedom of the village. As he watched, the animal jumped up, as it had at his window, to rest its front trotters on the windowsill of one of the cottages and be rewarded with a shower of potato peelings and old cabbage, which it scoffed down busily.

"Good morning," Sebastián turned round to Juan's twinkling eyes. "You see him? For one year he has the run of the village and everyone feeds him. He lives like a king. He is our fiesta pig and tomorrow he will be the finest morcilla in all of Asturias. Are you sure you will not stay? At least join the hunt this evening. Our final one will be our best ever."

"Juan, it would be an honour, but you understand that I have my instructions and Madrid cannot be kept waiting."

"Take this then," Juan said. "In case there isn't an opportunity later. A memento."

It was a long, bone-handled penknife.

"Thank you. Thank you."

"Pepita, is there bread already?" Juan said to a small woman hurrying by, her loaf wrapped in linen under one arm.

"It's coming out the oven now," she called back.

"Adiós, sir," Juan waved as he disappeared in the direction she had come from.

Outside the church with the tall tower, a man on a rickety ladder was hanging a string of lights high across the street. The hunt, the pig, the coloured lights: Miga was getting ready for the summer's feast that would honour their Lady of the Snows. That it would mark the rude end to a story going back to times before memory restarted a confusion in Sebastián's heart and he dived into the church to seek solace.

He peered into a dark space. Ranked pews extended much further back than he had expected and the gloom was such that the altar was quite hidden from view. Narrow steps to the high tower wound up to his left, while in a shadowy corner, next to a saddle, potatoes were piled high on a piece of blue plastic sheeting. Concentrating, he made out a murmur of voices and moved forwards down a side aisle. Where he might have expected incense, there was a smell of fireworks. The suggestion that the country people were less than ceremonious in their use of the place of worship, which was cool and dry, was reinforced in no uncertain manner when he passed by a confessional box. It wasn't the source of the voices and when, out of arbitrary curiosity, he pulled back the black curtain, he found the interior stacked with rifles. There were a dozen or so, stood upright and looking terribly old. A museum would have been the appropriate place for them, but little Miga didn't have a museum: it was one.

He followed the stone wall, walking noiselessly to the far end of the nave, where a door to the vestry lay ajar. He could hear the priest and another man talking, possibly Don Vicente, and he hesitated outside.

"...just the two left now."

"Since we got the youngster, yes."

"That was hardly sport."

"What were we supposed to do? He was scavenging almost daily."

"The female's past breeding age, but that's hardly the point anymore, is it?"

"She'll have to be poisoned. We can't leave her here and we can't take her with us. This is a terrible day, Father."

"The Lord giveth and the Lord taketh away, Vicente. Miga is an old soldier who has been instructed to lay down his arms and that is what he will do. We will have a Guard of Honour for our Lady after Mass and bearers will take her up as far as the Fountain of the Angel. After that, the hunt is on its own. The honour of the last kill should be open to all, do you agree?"

"Shoot on sight, yes. Whoever the Virgin favours. There'll be a gun each."

"Any trace must be eliminated completely. There will be outsiders coming. No trophies or mementos."

"It's the very last."

"How long do you think you'll need?"

"As long as it takes. They're older now, and craftier, but the old mine has long been their favourite hide-out. We'll try there first. Did you see the photographs the mayor has? That area is going to become a festering open sore starting Wednesday. Do we have to meet these Chinese? Presumably not. Nobody wants to."

"I don't think so. We'll know more after the council meeting. One thing I can tell you is that the relocation programme will mean splitting up the village completely. Families, you understand. Far and wide. Who's that?"

Sebastián knocked on the open door before pulling on it.

"Good morning," he said. "Excuse me."

"What is it you wish?" asked Father Raimundo.

"Pardon me, Father. I was hoping to hear Mass today and wanted to ask if there will be a service."

"Not until six. If you're still here..."

"Well, in that case, would you hear my confession?"

Father Raimundo and Don Vicente exchanged a look.

"I quite understand if—"

"You could but, young man," said Don Vicente. "Everybody knows."

Sebastián blushed. "I wish there was something I could do," he said weakly.

Back on the street, where the sun now depicted a fine, strong August morning, a welter of emotions took hold of him. If the whole village knew what he supposed had been a secret adultery with Beltrán's wife, how could he look the mayor in the face? But even that shock paled beside the secret of theirs that he had just learned. One that he hadn't for a moment suspected. It could, he thought, paradoxically be the one thing that might save Miga. If he reported it. If the media found out.

Bears. Cantabrian brown bears. Hiding out in the old mine, but coming down to the village to scavenge.

The region's rarest and most emblematic creature was the one that had never crossed his mind. Strictly protected by law, there were only a couple of dozen left in all these mountains. To hunt one was unthinkable—to him, to just about anybody—but these people didn't live in the progressive world of conservation and education about extinction. They might think they had a perfect right to make a bear hunt the highlight of the village fiesta. And all the more so now, since it was to be their final chance. But if Sebastián could prove the existence of bears—the conversation in the church suggested there were a pair—the mining project would surely be halted and in all probability cancelled. Nothing outranked the endangered brown bear in Asturias when it came to protected species and untouchable habitats.

The official reports were still fresh in Sebastián's mind. They had been, he thought, comfortlessly explicit. But there had been nothing, no mention of bears.

Just one confirmed sighting would be enough to declare the area a no-go zone.

His mandate, his official duty, was to carry out the mission and return to Madrid, but this new data altered the scenario, did it not? And to whom was his first duty? To his country. But what did that mean? His political bosses? Men and women who would come and go according to the colour of the government? Or these priceless animals, the last of their kind, which could still be saved? And Miga, too! Miga might now be fatalistically resigned, but that was no reason for him to be. Sebastián had a strong suspicion that Jaime de Abascal knew rather more than he had let on. He had an unformed notion that this might be the clandestine venue for highly illegal hunts and that he wasn't the first person from Madrid to know about it, or even to participate in one. He had certainly been suspicious about the oddness of his assignment. And now, thinking about it, about the unique cured meat he had been given at supper. "Now you are one of us," Don Vicente had said.

He needed to be sure, but nobody in the village was going to tell him anything. He couldn't ask Juan, and certainly not Miriam, whom he dare not see. The only person he could think of who might, just possibly, let on something, was the mad woman who wore red. The only one who had pleaded with him to save them.

He retraced the route to Josefa's house, where he had had lunch the previous day, and came to the spot where the villagers had been harassing the woman. One small house stood out for a certain indefinable squalidness and a fox's tail nailed to the front door. He knocked and then knocked again, grateful that there was no one around to observe him. The door opened and big eyes looked out at him, one of them purplish from a bruise.

"Could we talk? Inside?" he said.

It was dark and rancid and primitive. Sebastián felt immediately uncomfortable in his city suit. The rough granite walls by the hearth had been daubed with soot to make gross squiggles and faces. A bird in a cage on another wall flitted about, but didn't sing. He sat down at a central table piled with unwashed crockery, an open jar of honey, and wrinkly vegetables that cried out to be binned or composted, while the woman paced three steps back and forth, wringing her hands, murmuring to herself. She looked to be around fifty, but her condition and raggedy clothing made her seem much older.

"Since my companion left," she said, looking to him for comprehension.

"I would like to help. I don't know if you understand me."

She shook her head, but it wasn't clear if it was an answer or part of the nervous monologue she was having with herself.

"Are you here?" she said finally, looking straight at him.

"Yes."

"I am the bitch," she sobbed.

He looked around in some desperation, wondering if he should simply leave. The house might easily be a scene in a children's story about a witch. From a beam hung an iron cooking pot, a ladle, a roasting fork and a net of walnuts, and in a corner of the room was a fat, grey rabbit, silent and vigilant.

"You are a friend of the animals, right?"

"Oooohh," she crooned, and made as if to cradle an infant in her arms.

"The men are going to hunt today," he said. "I overhead them talking."

"My pretties," she said. "The lady without mercy. My boys."

"Tell me the truth. They're going after bears, aren't they?"

"My babies," she said. "They will be hungry. You must take them food!" She suddenly busied herself, getting together a chunk of ham, a blood sausage, bread, goat's cheese that she lifted dripping from oil in a jar and wrapped in leather, and a bottle of wine, all of which she stuffed into a flexible basket made of hemp.

"If I can find them still alive and take photographs, I might be able to save them, but they're notoriously shy. I think there's an old female held in captivity somewhere in the village. Do you know where they keep her?"

"The stranger," she said, sitting down opposite him and raising a hand in a little greeting. The reek of her unwashed ruddy clothes and body drifted across the table. "The stranger will do it."

She got up and went to the corner where the fat rabbit twitched awake. She seized it, broke its neck with a barely audible crack, and brought it to the table. Sebastián was seriously alarmed that she might be about to carry out some satanic ritual, laying out its heart and glistening bowels on the table top, but instead she stuffed the animal into the basket of provisions, tying the top closed with some twine, and stood back, evidently waiting for him to take it and go. He stood up, and for the sake of an amicable exit, took the basket by its long handles and left.

Further up the street, shortly before the steps that went up to Josefa's, was a water fountain. He took a long, cool drink and wiped a wet hand over his face.

His phone told him that it was eleven thirty. All he had to do was wait two hours for the meeting with the mayor and his council, receive the official response and return to his car, escorted by Pepe and Polo, and that would be an end to it. He could leave and no man would be any the wiser. But nothing was ever hidden from the divine conscience which appealed to him now. The hidden order, the greater mystery behind all worldly things, was at work here. He had been chosen for a reason and a duty: there were no coincidences. He had nothing personal against the Chinese as such, but that a godless nation should be allowed to poison the heart of all that was Christian and good in the very land where Pelayo had stopped the rot of Islam, was an iniquity he could not be a willing part of. The inconclusive interview with the mad woman didn't change anything. He had been led into sin and subsequently been handed a slim chance to save the village and redeem himself. An act, however hopeless, was asked of him.

He had already figured out from the surveyor's map in the dossier, and from simply walking around, that there were three ways into and out of Miga. The one he had entered by; the one down to the river he had taken with Juan; and if you carried on past the red woman's cottage and Josefa's, where he was now, another path eventually climbed away into the mountains. This third one led, after many twists and turns, to the mine, which was where Don Vicente had told the priest that the bears took shelter. Two of them. Fully grown males from the sound of it. Sebastián hoped the camera on his mobile would capture them from a safe distance.

He knew that he would have to be lucky to find them, but if the hunting party expected to, then why not him? The scale map he had studied earlier suggested that the mine was about seven kilometres away. Not a short walk. All the more reason to get going, then. He knew he ought to change into the old clothes Juan had lent him, but he felt a kind of superstitious suspicion about going back once his mind was made up. Sebastián put his faith in the Lord and set off.

After the steps up to Josefa's, the way dipped and he went by a crude laundry where a constant stream of water flowed through a series of sinks. A woman with a broad back who was heaving waterlogged sheets didn't hear his steps, or turn round. He continued past a small landfill to a low wall with a simple garden gate, let himself through and walked out. The path narrowed and rose like a challenge. Sebastián climbed rapidly until he knew that he had left the village well below. Not that he could see it. Just like before, when he had arrived from the other direction, it was seamlessly hidden from view by the forest's canopy. The day had grown hot, but the trees' welcoming shade encouraged him to soldier on, with little pause for rest. He took off his suit jacket and thought about stashing it with the basket behind a conspicuous, overhanging rock, but then thought better of it. He didn't much like the idea of carrying a decomposing rabbit with him, but he might be glad of the cheese and some bread later on. His mouth was dry, but he guessed correctly that there would be water in this aquifer-rich forest and he was soon rewarded by a pair of clear running streams and the sound of a heavier one some way above. He turned past the thick trunk of a chestnut tree and came to a little mill. Water tumbling from a small cascade just above it was slowly turning mill's wooden wheel before continuing contentedly on. Sebastián thought it was the prettiest thing he had ever seen. He cupped the falling water in his hands to drink and patted down his hair in order to cool off, waiting around a while to see if someone might appear, but there was no sign of anyone around.

The next hour, along a rocky and often crumbling path invaded by gorse bushes and brambles, was a test of both his stamina and his will, and more than once he was tempted to abandon what was conceivably an ill-advised exercise in self-castigation. But Sebastián knew that such doubts were the lot of any pilgrim, and he pressed on.

Instead of thinning out as he ascended, the forest grew denser. He went on up through its shade until he came to the top of a wooded ridge. Beyond was a rising valley, so thick with yews that it appeared dark in the afternoon sun. He couldn't swear to it, but he was pretty sure this was the high valley where the old mine was located. It ended, at a considerable distance, in a formidable vertical rock, but Sebastián guessed that he wouldn't need to go that far.

The path took him down to a dry gully and turned to follow the gully's contour, winding through a line of beeches until they ended at a broad and empty expanse of hillside. This steep slope of hill reached up to a high barn just below an escarpment. Even at this distance, he could see something hanging across the open doorway to the barn. He put down the increasingly weighty basket, which he had been carrying slung over his shoulder, and shielded his eyes with a hand. It was too far up to see anything clearly and the path didn't go that way, so he left the woven bag against a stone, together with his suit jacket, and began scrambling up.

It was hard going in the sun and halfway up he cursed, remembering Juan's binoculars in his jacket pocket. But when he looked again, he could see it. It was a carcase, skinned and left there to cure and dry in the mountain air. Not a large animal, it looked bigger for being tied upright to the four corners of the barn opening, so that all four limbs were stretched out as far as they would go and the ribcage protruded. The head had been cut off the youngster, so that it took Sebastián more than a few seconds to realize that he was looking at a human boy. Then he fell to his knees and was sick.

Sebastián's legs wouldn't let him back up, so he crawled. When he was about twenty metres from the flayed body, he took out his mobile and took pictures, before being sick again. There was still no signal, so the images remained pending when he pressed "Send" to Erica.

He got to his feet, standing in a quivering inertia, to see a man coming towards him across the hillside carrying a hoe. He was coming unhurriedly and steadily. If he attempted to run back towards the village, which was a doubtful choice, the man would easily cut him off on a diagonal downward course. Sebastián damned his shaking knees and ran the other way, down to the path, at which the man broke into a run himself, shouting. Sebastián's eyes were blurry but a kind of madness hurtled him along, missing every rock and gnarled root in his way, running through the trees as fast and as far as his lungs would bear, and then he jumped off the path, scampering and falling through gorse and briars to hit a rock and topple over and lie caught in the thick undergrowth, staying as still as his fear and his panting would allow. His ears strained to hear the sound of the man's boots on the stony path, but his head pounded too much and so he concentrated on not moving or making a sound, except to pull a bramble's thorn out of the back of his head. He wanted to whimper, but knew he mustn't. Minutes later, he thought he heard something on the path, which was only a short distance above him. He couldn't be sure. After that, he was certain that the man was waiting for him to move and give himself away and so he lay, painfully immobile, breathing through his mouth and unblinking. It was with infinite care that he scratched a nostril that was itching unbearably. Time passed. Eventually he could not hold the posture a moment longer and rolled onto his back, breaking twigs and causing a stone to roll down. He shut his eyes. Nothing happened. Nothing at all. Tension collapsed within him and he fell into the oblivion of sleep.

• • • •

HE WOKE WITH A START to befuddlement and a throat constricted with thirst, but above all to a feeling that something was wrong. He turned his head and found himself looking up the long barrel of a rifle, inches from his face.

"Get up," said the man. "Move."

It took him so long, being stiff and tangled up and awkwardly positioned on the steep slope, that he almost wondered if it didn't make more sense for the man to shoot him and leave him there. He eventually tore himself free of the briars and struggled wretchedly up to the path, realizing for the first time that he had twisted an ankle. There was a second man, also armed. In addition to a knapsack, he had Sebastián's fibre basket and jacket. The first man searched his pockets, taking his wallet, car keys and mobile.

"Now what?" Sebastián said.

"Don't talk. Don't make any sound. Walk."

He received a shove in the back and started moving.

Instead of going back to the village, they were taking him further up into the mountain. He stumbled more than once, tired as he was and his right ankle hurting, and yet with each submissive step he hoped against hope that his captors might have a change of heart. When they came to a clearing where a spring had been made into a fountain and tiled with religious images of angels, he was told to drink water. The two men, one around forty, the other his junior by some years, took turns to drink, keeping a gun pointed at their tall prisoner. The younger one pushed Sebastián off the stone on which he had sat with the sole of a boot.

"Keep moving."

After half an hour or so, they took a detour directly up the mountainside, which brought them to a camouflaged cave. The older man led the prisoner inside, where a rudimentary shelter had been set up, and sat him on the ground. He tied Sebastián's wrists and ankles with some twine.

"Now talk, fascist," he said, while the other man undid the basket. Both of them wore military-style clothes that were even more outdated than anything worn in the village. Neither of them, Sebastián realized, was the broad-shouldered farmer with the hoe.

"You're not them. You're not from Miga," he said.

"We're from Miga. Who are you? What are you doing here?"

"My name is Sebastián Elcano. I was sent from Madrid."

"What are your orders?"

"Basically, to tell the village that they have days in which to pack up and leave before the Chinese move in."

"The Chinese? Not the Russians?" The younger man was suddenly interested.

"They're going to reopen the mine."

"That's enough of your shit. What's your game? Who are you with?" The older man lifted his gun and aimed it at him. "Wrong answer and you're dead."

Sebastián's mouth went dry. He didn't know what to say. He didn't know the answer.

"Look," said the younger man, lifting up the rabbit and the leather pouch with the oily cheese. "This is from Mamá. She sent him."

"It's you," Sebastián croaked. "I mean: she's your mother. There aren't any bears. You're the bears."

"We are men! Fascist bastard!" shouted the older man, pointing the gun at his head again.

"No!" Sebastián objected. "I'm no fascist. I did vote—"

"Then what about this?" He brandished the bone-handled knife that Juan had intended as a parting gift.

"It was a present."

"Made from the skull of our father."

"Let me see," said the younger one, taking it. "It's deer bone. It's nothing." To divert the black anger in his older brother, he offered him the blood sausage. The man accepted it, taking another knife from his back pocket in order to share it between them, but he remained unappeased.

"He looks like an officer," he said chewing, sitting down cross-legged opposite Sebastián, with the gun at his side.

"I didn't know there was anyone up here. When Don Vicente and Father Raimundo talked—"

"Son of a bitch," the man spat at the name of the priest. "What did he say?"

"I thought they were talking about a bear hunt. The village is coming tonight. For both of you. Look, I saw what they did. The boy..." Sebastián lowered his eyes.

"His name was Pedro."

"That's when I ran."

"We saw."

"I'm sorry."

"Someone has to pay."

"I agree. Or there is no justice in this world."

"Justice," the man raised his already blood-stained knife to Sebastián's throat.

"Fermín, leave off. Give him food. Give him food and leave off, for fuck's sake," the younger brother raised his voice. "Can you fight? Do you know how to shoot?"

"My girlfriend does."

The three words had a magical effect. Fermín's fierce look softened and he roared with laughter. "His girlfriend does. What a fairy. He runs away from a fat man with a hoe."

"She drives better than me, too," Sebastián said, but didn't earn any more laughter.

Fermín got up and went to the mouth of the cave with Juan's binoculars. When he came back, he sat and went through Sebastián's things again.

"What's this?"

"Euros."

"How much in pesetas?"

"I don't remember. I think it was a hundred and sixty-six. Each."

"There's no matches," the younger fellow complained, emptying the basket. "She always forgets tobacco and matches."

"What does this do?" Fermín held up the white oblong of Sebastián's iPhone.

Sebastián hesitated. If the man really didn't know, the truth would be too improbable and it might rekindle his ire. "It's a torch," he said.

"Show me." He motioned Sebastián to turn around and cut his hands free.

Seb had recently downloaded a LED app which lit up the wall in the dark recess of the cave with a strong beam of light.

"Tell me more," Fermín said, more curious now.

"They think you're at the mine. That's where they'll be looking."

"We like it better here. It's dryer. I'm Mateu," the younger brother cut a hunk of bread and placed it in front of their prisoner.

"Sebastián," he replied. He reached for the bread and found his wrist held in a strong, countryman's grip.

"I don't like you," Fermín said. "Or those gentleman's shoes you're wearing. You don't add up. You don't belong. You're a spy."

"No." He shook his head. The other man smelled sour close up.

"Are you with the government?"

"Yes. But I am disobeying orders in coming up here. I will be dismissed on my return."

The grip tightened, twisting his wrist so that Sebastián screwed up his face in pain.

"So why do it?"

"I felt it was my duty before God."

Fermín let him go, laughing again. "A good Catholic! Now I really have seen it all. Alright. But one false move and I will reunite you with your God."

They were silent for a minute, eating cheese and bread, getting the measure of each other. When Sebastián saw how ravenous they were, he curbed his own appetite.

"How long have you been up here?" he asked.

Fermín scowled. Either he took this imposter out and shot him, or he took him at face value and let the extraordinary chance to speak to another human being continue into the night. The hopeful look on his brother's face didn't help him decide either way.

"I was thirteen," he said, "when the fascists drove me out to join my father and my older brother. Mateu had only just been born then. They kept him in the village until my brother and then my father fell. Now he's here."

"But why haven't you escaped? To freedom?"

"To France?" Fermín scoffed. "Impossible. At least we can survive here, just about. Did you bring tobacco? Goddamn." He tore off some more bread and stuffed it into his mouth with another slice of sausage. Then, not without misgivings, gave some to Sebastián, before working the cork out of the wine bottle and drinking back a couple of swallows. "A hunt is it? How many of them?"

"I don't know, but they'll have a gun each," Sebastián remembered from the conversation in the vestry. "And first they'll carry the Virgin to the Fountain of the Angel."

"We'll take them there. We'll be waiting."

"You're going to fight the whole village?"

"We are," the man smiled, scratching inside his trousers. "You, too."

"But you haven't got a chance."

"You said the Chinese will be here in a matter of days."

"On Wednesday, yes."

"So they are coming to finish us off before they retreat."

"Well, something like that." Sebastián was at a bit of a loss. "Yes," he said finally.

"I don't see that we have a choice. Mateu?"

"Death to the fascists!" his brother said, holding his rifle high.

They ate the ham with blueberries and drank some more wine. Mateu played a tune on a banjo with three strings while his brother went outside for a dump, taking his gun with him. When Fermín returned, he looked darkly thoughtful.

"Come with me," he told them both and said something in his brother's ear.

Sebastián got up with a dignity he did not feel. They left the cave and climbed up above it, where a promontory provided a good look-out point and a nasty drop. Fermín stood back with the butt of his gun on the ground and his hands around the muzzle. Mateu loaded his own rifle and readied it. Nobody spoke. Sebastián's fear made him obedient and he despised himself for it.

"Sight it like this, hard against the shoulder, and just squeeze the trigger, nice and gentle. Firm on the shoulder, gentle on the trigger."

He handed the weapon to Sebastián, whose heart was jumping.

It was heavy and unwieldy. When he had gone through the motions, repeated by Mateu, and pulled on the trigger, he was glad that it didn't go off. There was obviously no need to trust him yet, or waste ammunition. And they wouldn't want to draw any attention, even at this distance from the village. Not even to execute him.

When they returned to the cave, Fermín wanted to get going already. Sebastián told him that the sortie wasn't due to commence until after six o´clock Mass and showed him the time on the mobile, but the senior of the two maquis wasn't interested. He declared that he would borrow the binoculars, but handed the rest of Sebastián's things back to him. "We are not thieves," he said.

When they reached a vantage point behind a rock, from which they had a clear view of the Fountain of the Angel, Fermín left Mateu to watch over their indeterminable prisoner-companion and went to check on any movement from the village.

"What do you live on?" Sebastián asked, by way of making conversation. He wanted to be alone with his own thoughts but he was afraid to be.

"It depends on the time of year. We trap rabbits, birds. Now and then a boar. Winter is hard now. They used to let us steal vegetables. Potatoes and onions and raddish and carrots, and around Christmas time there would be a goat or a sheep left tied up by the fountain. But last winter we got nothing. Pedro was still with us then. He was always a daredevil, the young'un. One night in January, he went down into the village itself, when it was asleep. The sheep and goats were too well locked up, but he knew where the goatherd kept his dogs, so he let them out, all five of them. They thought they were going to work and followed him up as far as the washerwomen's place, where they started getting nervous, because they didn't know him. He killed them all there and then. He got badly bitten. He carried the biggest one back to the mine and we ate meat for the first time in a month. A week later, he went back and stole some eggs."

"Then they killed him." Sebastián realized that he hadn't heard a single dog bark in the entire time he had been in Miga. Two days which now seemed an age.

"They would have got one of us anyway," Mateu said. "Fermín had been expecting a big hunt, because there hadn't been one for years. They had a helicopter, you know? And a lot of outsiders with Juan and the doctor and El Polo. We spent the first night in one of the shepherds' huts way up above the oaks in the snow. We didn't dare make a fire, and we slept together for warmth, but still we froze. We had no food, just snow to eat. We didn't stand much of a chance. In the morning, Fermín said he knew where the shepherds kept a stack of potatoes and some cured beef. He told us to stay where we were, in the hut. He was obviously lying. 'You're going to get killed.' I told him. After a while, we heard shouting. The hunting party was hurrying through the trees after Fermín. But then one of them, Polo it was, saw the tracks in the snow we had made the night before and brought the leaders of the hunt to within sight of the hut. Pedro and I made a break for it and ran but there was no tree cover.

They waited a long time for the guest of the hunt to fire and he needed eight or nine shots but he got Pedro in the end. I stopped and waited for my bullet but it never came. They came and took Pedro and just ignored me. I went back down to the mine and eventually Fermín made it back, too."

"Did you recognize the guest of the hunt?"

"I only know people from the village. That's an Egyptian vulture," Mateu pointed at a bird with a bow-shaped wingspan.

"Would you know him again?"

"He killed my brother."

When Fermín returned a half hour later, Sebastián had seen an alpine sparrow and a red-billed chough, but the conversation with Mateu had otherwise dried up.

"They're nearly here. Fifteen of them," Fermín said.

"Shouldn't you show me how to reload?" Sebastián asked.

"Your gun has two cartridges. There aren't any more," Fermín said. He went to take up position on the far side, from where they could see his signal. The three of them lay belly down with the guns in position, trained on the fountain where they expected the hunters to halt and rest.

A slow drum, drum, drum announced the arrival of the procession, which was led by two armed men, two drummers and a parishioner in a white surplus swaying incense from a pole. Then came the Virgin of the Snows herself, whose plaster image on a throne was carried on the shoulders of four villagers in red berets, the priest and Mayor Beltrán, with Captain Echevarría and the three other Civil Guards bringing up the rear. They all wore or carried rifles, apart from Father Raimundo. Once they had reached the stopping place, they carefully lowered the inanely smiling figure of the village's patroness to the ground and crowded round the water fountain to drink. Osvaldo Beltrán, improbably suited for the occasion, wiped his face with a handkerchief. At this altitude the day's heat had dissipated, but the climb had been a chastisement for the man.

It was the mayor himself, Mateu now whispered to Sebastián, that he should designate as his target. As if in a dream, Sebastián shifted the barrel round a few degrees until he could see the man's bald patch in the crook of the gun's sighting. If they killed six men outright with two shots from each gun, that would leave nine combatants. Eight, if one discounted the priest. What then? It was absurd and he was terrified, but he couldn't stop his mind from doing the mathematics. Fermín hadn't elaborated any plan and Sebastián doubted that he had one, but at least when he looked over, the man had his hand held up to indicate that they should wait while the hunters lined up for the priest's blessing. Sebastián took hold of himself. He took aim again, hating he knew not who for putting him where he was now. He lined up the crook with the bead at the rifle's tip, as Mateu had shown him, and when Fermín fired he mouthed "Forgive me" and squeezed the trigger.

Captain Echevarría fell, as did the man he had seen on the ladder, Pepe's father-in-law who had been putting up the fiesta lights, but perhaps the greatest consternation was caused by Sebastián's shot, which exploded the plaster head of the Virgin of the Snows, blitzing the hunting party with thousands of tiny fragments. De la Fuente of the Civil Guards and two other men were blinded. Mateu fired again and the doctor collapsed, clutching his stomach, but Fermín's rifle had jammed and he ran down roaring to attack hand-to-hand. To Sebastián it all seemed to be happening in slow motion. He found himself looking straight at Juan and motioned with his rifle to tell him to get away, whereupon Mateu punched him, taking the gun and firing its other bullet into the mêlée around his brother, who was being clubbed to the ground and bayoneted by Don Alfonso. Juan jumped down the slope of the mountain where a juniper bush saved him from falling to his death.

Sebastián's arithmetic hadn't been far off, not that he had had the time to count them. There were seven men, including the incense-bearer, who came after the two remaining assailants, climbing up above the fountain towards them, urged on by the screaming priest.

The guerrillas ran together, leaving the useless, heavy guns behind them, up the mountainside seeing as they could not go down, into an evening that refused to darken, until their strength and their luck ran out and Pepe stood over them, waiting for the mayor to catch up and issue the command.

When the order came to escort them back to the village, Sebastián nearly laughed. During the march back, the posse sang songs and did what they wanted with the rebels. He and Mateu were paraded through the streets before being chained to the floor of what could only be described as a dungeon, while all of Miga raged in jubilation outside the high barred window.

• • • •

THERE WERE TWO IMMOVABLE dates in the year when the village did not sleep.

One was Saint Sylvester, the last day of the year, when the priest nailed up in the church the New Year's calendar with red days marked out as fiestas, a bonfire blazed all night in the square as they drank orujo and the pipe players blew their hearts out.

The women would dance their *orri-orri* and the one male in the dance, after being collectively spurned once, then twice, would grab a maiden and carry her off, tramping through the dirty snow in the streets to a stable manger, which would be laid ready with blankets, and sometimes also contain a surprise thought up by his friends, such as a mattress of pine cones, or a piglet. Like every other village male between pubescence and infirmity, Polo had been the man in the dance, but only once and that was a long time ago and then he had taken Elsa, the pretty one. After that, he had only ever had his cousin to screw and then she had died along with the baby when it was born. There were fewer neighbours in the village all the time.

The other night-long celebration, and the best, was this summer's eve of the Virgin. Polo had been bitterly disappointed to miss out on the hunt and, worse still, on the fiesta, whose existence at this remove could only be sensed by occasional pyrotechnic booms. Pepe had promised to bring a cup of hot pig's blood in the morning and relieve him, but it would be largely over by then. Polo had a lonely night ahead of him, with nothing to do but stare at the stranger's vehicle on the other side of the gate, follow the sliver of moon across the sky and strain his ears for sounds from the village. His only consolation was to have the spirits of the forest for company. Some were good and some desired him harm; some moved about and some lived in the permanent things of the woods. There was a certain tree stump that he took care to avoid and a rock that brought him luck when he touched it twice. He would feel more akin to them as the night deepened and knew they wanted to tell him things. On special nights, the Old One would sometimes halt briefly from stalking by on his goat legs and send him a present in the form of dormouse or a badger, which Polo would pin to the ground with a long iron spike.

So when, far into his watch, a person came walking up the track and it was a barely dressed girl, the very image of a pixie with her shorn hair, he wondered very hard if she was a gift from Busgosu. She took a great interest in the car, which she tried to get into, and played with a small light, which she then listened to as if it might tell her something. Polo watched fixedly from his guard post in the shadow of an elm.

• • • •

ERICA'S RAPID PROGRESS from Madrid had been frustrated at the very end by the confusing GPS signal being transmitted from Sebastián's car, which suggested that it wasn't on any road at all. Assuming a margin of error in the coordinates, and having driven along the only road in the vicinity without seeing any other vehicle or hint of human habitation, she had then tried branching off at distant junctions in case the roads were incorrectly mapped, but this strategy only took her on long detours away from the pulsating dot on her mobile screen. It occurred to her that the tracking device might have fallen off Sebastián's car, or even that the software might be faulty and be misdirecting her to a spot where there was nothing but bushes in the middle of nowhere, whereas her boyfriend was in fact over four hundred kilometres away, at home and in bed, which was where he was supposed to be. But she had no choice. She had to keep going and keep looking, even though it was the dead of night and she was distraught and scared. The name of the village was Miga, Sebastián had told her, but Miga didn't show up on any map or any other online record. She eventually found herself back on the one narrow, winding lane that came within three kilometres and a half of the beckoning dot and decided to stop where she was.

Had she passed along the road a day earlier, she would have seen a gap in the hedgerow through which a vehicle with high clearance, like the one she was driving, might pass with care. But before the hunt began it had been closed off and concealed by brushwood and branches. The village wasn't prepared to admit any more visitors. The top gate would be guarded as always, but Polo could be reliably left to that duty on his own.

The series of tight bends that wound steeply down made it a hazardous place to abandon a car, but she resisted all her police training and left no warning lights on, simply tucking the car as close in to the hillside as possible. She got out of the car on the passenger's side and started to look for a way up. She walked up and down the moonlit road, peering up to the forest darkness that she was somehow going to have to climb through. The incline on its own presented an almost insuperable barrier and wild, thorny vegetation, packed densely between the trees, completed the deterrent. She went back to the car to check her bearings a last time and prepare herself psychologically for whatever came next. Humidifying wipes that she found in the glove compartment were enough to clean off most of the dried sweat and blood on her skin, so that she was almost presentable, apart perhaps from the look in her eyes. But her summer shoes were back at the Camp along with the useless flip-flops, and to tackle the sheer hillside barefoot was not something anyone in their right senses would contemplate. Erica resolved to try anyway.

It was hard, painful and lonely. A lot of the time, it was all she could do to stop herself from slipping back down. Where the climb was not totally obstructed, she was caught by the unforgiving trees and scrub. Her feet and legs and arms were constantly grazed and scratched and poked, and the going was very slow. Erica told herself to keep her nerve, only to find the way irretrievably blocked by a treacherous, rushing stream and a sheer rock face. All the way back down to the road, to which she had to jump the last couple of metres, she fought the self-reproof of knowledgeably doing something slightly insane.

Before making a second attempt, she returned to the car and tore up a large chamois leather into strips to bind her sore feet. After twenty minutes resting in the expensive-smelling interior of the patrol car, so comforting and ergonomic after her encounter with raw nature, she figured that she wasn't about to collect her thoughts or have a brainwave, so decided to set off again. The only supplies in the car were a bottle of water and some mints, so that's what she took. She thought about taking the gun from under the driver's seat, but then couldn't think why and left it.

This time she walked along the road, past the corner where the water hurtled down from the impassable channel above, and kept walking for some time until she came to what appeared to be a less daunting ascent through a dim coppice of beech. It soon turned into the blackness of a tangled thicket and her battle with wicked briars and branches resumed. Only the soft leather bandages wound tightly around her feet saved her from having to give up and turn back again. By the time she had struggled a way through to more manageable terrain, her summer camp T-shirt was shredded and even her forehead had been caught by prickles and bloodied. She started to move a little quicker, now down, now up, through the clearer, rocky forest of conifers and kept an eye on the mobile's map, which showed her as heading more or less in the right direction. Erica sang in a determined whisper to keep herself going and desperation at bay. Any forest sounds, even the strident cry of a fox, were a welcome distraction from her monotonous anxiety. An owl's call reminded her of her dream in the well, when the bird had flapped on ahead into the tunnel after the indefinable promise of the kaleidoscopic display, and she clung to the dream image now as a scrap of meaning in an otherwise meaningless night.

After forty minutes of unhappy toil against an unfeeling, invisible foe, an unannounced drop caused her to fall into a dell and crack her head against a tree root. Erica cried quietly to herself. She found that it had the effect of clearing her head. The more so when two distinct explosive thumps gave her reason to hope that she might not be alone in the mountains. She sat up and checked the mobile navigator. It told her that she had come within eight hundred and fifty metres of Sebastián's car, west by north-west. She got to her feet and clambered up the slope of the dell to what was more even ground and easier going through the trees, and then she was out under a murky night sky at the edge of what seemed to be a limitless, unfarmed field.

Erica shivered and rubbed herself. She was damp and smeared with dirt and the northern summer night had turned cold. The white dot continued to blink on her screen and she trod directly towards it across the sloping field.

• • • •

AS THE NIGHT WORE ON, Mateu and Sebastián heard the mood of the fiesta rise and fall, now roused by impromptu shouts and the jangling tunes of musicians, now sinking into the sobriety of mourning, only to be rekindled with growled oaths in the crackling of the great fire in the square and sustained in a lowing of joined voices. They were aware of periodic visits, of people coming to their prison's door and peering through the grating at them, two chained men who neither talked nor slept, sitting against the stone wall. It seemed a long time coming, but once a decision had been taken, no time was wasted. The door, hanging heavily on its hinges, was opened and Juan came down the steps. He stood looking down at them, hands on hips.

"Who wants to go first?" he said cheerily.

For some time, Sebastián had done nothing but gaze at his ruined shoes. He was oddly relieved to be able to do something else. He looked up at Juan and raised his arm as best he could.

"Very good," Juan sounded pleased.

As he and another man removed his chain and lifted him up from the ground, Sebastián said an "Adiós" to Mateu, who said nothing and would not look at him. The gaolers helped him up the steps and out into the square, where he was presented. The villagers standing around the fire gathered together into a huddle and hurled abuse at him. Sebastián heard the words, but they meant nothing to him. Almost immediately, he was marched off down the street, followed by the mob, some of them carrying burning sticks. They passed by a mule drinking from a large pail, roped to Fermín's body which lay like a heap of dung behind it. There was an animated scene where the red woman was being tossed from one man to another, but even this stopped to follow the main event. They were met at the church entrance by the priest in his robes and a fractured torso which was all that remained of the Virgin of the Snows. The priest stood aside. At the foot of the spiral staircase to the tower, which was only wide enough for one person to pass at a time, Sebastián showed a moment's reluctance and received a rifle butt in the back of his skull. The pain disabled any lingering thoughts he might have had. He climbed the multitudinous stairs, his twisted right ankle hurting again, and while he bridled at the muzzle of the gun being repeatedly jammed into his back, he kept going up, one step at a time, round and round.

A single bell hung down from the crown of the tower, which was otherwise open to the elements and surrounded by a low wall. Two men seized hold of his arms and a third crouched behind him to tie his wrists and ankles with cord. He was lifted up and carried to the edge, to look down on the village looking up at him in expectant, tentative silence. The great black pig, a dark patch in a dark night, and a small goat were tethered by ropes to heavy iron rings in the church wall. "My boy, my boy!" rose a woman's cry, to general jeering and laughter. "It's not your boy, you donkey." The mad woman was down there, too, restrained as he was, gripped as everyone was.

"Hear my confession, father," Sebastián said.

"This is a very old church," the priest said. "The tower was added much later, but the building, the main structure, is ninth century; one of only three remaining from the reign of Ramiro the First." His face shone in the night. "When we abandon Miga on Tuesday, the church will be destroyed. We will not be leaving to the heathens either our house of prayer or our dynamite for their mining. Normally we throw off the goat, you understand, but such a unique occasion calls for something special."

Sebastián, already immobilized, felt the grip tighten. He was pressed up against the low wall, which came up to his knees. He closed his eyes.

"For our many sins," began the priest, when *ping, ping, ping, ping, ping, ping, ping, ping, ping, ping* went the iPhone in Sebastián's trousers.

"Wait."

The peremptory order did not cause a release of the grip on his arms and belt, but his feet were still in contact with the floor. Father Raimundo fished the white phone out of the outsider's trouser pocket and saw that a series of messages had been received and sent, including photographic images. This high tower was the priest's private domain. Not even the mayor was permitted to climb up to his sanctum. As far as he knew, it was the only location in their mountains in line with a signal that enabled a modern telephone to work. It was a secret place where he alone communicated with the greater world beyond Miga, that cesspool of power, vice and corruption which had engulfed the purity of national principles.

Two of the photographs were unfortunate. He had to think about this. It could complicate matters.

"Take him down. Put him back."

At the foot of the tower, unsatisfied but not displeased, conjecturing that the ploy was a means of playing with the victim's emotions and extending his agony, the villagers made way and Sebastián was steered back to the cellar. His handlers took him past a man named Miguel, who had given Fermín death at the Fountain of the Angel. It had been the young man's first kill and he sat now on the ground, speechless, staining the earth red with the wet, dripping viscera draped over his head and shoulders for his blood wedding.

When Mateu saw his fellow prisoner brought back in, his look took on hope, only it was his turn to be manhandled out of the hole and led off to the church. Fear had turned Sebastián's mind a blank, but his ears still heard. There came a moment when the distant voices went very quiet, except for a single wail. There was no way he could have heard it—it was simply too far away—but in his imagination he heard the clatter and the smack of limbs and skull.

The door opened and Juan entered, followed by Father Raimundo and the Mayor. By way of preface to their conversation, the priest slapped him hard in the face.

"Who is Erica?" he held up the iPhone. "Your girlfriend?"

"She's a policewoman," Sebastián stated. "My girlfriend," he continued, when he saw that they wouldn't believe that on its own, "is a policewoman."

Making sense of the activity on the mobile had proven troubling to the priest. This Elcano and this Erica had clearly wanted to speak to each other and urgently, and yet no calls had been connected. Photographs, very embarrassing ones, had been sent but not yet received. They couldn't, however, be cancelled.

"Where is she?"

"Madrid."

"Son of a bitch," Mayor Beltrán kicked Sebastián in the side of the head. They filed out, leaving him with a ruptured ear drum and blood trickling a thin red line beside his tears. A tiny hope pulsated an additional pain in his sorry head. A hope that went to work, stringing out a narrative to justify itself.

He had heard his iPhone connecting to a 3G network, receiving and sending messages to Erica. Pictures of the boy, presumably the last and youngest of the red woman's sons. Probably educated in isolation by a village itself cut off from time, groomed from an early age like his father and brothers to act out the role of Republican resistance fighters in the Asturian hills—some fifty years after the last of them had been gunned down—as a theatre for the amusement of hunters playing at being Franco's doughty troopers. Hunters from a very particular class of people, who had rank but no names. He guessed that the boy, Pedro, Miga born-and-bred, had been inculcated with the same ignorance about the outside world as Fermín and Mateu, given the same old, ill-fitting Republican uniform, and sent out to survive with them. Allowed to subsist for long, undisturbed seasons, smuggled an occasional basket of produce by their unhinged mother, even supplied with provisions by the village to ensure that the quarry remained alive in the mountains, ready and waiting for the day that certain very important guests arrived.

But would the images be legible on a small screen? Without any words to accompany them, would Erica look closely enough to see what it was? Stretched out on the barn door like a tortured animal, flayed and left to cure as meat in the cold mountain air.

• • • •

FINDING THE BLACK CAR in such an improbable location gave her mixed sensations of elation and confusion. It was locked up and cold. A closed gate that presaged a dark track was the only and obvious way that Sebastián could have gone on from here. She tried phoning him once again and, once again, the call jumped to his voicemail. There were messages from him, but they were in the form of images that rolled round and round interminably and refused to download into focus.

When the creature climbed over the gate, Polo didn't know what to do. He was nervous in the extreme. On the one hand, he had a clear-cut duty to stick to his post and not let anyone pass. On the other, it was the night of Our Lady and anything could happen, even a visitation from a woodland being. She was surely harmless or surely dangerous. She was pretty and half-naked. He decided to let her go on and not hurt her unless he had to.

After the ordeal of the forest, the track was a simple if not painless hardship. She was very tired now. She was starting to imagine things and the soles of her feet suffered on the granite rock. Once, when the binding on her feet came loose and she stopped to retie it, she thought she perceived a figure behind her. She even turned the light of her mobile in its direction, but all that shone was the night's dark nothingness. Erica went on, hobbling, up the path to a ridge, where the doubting void inside her was finally answered. A faint sound of merriment and music reached her ears. A wavering light suggested a fire, quite strange in the parched forest.

Step by limping step, she made her way down through the trees until, like Sebastián before her, she came to the furtive wooded dwellings of Miga and walked along its main street, finally becoming certain of the presence of someone at her back. She turned. A tall, angular youth or young man hovered there, waiting for her to continue. There seemed no point in giving it or him much thought, so she walked past the rickety cottages towards the noise and the light, to be greeted by the warmth of an orange-and-yellow bonfire baking in the village square, a sweet smell like burning pork, and dozens of scared, excited eyes.

The priest's emergency conference in the village hall with Don Vicente, Don Alonso and Beltrán was interrupted by two agitated women, whose gesticulating and insistence made further conversation impossible. They shooed the men outside, where they saw a sight that they did not know what to make of. Here was an unknown woman, barely clad, with no hair to speak of, presenting an image of suffering to Miga's paltry but devout populace, half of whom were kneeling before what they decided must be the Virgin herself, come in the true flesh to take the place of the icon destroyed on her sacred night.

The woman saw them and walked, as if afflicted, towards where they stood. "Hi," she said. "I'm sorry to bother you. I'm looking for my boyfriend. His name's Sebastián. I saw his car back there and I didn't know where else to look. Is this Miga?"

When she was shown into the dungeon, Sebastián instinctively went to raise a manacled hand in greeting, but found that he could only stare at her in disbelief. Part of him felt that she should really have known that the gravity of the situation required her to be in police uniform, and he didn't know how she had made it there so quickly, but like a child whose parent has come to fetch him from dire trouble, he wasn't going to argue.

Seeing him there, set in chains, on his own in the cavernous cellar and illuminated by a solitary candle, Erica felt a vast relief swelled by the amusement of seeing him in a worse pickle, here at least, than she herself was.

"That's him," she told the men. "What on earth have you done?" On closer inspection, he didn't look too good.

"Are you with him?" she was asked, and on replying in the affirmative promptly found herself sat alongside Sebastián, with her limbs pinned to the wall and stone floor by the same strong chains. Outside, after a careful examination of her phone, the priest gave thanks to the wisdom of the Almighty and tossed it to be consumed by the fire,

"Sebas?" she said to him, no sooner than they were alone. "Are you alright? What happened to you? What's this all about?"

He looked at her in a way she had never seen before. "I'm sorry," he said quietly.

In spite of everything, she felt calm. At least she had found him. "It's OK. Talk to me," she said. "Whose sensibilities did you offend this time?"

He was saved from answering by the cellar door being pushed open again. A woman, raising the hem of her dress so that it wouldn't catch on her shoes and cause her to trip, came down the steps into the shadowy cellar. She approached them and stood briefly above Erica in quiet composure, her head inclined to one side, appraising her, before squatting down with her ankles either side of Sebastián's outstretched legs. Smiling at him, Miriam lifted her dress and waddled forwards on her high heels, shoving her bare cunt into Sebastián's face and holding him there by the ears, laughing as he tried to free himself and then stopped struggling.

Two, maybe three long minutes later, she had finished. With the briefest of glances at the woman, the mayor's wife pushed herself up and rearranged her yellow cotton dress.

"Your son will be a fascist," she told Sebastián, not bothering to close the door on the way out.

Erica, appalled, had turned her face to the wall, and he couldn't stifle his panting for breath. It seemed better, almost, that Pepe should come for them. He took them up the cellar steps and outside, where El Polo and the two Civil Guards, López and Soto, waited in the darkness to escort them. El Polo stepped forward to gag them. A few villagers were lying around, drunk or asleep, or both. Others, disabused of Erica's divinity, eyed them coldly as they were led past the bonfire, on which two skeletal figures lay glowing phosphorescently. They were pushed forwards under the bunting, under the fiesta lights and up the street, passing by the red woman's cottage, passing the steps to Josefa's, where Sebastián had had such a filling repast and a view that cried out to be shared. They left behind the washhouse, where Pedro had killed the dogs, to leave Miga by the gate to the high path. Sebastián's hands were tied behind him but he could look round and see Erica, her head bowed. She had silently but vehemently refused a blindfold, but would not look up, either. Juan was back there following, and a couple of village men he had not met.

The morning was coming on. He wanted to tell her, for the sun to show her the pretty mill that they trudged by. Birds swooped low across their path and Sebastián felt the poorer for having no idea what they were, for not having spent more time learning in the company of Mateu, or Juan. He knew this way and pressed on obligingly, even now. The blood beat in his ears and Erica stumbled. They were nearly at the rim of the hill that Sebastián knew would bring them to the ancient yews, the deep, deep forest that was just days and hours away from invasion by the technicians and earthmoving vehicles of the mining concern, when they took a sharp left along an overgrown path that wasn't used any more. Soto had to use his bayonet to clear a way through. It brought them at last to the edge of a high cliff, below which, had they been standing there at a later hour, they would have seen nesting vultures launch and rise on invisible thermals, before circling down.

Did you love *The Asturian Campaign*? Then you should read *The Ministry of Flowers*[1] by Guy Arthur Simpson!

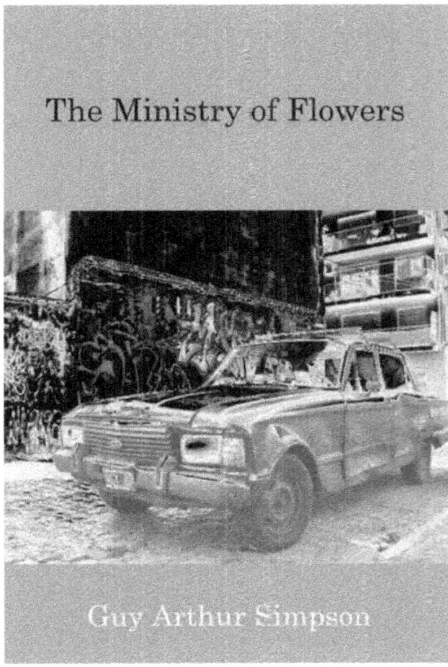

[2]

Lorenzo is worried about the city.

Everyone else is worried about Lorenzo.

Decay and chaos blight the sprawling metropolis and he suspects that the flowers are to blame. Although maybe the cardboard collectors are mixed up in it as well.

The president will know: and Lorenzo means to find out.

novella ~ 20,000 words

Read more at www.guysimpson.com.

---

1. https://books2read.com/u/bpOzjJ

2. https://books2read.com/u/bpOzjJ

Milton Keynes UK
Ingram Content Group UK Ltd.
UKHW041809170923
428861UK00002B/25

9 781916 106154